A Match Made in London

The School for Spinsters
Book One

By Michelle Willingham

DRAGONBLADE
PUBLISHING, INC.

Dearest Reader;

Thank you for your support of a small press. At Dragonblade Publishing, we strive to bring you the highest quality Historical Romance from some of the best authors in the business. Without your support, there is no 'us', so we sincerely hope you adore these stories and find some new favorite authors along the way.

Happy Reading!

CEO, Dragonblade Publishing

Additional Dragonblade books by Author Michelle Willingham

The School for Spinsters Series
A Match Made in London (Book 1)
Match Me, I'm Falling (Book 2)

Prologue

London, 1816

"I'M HERE TO see Mrs. Harding," Violet Edwards told the footman. "I-I have an appointment."

She twisted her hands together as he led her inside, the fear rising in the pit of her stomach. The man led her to a small sitting area and said, "Wait here, if you please, Miss...?"

"Edwards," Violet finished. She didn't know if the headmistress—if one could call her that—would be able to help her. But after three Seasons without a single suitor, she saw no alternative but to enroll herself in Mrs. Harding's School for Young Ladies.

The not-so-polite name was the School for Spinsters.

Rumor had it that Mrs. Harding took only a few students each year. Violet had witnessed one transformation when her friend Felicity had disappeared for a few weeks, only to return, find the perfect husband, become blissfully happy, and now, she had a child on the way.

Violet's cheeks burned, for she wanted that, so very much. True, her looks were only average, and certainly she would never be a great beauty. Her dowry was pitiful. But that wasn't the real reason why men didn't want to marry her—it was her stutter. An invisible weight sank down on her shoulders with the unspoken question of whether she could ever overcome the problem.

Another gentleman entered the sitting room. He looked to be

in his thirties, and he had light brown hair with kindly blue eyes. "Miss Edwards, I am Mrs. Harding's secretary. Cedric Gregor is my name. If you'll just follow me into the study, we will discuss your situation with the headmistress of our school."

Violet walked alongside the gentleman, keeping her eyes lowered. With every step, her fears only multiplied. Even now, she felt her eyelid beginning to twitch while a ringing noise resounded in her ears. She took deep breaths to stop herself from growing faint. That was the last thing she needed right now.

When Mr. Gregor led her inside, she was surprised at Mrs. Harding's appearance. The woman looked to be only a few years older than Violet herself. Yet, when she glanced into the headmistress's eyes, she saw the mirror of someone who had endured suffering.

Mrs. Harding glanced up from her correspondence and re-garded Violet. "I received your letter, Miss Edwards. I am Rachel Harding, and you've already met my secretary, Mr. Gregor. I presume you have come about enrolling in my school."

"Y-y-yes." Violet wanted to curse herself, but her stammer only worsened. She cleared her throat and tried again. "I-I-I've brought money f-for the tuition," she said, placing her reticule on the desk. "I've saved my p-pin money for over a year."

She bit her lip, wishing to God she could rid herself of the stutter. Although Mrs. Harding waited patiently while she spoke, Violet could see the sympathy in her eyes. She lowered her head again, her shoulders slumping while she waited for the woman to answer.

"Tell me more about why you have come to seek my help," the woman said gently. "What is it you want to learn from my school?"

Violet tried again, but whenever she got nervous, her stutter seemed to grow even more impossible to control. "M-my mother doesn't believe I will e-ever marry," she managed. "I was hoping to f-find a husband of my own. I've heard you c-can help women who have…very f-few choices."

Mr. Gregor's expression tightened at the sound of her voice, and Violet turned away from him. No doubt he was disgusted by her speech.

"And do you consider yourself one of those women?" the headmistress prompted.

Violet nodded. She had grown so accustomed to being a wallflower, she could barely remember the last time anyone had asked her to dance. She couldn't truly say she was a woman with few choices—she was a woman with no choices at all.

"You lack confidence, don't you?" Mrs. Harding said. Violet wasn't certain how to respond to that, but then the matron continued. "There's nothing wrong with your appearance, aside from that boring gown."

She glanced down at the dove gray bombazine, wondering if the woman's remark was sincere or a test of some kind. "It's f-far more than that. I can...barely speak. No gentleman wants to marry me."

It would be easy enough to change her gown and her hair. But confidence was something she'd never had. Nearly everyone mocked her stutter, and it was easier to simply retreat from the ballrooms and hide in the shadows. Which, of course, made it impossible to meet a man to marry.

"What does your father think?"

Violet shook her head. "He d-died years ago."

Mrs. Harding tilted her head slightly. "Did he have a title or any wealth at all? Does he have an heir who is responsible for you?"

"He was only a baronet. My younger brother inherited his title and the house."

The memory of her father brought a soft warmth, mingled with regret. Arthur had made many friends among the members of the *ton*. Violet believed it was the reason why they still received invitations to balls or dinner parties—certainly not for her mother's sake.

"What sort of husband are you hoping to find?" Mrs. Harding

was starting to take notes, which made Violet feel slightly better. She might actually be able to join this school, if the headmistress decided to accept her.

"Someone kind," she answered. "He doesn't h-have to be very handsome as long as he is a g-good man."

"Do you not believe you are capable of winning a handsome husband?" Mrs. Harding asked.

Violet shrugged. "Of course not. H-handsome men don't want to c-court a woman like me."

The matron stared at her for a long while, as if trying to make up her mind. "I cannot accept every young woman who seeks my help," she said slowly. "While I believe you may benefit from our tutelage, I have a task for you first. If you succeed in this, then we *might* be able to accept you into our school." She emphasized the word, making it clear that she had not yet made a decision.

"W-what sort of task?" Violet asked. She couldn't imagine anything they could possibly want from her. She was genuinely curious.

"You must attend a ball this week," Mrs. Harding announced. "Send word to me which one it is, so I will know that you have kept your word."

"M-my mother is forcing me to attend Lady Shelby's ball in two days," Violet admitted. She wasn't at all looking forward to it, but then again, she had never liked social gatherings. They were a means to an end, not something for enjoyment.

"Very good." Mrs. Harding scribbled a note to herself. "Now then, your task is this: I want you to study the most popular ladies. Look at the ones who are asked to dance by dukes and viscounts. I want you to find out what these women are doing to attract the attention of high-ranking gentlemen. And by that, I do not mean her appearance. I mean her mannerisms. Her behavior and the way she smiles or glances at a man. Do you think you can do this?"

Violet nodded at Mrs. Harding before glancing down at the carpet. This was an assignment she could easily manage. It was what she always did anyway—she stood against the wall while watching the other guests.

"Good. Return to me next Tuesday and tell me what you've learned." The headmistress paused a moment and then said, "One more thing, Miss Edwards."

"Yes?" she whispered.

"Look up at my face when we speak."

Violet felt a flood of color in her cheeks, but after a long pause, she did. Mrs. Harding studied her closely, and with each moment, Violet's discomfort grew. "When anyone speaks to you, do not look at your hands."

She nodded again and looked downward out of habit. But this time, she forced herself to look up again.

"Good. You have now had your first lesson. Return to me in a week's time, and we shall see if you can earn a place in my school."

A flood of hope suddenly rushed through Violet as she reached for her reticule and stood. Though her cheeks were still flushed, she agreed, "I will. And th-thank you."

RACHEL HARDING SET her pen down, giving herself time to think about what Miss Edwards needed. After she'd been widowed three years ago, she'd vowed that no woman should ever have to endure an arranged marriage like her own. Because of it, she'd opened a school for young women who had difficulty finding a husband. It didn't matter that her establishment had been nicknamed the School for Spinsters. If that meant the right ladies arrived on her doorstep, so be it. Rachel prided herself in finding a match for any unmarried young woman who was facing the same nightmare she herself had endured.

There was tuition, of course, but it was mainly to ensure that the young woman was serious about her quest to find the right husband. Most believed that finding a husband was about transforming her appearance, becoming beautiful and wearing fine clothes to lure the perfect man.

But finding a husband had nothing to do with physical beauty. It was about the young woman's inner transformation. She had to believe she was worthy of being loved, and she had to develop her confidence. That was Rachel's true purpose. Although, sometimes a few wallflowers needed to feel beautiful first.

Cedric Gregor's role in the matchmaking was just as crucial, for he spent time in the gaming hells and ballrooms, finding out which men were appropriate for marriage and those who should be avoided. He was her dearest friend and an excellent business partner. He was discreet in his preference for men, which made him perfect for finding the right gentlemen for her spinsters.

And Miss Edwards would indeed be a good candidate.

Demure and shy, Rachel thought. *But it's more than that. She's trying to hide from the world.*

Her stutter was a problem, yes, but not the greatest one. It was the young woman's insecurities that hindered her the most.

Her door opened wider, and Cedric returned. "What do you think? Can we help her?"

Rachel shrugged. "It's possible. But we need to watch her further. She will attend Lady Shelby's ball on Thursday. We will go and observe her behavior. And in the meantime, it would be good if you could start searching for an eligible bachelor. She wants someone kind, and his looks don't matter."

Cedric smiled. "Consider it done."

Rachel picked up her pen again, trying to press back the rise of excitement. It would be a challenge, yes. But she felt confident that they could succeed.

Chapter One

"**Y**OU KNOW WHAT you have to do."

Damian Everett, the Earl of Scarsdale, kept his gaze averted from his father. Yes, he did know his responsibilities, all too well. He had to set aside his old ways and become the practical son, the one who saved his family from ruin by choosing the wealthiest bride in London. He acknowledged the marquess's remark with a simple nod.

"Then stop standing here and go convince the chit to marry you." His father's impatience was palpable. Which likely meant that Jonas had lost even more at the gaming tables yesterday.

Hence, the reason why Damian was courting the most irritating woman he'd ever met—Lady Persephone Camden, daughter of the Duke of Westerford. She gathered suitors like rotting meat collected flies, and she reigned over them with a calculating smile.

Damian obeyed his father's demand and crossed the room to join the others. Resentment festered within him that he had to play this role. Several gentlemen moved out of his way as he neared Lady Persephone. Mostly because he had a reputation as a fighter, after he'd defended a few ladies in the past from unscrupulous men.

"Good evening, Lord Scarsdale," Lady Persephone purred as he moved to her side. "I'm so glad you're here tonight."

He eyed some of the men surrounding her, and most took a step back. "Don't you grow bored of all your admirers?"

She laughed. "Not at all. It makes the task of choosing a husband so much more exciting."

And didn't he recognize that? It was a game to her, playing one man against the other. She truly didn't care which man she flirted with or teased.

"I'll dance with you later," he said. "We'll talk more then."

At that, she shot him a look of false dismay. "Oh, dear. I'm afraid my dance card is full, Lord Scarsdale."

Damian refused to engage in her ruse. "I'm sorry to hear it. Another time, then."

"Giving up so easily on me, are you?" she chided. Then, she turned to the elderly man standing behind her. "What's your name again, sir?"

"Er—Nigel Dryden, my lady." The elderly man appeared confused but somewhat intrigued by her interest.

"Oh, yes, that's right." Then Lady Persephone studied her dance card and said, "You won't mind if Lord Scarsdale takes your place, will you?"

"I…well, that is—"

"Good," she smiled, crossing off his name. "That's settled then."

Mr. Dryden appeared uncertain, but he had no other recourse. "As you wish, my lady."

But Damian could see the gleam of excitement in her eyes. She loved the sense of power and control over men and did as she pleased, no matter the consequences.

"Which dance is it?" he asked. Not that he truly cared.

Persephone told him, and with a nod to her, he departed. The less time he spent in her company, the better. In truth, if he did somehow convince her to marry him, he planned to live at the Scarsdale estate. She could remain in London, far away from him.

It bothered him that he had to pursue such a woman. He didn't particularly like Lady Persephone. And yet, he would do what he had to for the sake of his sisters, Melanie and Regan.

They were the reasons why he was sacrificing himself upon the altar of marriage. They hadn't deserved their dowries to be gambled away by their father. Melanie should be here now, making her debut in society. She should be dressed in white, surrounded by suitors and smiling. But unless Damian found a way to change their circumstances, it would be at least another year, if not longer, before he could restore her dowry.

As for himself, he'd never particularly cared about a wife or a family. Why should it matter if he wed someone like Persephone? It was little more than a business transaction, one where the young woman's dowry would give his sisters the futures they deserved.

And he would do whatever he had to, for his family's sake.

Damian returned to the opposite side of the room, acknowledging a few friends as he passed. Near the doorway, he spied a young lady who appeared as miserable as himself. She had brown hair and wore a garnet-colored silk gown. A string of pearls hung around her throat, and despite her painful shyness, she did have a lovely face. It was the face of the innocent girl next door, one he suspected wouldn't know how to be cruel if her life depended on it.

And yet, he sensed her terror. She was clenching her gloved hands, taking slow deep breaths. He fully understood her desire not to be here, and a part of him wished he could leave as well.

The young woman's eyes were downcast, but he saw her murmur to herself before she raised her chin and looked around. Almost as if she'd scolded herself. She pasted a smile on her face, but she clearly wasn't happy to be here.

He understood that feeling all too well.

With a sigh, he realized that his dance with Persephone would begin soon. He had to stop brooding in the corner and face the reality of courting the woman. He had no other choice, and it was time he accepted it.

VIOLET HATED ATTENDING balls, but they were a necessary evil toward her goal of finding a husband. Most of the time, the gentlemen overlooked her presence. Today, however, it didn't seem so dreadful since she had a task to complete. This event was not about standing in the corner and feeling miserable because no one had asked her to dance. She was here to gather information, and somehow, knowing that she was here to observe, made it a little more bearable.

Their names were announced before they entered the ballroom. Violet's younger brother Daniel escorted their mother, along with her sister Charity. Violet was perfectly content to walk behind them for it was easier to remain unnoticed.

At least, it was, until her mother demanded, "Stop lurking, Violet, and come stand beside your sister."

She obeyed, keeping her head lowered. Then she remembered what Mrs. Harding had told her—that she should look at the person's eyes. She risked a glance at her sister, and Charity offered a silent look of support. It gave her comfort, and she was grateful for it. But when she turned to meet her mother's gaze, there was only disgust in Thomasina's expression.

She hates me, Violet thought. *Because I cannot speak properly.* It wasn't a surprise, really, but sometimes she wished her mother weren't so embarrassed by her.

The musicians began to play a country dance, and Violet watched the young women who were asked to dance. She saw Miss Green on the arm of Viscount Leighton, and the young debutante smiled at him. She simply exuded joy, as if she could not be more delighted to dance with him.

Interesting.

Personally, Violet had always experienced terror that twisted her insides apart when she'd been asked on a rare occasion to dance with a gentleman. It was usually someone too old, too poor, or someone who made her skin crawl. She'd never had the opportunity to dance with someone handsome.

For a moment, she studied the young men and women, wondering whom she would choose if she actually did have a choice. Then her gaze settled upon Damian Everett, the Earl of Scarsdale.

You've lost your wits, she warned her brain. Lord Scarsdale had a reputation of being an incorrigible rake. He had a wicked smile and a way of making women blush. Violet had heard rumors that he'd had dozens of mistresses and if he merely crooked his finger, any woman would succumb to his charms.

He was...watching her. Why on earth? She blinked in surprise, and he smiled at her. Those deep green eyes held a sleepy look, as if he were imagining even more sinful deeds.

Her mouth went dry, and her heartbeat quickened. My goodness, but he was handsome. He was taller than all the men in the ballroom with dark blond hair that was longer than fashionable and a muscular form. His face had a strong jaw and those green eyes held her captive.

Then she saw another young woman emerge from behind him. It was Lady Persephone, Violet was fairly certain. The debutante crossed over to the earl, and he took her hand and kissed it. Of course. *That* was who he'd been smiling at. Not her. Violet breathed a sigh of relief, but then her thoughts began to wander. What would it feel like to have a man kiss the back of her hand? Would his mouth be soft? At the very idea, her skin tightened with goosebumps.

"Violet, are you all right?" Her sister Charity was staring at her. "You've gone red."

She fanned herself furiously. "It's just the heat." But her sister's interruption was welcome. She needed to stop imagining what would never happen and instead focus on her task at hand.

Smiling, she decided. That was what Miss Green had done. She'd smiled at the viscount, and he had smiled in return. It was a good trait to add to her list. Violet took her empty dance card and scribbled the word "Smile" upon the first entry. It wasn't as if she would ever be adding any names to the card, so she might as well put it to use.

Within moments, her brother and sister abandoned her. Charity had been asked to dance by a neighbor's son, while Daniel had gone to speak with some of his friends.

Violet envied them their escape, but she remained by her mother's side as ordered.

That is, until Lady Ross appeared. The older woman was Thomasina's best friend, and the pair of them had matching sour expressions while they gossiped about the *ton*. Violet started inching away from them to watch the dancing again. She saw another young lady walk past a handsome gentleman, and the lady exchanged a coy look with him before she dropped her fan.

The man picked it up, of course, and then they began to converse. Violet took out her pencil and scribbled "Drop fan" on her list. It intrigued her to realize that the women truly were not helpless or waiting to be asked to dance. They encouraged the man to join the chase. Fascinating.

What would happen if she smiled at a gentleman and dropped her fan?

He would likely pretend he hadn't seen it and would walk away. No man wanted a woman who couldn't even speak a single sentence without stuttering.

It wasn't as if she hadn't tried for years to overcome it. But the more nervous she became, the worse the stutter got. Sometimes around Charity, she could speak without one, but that was only because her sister knew her well and never teased her.

Her mother was still conversing with Lady Ross, so Violet seized her escape and pretended to go in search of lemonade. Along the way, she passed by another heiress, Lady Ashleigh, and a few other women she didn't recognize. Violet didn't miss their whispers, and without really meaning to, she lowered her head to continue walking past them.

Only to bump into a solid wall.

Violet bit back a yelp and realized that no, it wasn't a wall. It was Lord Scarsdale. How mortifying.

"S-s-sorry." She moved backwards so fast, she nearly stumbled.

He caught her elbow before she could fall toward the refreshments table. "Are you all right?"

I've nearly knocked over the most handsome man in the ballroom. No, I'm not all right. I want to crawl into a hole and die.

"I-I-I'm f-f-fine," she stammered, backing away without looking up. Oh, Lord, the stutter was worse than ever. Now she sounded like she couldn't speak at all. Could there be anything more humiliating than to bump into the most handsome earl in the room?

Behind her, she heard the titters from Lady Persephone and Lady Ashleigh. "G-g-good," Persephone answered. "Y-y-you should w-watch where you're g-g-going."

Her face burned, but Violet said nothing. She'd grown accustomed to their taunts over the years. The young ladies were not known for kindness, and they seemed to delight in their superiority over others. Instead, Violet hurried away from them, trying to regain her composure.

She found a place in the alcove where she took several deep breaths, calming herself. *You're not here to find a husband tonight. It doesn't matter.* And truthfully, Lord Scarsdale probably hadn't noticed her much. Violet rather hoped he would forget she was alive, which was quite possible.

When she glanced back at them, she saw Lady Persephone smiling warmly at Lord Scarsdale. He returned it as he handed her a glass of lemonade.

Everyone knew that the earl had been courting Lady Persephone for most of the Season. Her father was a wealthy duke, and she could have any man she wanted. And who wouldn't want the wicked Lord Scarsdale? Some whispered that Scarsdale's father, the Marquess of Trent, had fallen upon hard times. The earl would want to marry someone wealthy if that were true.

And Violet was definitely not in that category. She had enough pin money to afford her tuition at the school, but not much else. She was gambling her own future in the hopes that, somehow, she could find a husband.

She forced herself to watch them, wondering how someone as cruel as Persephone could get any man she wanted. The woman was never nervous or uncertain around gentlemen, and she moved around the ballroom as if she owned it. Confidence, Violet decided, was another attractive trait to gentlemen, and it was not one she had ever possessed. She scribbled the word "Confidence" on the empty dance card.

Didn't Persephone's suitors recognize her cruelty? Or did they just not care because she was beautiful? Maybe money was the key to finding a husband. Which made things even worse because Violet wasn't certain she even *had* a dowry. Her mother seemed to have given up on the idea of her finding a suitable match.

But there was still time. She might be a spinster, but there was always hope. She scribbled the word "Money" on the dance card and read it once again. It seemed that smiling, flirting, confidence, and wealth were the common elements of a popular heiress.

Was it possible that she could learn any of those? She saw another gentleman walking toward her. He was reasonably attractive and not too old at all. A reckless side of her wanted to act.

Don't do it, her brain warned. *This isn't a good idea.*

But she had to know. Was it possible that she could mimic the debutantes' behavior? She had watched them, jotting down notes about what they had done to capture a man's attention. What if she'd simply been sabotaging herself by remaining a wallflower all these years? What if...she attempted to smile at this man or even flirt? Would it work?

Violet ignored her brain's frantic attempts at common sense and heeded her heart's reckless urging. She would try it. What did she have to lose, after all?

And so, she stepped away from the wall and took a step closer to the gentleman. She lifted her chin and met his gaze. He appeared confused at first and glanced behind him. Then Violet smiled in welcome and deliberately dropped her fan.

The appalled expression on his face was like a physical blow. He saw the fan, looked back at her, and turned to walk away in a hurry.

Violet's spirits sank as she reached for her fallen fan. Her cheeks were burning, and she retreated to the alcove. Clearly, there was more to this than following a list of rules.

Though she knew it wasn't a good idea, she started watching the Earl of Scarsdale. He laughed at something Lady Persephone said, and Violet wondered what it would be like to have a man look at her in that way. It was such a ridiculous idea, especially after her most recent experience.

And yet...she longed for that sort of companionship. What would it be like to attend a ball with a husband, to smile at him across the room and see him return it? Perhaps dance with him, knowing that they would return home together later. She might rub his shoulders, and he might rub her feet if she was exhausted from dancing. She smiled wistfully at the image.

Lord Scarsdale led Lady Persephone to the dancers, and she was caught up by the sight of his hands upon the young lady. His gloved palm pressed against Persephone's back, and he stared into her eyes with bold interest.

Violet opened her fan, for it was growing warm in the ballroom. But even fanning the air did nothing to diminish her wayward imagination. For a moment, she envisioned that *she* was in the earl's arms. That it was his hand upon her waist, his other hand clasping hers.

His face was close to Persephone's while he spoke to her. If he moved any closer, he could steal a kiss from the lady. What would that be like? Violet wondered. She'd never kissed anyone before.

She sighed and decided to return to her mother's side, for she'd experienced enough longing for the evening. She had her list prepared for Mrs. Harding, and when she returned on Tuesday, she would bring it with her.

Just as she walked over to them, she overheard Lady Ross saying to her mother, "So have you made the arrangements yet?"

Arrangements for what? Violet took a slight step backwards, trying to remain inconspicuous.

"I have," her mother answered. "My mother-in-law is expecting her." With a sigh, Thomasina added, "Since she will never find a husband, I think this is the best solution for everyone. She will be a companion and care for Annabelle during her illness."

Violet stiffened, and she wondered if she'd heard her mother correctly. Thomasina planned to send her away? To be a companion to the grandmother who despised her?

"I imagine that will set your heart at ease," Lady Ross continued. "It's the perfect solution for everyone. When does she leave?"

"By Friday next," her mother answered.

Though she knew she ought to stay out of the conversation, Violet couldn't help herself. She approached the women, needing to know if it was true. "Who is l-leaving by F-F-Friday next?"

"Y-y-you are," her mother taunted.

Violet paled. No, this could not be happening. Not when she'd worked so hard to become one of Mrs. Harding's pupils. She could not imagine leaving London.

"Why?" she managed to whisper.

"Because your grandmother needs someone to care for her until she dies, and it will not be me. You have no chance of being married, so I believe this will suit everyone."

It doesn't suit me, Violet thought. But then, her mother hardly cared about anyone but herself.

"What about m-my dowry?" she whispered, trying to hold back hot tears.

"You won't be needing it. If I give your dowry to Charity, it will help her chances immeasurably."

Violet said nothing but lowered her head to stare at her feet. She didn't want to hear any more of this, for now the truth was clear.

Becoming a pupil at Mrs. Harding's School for Spinsters was her last and only hope.

CEDRIC EXCHANGED A glance with Rachel Harding. "What do you think?" They had been watching over Miss Edwards for the past few hours, unbeknownst to the young lady. Poor girl. He'd seen the way Lady Persephone and Lady Ashleigh had treated her. He felt sorry for Miss Edwards, but she might be beyond their help.

The widow appeared uncertain. "I think Miss Edwards has a lot of work before her if she wants to transform herself. She has no confidence whatsoever."

"Is it any wonder?" From the way her own family behaved, they treated the girl like dirt. "I can understand why she came to us for help."

Rachel was watching over the young girl, her face pensive. "I just don't know if it's possible. And I don't want to raise her hopes if she cannot do what is necessary to succeed."

Cedric agreed with her on that. But he admitted to himself that he did like the girl. He'd seen the way she'd tried to smile at a gentleman. And even though it hadn't worked, at least she'd made an attempt. She might have the courage that was necessary.

Mrs. Harding turned back to him. "Was there a gentleman whom you believe would suit her?"

The logical choice was a dull gentleman with few prospects. And yet, Cedric found himself wanting to play fairy godfather. What would Miss Edwards do with a gorgeous creature like the Earl of Scarsdale? Would she faint? Or would she rise to the challenge?

Though on the surface, it might seem like a ridiculous idea,

Cedric trusted his own instincts. He hadn't missed the way Miss Edwards had gaped at the man, and her embarrassment had gone deeper than the unexpected stumble. The earl had also been kind to her, despite the pair of predatory females who had shamed the young woman.

"Lord Scarsdale," he predicted. "He might suit."

"He's too far above her," Mrs. Harding predicted. "But I'm willing to think about it. Why did you suggest him, and what do you know about his background?"

"His father, the Marquess of Trent, has a gambling problem. He's relying on Scarsdale to marry well."

"Miss Edwards would not bring him the wealth he needs," she argued. "I'm not certain I agree with your choice."

Cedric shrugged. "She's not what he needs in terms of a financial transaction, I agree. But as far as a match?" His gaze focused on the earl. "I don't know. There's something there."

"I doubt it," she answered, "but he may be of use. When it comes to teaching her how to speak with handsome gentlemen, that is. Right now, she's far too nervous."

Cedric could see the wheels turning in her mind. There was no question Miss Edwards would be one of the greatest challenges Rachel had ever attempted. It would be a monumental undertaking. Yet, he wanted the spinster to find her own happiness. And whether it was with Scarsdale or another gentleman…time would tell.

"I'm going to find out more," he said, inclining his head in farewell before he walked toward Scarsdale. The earl was standing with a small group of men, along with Lady Persephone and Lady Ashleigh. Persephone stood closest to him with a half-smile on her face. The earl was also smiling, but it didn't meet his eyes. Instead, it appeared that he was merely putting on a façade of amusement. Cedric walked past them, but then he lingered nearby to eavesdrop.

"I THINK WE should have a wager," Lady Persephone was saying. "This evening is rather dull, don't you think?"

"And what is this...wager you're proposing?" Damian asked. He had a bad feeling about her suggestion, for there was a satisfied gleam in her eyes.

"I think you should ask Miss E-E-Edwards to d-d-dance," she suggested. "If she says yes, then you must dance with her and let her believe you are interested."

He didn't like her suggestion at all. Clearly, her intent was to make fun of the young woman, and he wanted no part of that.

"Persephone, that's cruel," Lady Ashleigh argued. "Why would you want to do that?"

At least one of the ladies had a conscience, Damian thought.

"It's not cruel at all," Persephone continued. "After all, she's dancing with Lord Scarsdale, one of the most notorious rakes in London. She should be fortunate to even have a minute of your attention." With a sly smile, she reached out to touch his arm.

He wanted to pull away, to chide her for suggesting something so petty. And yet, he knew that Persephone would only sulk and play the victim.

Part of him wondered what he was doing, courting a woman like her. Was she always so vindictive? He wanted to believe that Persephone was different in private. Perhaps she'd been so coddled, she had no idea how the rest of the world lived. Maybe she simply needed to break out of her spoiled existence and learn a little humility. If she saw the suffering that others endured, would that change her outlook? He wasn't certain.

Damian covered her gloved hand with his own. "You don't really want me to take this wager." As a distraction, he changed the direction of the conversation. "And you never said what I would win, if the lady refuses." He kept his voice low and teasing, as if he were hoping for a stolen kiss.

Persephone gave a musical laugh. "Why, you may pay a call upon me in the morning."

"Not good enough," he countered. "I was planning to do that anyway." He paused a moment, pretending he needed to think about it. "I know. You should tell your father that you've chosen me as a husband." He sent her a flirtatious smile, even knowing that it was too much to ask. He'd already formally proposed to her a month ago after asking the duke for permission. Unfortunately, Persephone was enjoying her role as the most sought-after debutante, and he sensed she had no intention of choosing a suitor yet. "We could be married by special license," he suggested. "Or I could steal you away to Scotland."

But Lady Persephone swatted him lightly with her fan. "It's entirely too soon for me to decide, and we both know it." Even so, he could see how delighted she was at his suggestion. She believed (mistakenly) that he found her irresistible. But he hoped the conversation had successfully diverted her attention away from tormenting Miss Edwards.

"How much more time do you need?" he asked lightly.

"I'm not certain," she teased. "But perhaps you could show your devotion to me by taking my wager."

It irritated him that she still wouldn't let it go. And so he countered, "It's a boring wager." Not to mention cruel to the girl. Though he kept his tone light, he shook his head. "I'm sorry, but I'm not interested."

Lady Persephone was pouting at his dismissal. "And what would it take to gain your interest?"

He shrugged. "I've already answered that question. And besides, I don't believe in humiliating young women."

Persephone's expression soured at his refusal. But then, a moment later, her face shifted, and she changed her tone. "I don't know, Lord Scarsdale. I think you should reconsider asking her to dance. Miss Edwards *is* a lovely woman, after all."

She wasn't listening to him, so he decided to put a stop to her ploy. He wasn't going to be a part of her vindictive plans.

"Nothing in this world would make me interested in dancing with Miss Edwards. No matter what you might say." He wanted that to be perfectly clear, and then he saw Ashleigh wincing. From behind him, he heard a slight gasp.

Then he realized why Persephone's face had widened in a delighted smile. He turned around, and Miss Edwards's stricken expression made him feel like he'd taken a blow to the stomach. "I d-d-don't want to dance with you either, s-sir." Then she hurried away toward the terrace.

Damn it all. Now he'd hurt her feelings, and the young woman knew nothing of why he'd said it.

Lady Persephone laughed gaily, as if she loved this turn of events. "G-g-goodness me," she mocked.

Damian kept his face neutral, though it took an effort not to reveal what he thought of Persephone's cruelty. Although her dowry was enough to solve every financial problem, was it truly worth it? He was starting to wonder. Was she truly that selfish and coldhearted? Or was it ignorance? Regardless, he had to be careful. Persephone held the power to end his family's debts with one wedding vow.

Damian quietly excused himself from the ladies and went to find Miss Edwards, intending to apologize. It was probably an exercise in futility, but he wanted to try. She'd only overheard part of the conversation, and in that moment, he'd sounded like an utter bastard.

Well, he probably *was* an utter bastard, but he still hadn't meant to hurt her feelings. His words had come across far more malicious than he'd intended. She might not accept his apology, but he wanted to find her and at least explain what he'd meant by the words.

He looked around for some sign of Miss Edwards and started to walk toward the terrace. Outside, it was dark, and there were a few couples strolling in full view of the doors. Somehow, he doubted the young lady would venture alone into the darkness of shrubbery.

Instead, he followed his instincts and turned down a small hallway where he found her crying in the corner. The sight bothered him deeply, and he knew he was the cause of her tears. He'd never meant to insult her, and seeing her cry made him feel like he'd kicked a puppy.

Damian hesitated a moment, wondering how to begin. If she saw him approach, she'd likely run away. And so, he kept his footsteps light, hoping he could apologize from a short distance and then leave her alone.

He saw a crumpled dance card upon the floor. Likely it was hers. He bent to pick it up and then tucked it in the pocket of his waistcoat. He started to take another step toward her when someone seized his arm. He turned and saw his father. Jonas glared at him and shook his head. "Come with me."

"I was just—"

"You were about to ruin all our plans, weren't you?" The marquess gripped his arm and led him back down the hallway. Damian stiffened, but he followed his father for the sole reason that he didn't want Miss Edwards to overhear the marquess's thoughtless remarks. She'd been through enough.

"I won't have you insulting the daughter of a duke while apologizing to that bit of nothing in the corner." Jonas was slightly unsteady on his feet, and Damian could smell the brandy on his father's breath.

"Your sisters are depending on you," his father continued. "Unless you marry well, they have no dowries. No fortunes."

"They would still have their dowries if you hadn't gambled the money away," Damian said beneath his breath.

But his father heard him and laughed. "Haven't I been trying to win it all back? One day, I might succeed."

"All you do is lose," Damian said. They were so deeply in debt, he'd pleaded with his friends to prevent his father from playing cards again. He'd spoken to the gaming hells and clubs, promising to pay them back, as long as they did not let the marquess enter. Some had agreed, but others had simply ignored his request. Because of it, his mother had been forced to quietly sell off her jewels.

"The only thing you have of value is our family name," Jonas continued. "My title will pass to you, and your bride's wealth will restore it all." His father clapped him on his back. "You have your choice of the ladies. Choose wisely. But not the Edwards brat. Never her."

His father swayed slightly before he went in search of refreshments. Damian waited until he'd gone, before he turned to walk back toward Miss Edwards. The lady was no longer weeping in the corner, but she remained in the shadows, out of the public view.

In a low voice, he murmured, "I am sorry for what I said, Miss Edwards."

"No, you're n-not." She stepped forward until she stood beside him. "You m-meant every word of it."

"You didn't hear what I said before you arrived—only the last part. I had no interest in dancing with you for the sake of a wager. That's not fair to you."

She grew quiet for a time, so much that he turned back to look at her. Wariness was stamped on her face. "I don't believe you."

"It doesn't matter whether you believe me or not. I am sorry that you misunderstood me, so I'll apologize for that. But I won't apologize for not wanting you to be humiliated. No one deserves that."

"Are you finished?" she asked.

"Not quite. Take my advice and stay away from Lady Persephone and Lady Ashleigh," he said. "They're not your friends."

"I am w-well aware of that." She cleared her throat. "And neither are you."

He probably deserved that, even though she didn't believe him. Her flare of courage quickly died away when he continued to stare. Miss Edwards glanced down at her feet and turned away to disappear into the hallway.

After she'd gone, Damian turned his attention back to the ballroom. He'd done what he could to apologize. If she despised him, so be it. His father had been right. His greater concern right now was to find a wife who could help dig them out of the mountain of debts. His sisters were counting on him.

And he could not fail in this.

Chapter Two

Three days later

VIOLET RETURNED FROM afternoon tea, only to find her maid Elsie packing a trunk with all her belongings. "W-what is happening?"

"Mrs. Edwards said I should pack for you," Elsie answered. "You're to leave for Bedfordshire in the morning."

Bedfordshire? Horror washed over her at the prospect. How could this be happening so soon? Her mother had given her no warning whatsoever, aside from the conversation Violet had overheard at the ball a few days ago. She'd been convinced she would have at least until Friday next to make her plans. But tomorrow?

"W-why so s-soon?" she asked. The fear and disbelief twisted her stomach into a knot.

"Because Mrs. Edwards says you might as well leave now. Your grandmother needs a companion to feed her, dress her, and help her use the chamber pot," Elsie answered.

"Why me? She could hire a maid for that."

Elsie shrugged. "I don't know. But she wrote to Mrs. Edwards about it, weeks ago."

So, they had been planning this for some time and had not told her. Of course, they hadn't; they didn't want her to have any alternatives.

Thank goodness, she hadn't told them about Mrs. Harding's school. They would have died of laughter and forbidden her to leave the house. Violet couldn't risk them learning about it. And now, she would have to throw herself upon the mercy of Mrs. Harding in the hopes that the headmistress would let her stay.

"Are they still attending a ball tonight?" she asked.

Elsie nodded. "But I don't know if they...mean for you to come."

Honestly, Violet was more than happy to stay behind. "Oh." She tried to pretend as if she were disappointed. Inwardly, she was rejoicing, for this was an opportunity.

In the meantime, she would have to protest, cry, and then feign reluctant obedience to her mother's plans. Thomasina would be suspicious otherwise. But when her mother left for the ball, Violet had every intention of making her escape.

The greatest challenge would be hiring another coachman to take her to Mrs. Harding's establishment. If she asked her own driver to bring her there, her mother would know where she'd gone and demand that she return.

It had to be someone they would never see again. Perhaps a hired hackney. And if she wanted to escape, it had to be tonight. She would wait until they had all gone and then order the driver to take her to Mrs. Harding's residence.

Her heart was pounding at the thought of all the things that could go wrong. "After my mother and sister have left, tell a f-footman to bring my trunk downstairs," she ordered Elsie. "B-beside the front door."

Elsie appeared uncertain about the orders, but she nodded. "I'll ask Mrs. Edwards."

"No, don't. Just have the footman do it after they're gone." Her escape plans would be difficult enough to manage without having to bring the driver inside to fetch her trunk. Better to have it waiting by the door.

Elsie folded the last petticoat, leaving only a nightgown, and a traveling day dress for the morning. She paused a moment and said, "Mrs. Edwards didn't say that I am to go with you."

Violet shook her head. "N-no. You w-won't go with me."
Especially not where she intended to go.

"I'm sorry about this, Miss Edwards. Is your grandmother so terrible then?"

Violet only nodded. "Worse than y-you can imagine."

She thought back to the last time she had seen her grandmother at Christmas. Their family had been invited to a holiday ball, and Violet had been rather excited about it at the time. There would be festive music and gifts exchanged. Annabelle had come to visit, but while Violet had begun preparing for the ball, her mother had said, "You can put your gown aside. You're not going any longer. You'll stay with Annabelle instead. She has decided she's tired and wishes to stay at home."

"But why do I have to stay with her?" Disappointment had welled up within her. "Couldn't she simply return to her bed?"

"She needs someone to watch over her, and it won't be me," Thomasina had answered. "You're going to ensure that Annabelle stays out of trouble."

Disappointment had weighed upon her shoulders, for this was the only ball she'd been looking forward to. But she'd resigned herself to the fact that the grandmother she barely knew might need her.

Hours later, after everyone had left, she went to join her grandmother in the parlor. Annabelle still wore black, for she'd been in mourning for years. Though she pretended to be feeble, there was nothing frail about her mind.

Violet murmured a greeting, and her grandmother demanded, "Speak up. My old ears don't hear as well as they used to."

"I-I said g-good evening, G-Grandmother."

Annabelle gave a sigh of disgust. "After all these years, you still cannot speak properly?"

Embarrassment made Violet's cheeks burn. What was she supposed to say to that?

"I thought you'd have grown out of all that by now, but you

haven't, have you? I can see why your mother didn't bother taking you to that ridiculous ball. No one will wed a girl who cannot speak and can't even look anyone in the eyes. You'll never marry anyone, will you?" Annabelle raised her chin, and her blue eyes glared at Violet. "Now if you had been my daughter, I'd have ordered someone to slap you every time you stuttered. *That* would fix the problem. Spare the rod and spoil the child. That's what Thomasina's done."

Violet started to turn away, hoping to escape to her room, but Annabelle hadn't finished yet. "Sit down."

She didn't want to, but she had the feeling that matters would only be worse if she left. Instead, she chose the seat furthest away from the woman and wished fervently that she had embroidery of some kind. Any kind of distraction was welcome.

"Look at me," Annabelle commanded.

With reluctance, Violet did. Her grandmother stared at her and said, "You're terrified of everyone and everything, aren't you? I think there's little chance you'll marry. Unless you find another idiot who has even less money than my son did. Heaven knows, Arthur was never anything but a wastrel, God rest his soul. I *had* hoped that marriage would change him, but..." Her voice trailed off with an angry sigh. "Obviously, I was wrong. And it seems that there's no hope for you, either. Unless there's a backbone buried in there somewhere? I doubt it."

"Y-you're wrong," Violet blurted out. "I still have t-time to find a husband."

"And with a little more time, pigs might sprout feathers and wings," she taunted. "No, my girl. You'll come live with me until I die. And one way or another, we'll beat that stutter out of you. You might have bruises for a time, but I promise you, eventually, you'll stop."

No doubt she meant it. Her grandmother lived like a pauper, but she did have several servants who were paid to obey her wishes—and they wouldn't hesitate to follow Annabelle's orders. God help her, Violet had to find a way to escape and avoid living with her grandmother. Otherwise, she would suffer beatings every time she opened her mouth.

Somehow, she would find a way to escape. And the sooner, the better.

"How bad is it?"

Damian sat across from his friend Graham, idly tracing the rim of his pewter cup. "He went out last night. I'm not sure how much money he lost." Damian slid a bank note across the table. "Take this and invest it in one of your ships."

"You can't afford this, Damian."

"I don't see another alternative," he pointed out. "We're going to have to sell off all our possessions. This money is mine, and if the investment pays off, it may help my mother and sisters."

He wasn't going to wait around for his father to lose everything. It was only a matter of time, and this investment was his last, desperate hope of saving them.

"It's a risk," Graham pointed out.

And he knew that. But Graham Hannaford hadn't become one of the wealthiest men in London by playing it safe. Damian trusted his friend.

"Let me see if I can find a safer investment," the man offered. "Something that is guaranteed to turn a profit."

"There may not be time for that," Damian answered. "Just use your judgment."

Five hundred pounds might not earn a large profit, but he had to start somewhere. He had to distance himself from his father and make his own living. And it wasn't as if he could go out and find employment elsewhere.

A grim sense of foreboding settled in his gut. Whether he liked it or not, his father was right. Marrying an heiress was the quickest solution to his problem. And though he personally thought Lady Persephone and Lady Ashleigh were spoiled brats, they *were* wealthy brats.

He despised being dangled like a fish. But what other choice did he have? Only last night, he'd caught his mother weeping alone in the dining room. He'd let Clara be, knowing she didn't want to be seen. But he had to do something. And if that meant sacrificing himself, so be it. But in the meantime, he intended to fight back against his father's gambling.

"I hope this will be profitable for you," Graham said.

"So do I." He raised his cup in a toast, and then his friend stood to depart.

"I will take care of this today," Graham said. "Thank you for your investment."

After his friend departed, Damian finished his drink. He was about to leave when another gentleman stepped forward. The man was fashionably dressed in a single-breasted, russet-checked coat, a tan waistcoat, and dark trousers. In one hand, he carried a black walking stick.

"Lord Scarsdale," the man greeted him. "I am Cedric Gregor. Our paths may have crossed a time or two. We were both at Lady Shelby's ball the other night, I believe."

Damian thought he might have recognized the man but wasn't certain. "Perhaps."

Without asking, Mr. Gregor sat across from him. Then he handed him a card with an address printed upon it. "I realize this is…unusual for me to be approaching you. But I think I could be of some help. I understand your father has fallen on hard times."

"It isn't polite to eavesdrop," Damian said and didn't take the card.

"It's not eavesdropping when it's common knowledge." Mr. Gregor met his gaze. "I have a possible task for you that would be financially beneficial, should you take advantage of my offer."

Damian recognized a potential swindler when he saw one. The man had obviously witnessed him investing in Graham's shipping venture and thought he would try to do the same.

knocked on the door. Her stomach twisted with fear, and she stared down at the threshold.

What if she doesn't take you as a student? What if she sends you home?

She didn't want to think of that, for there was nowhere else to go. No, she would find a way to convince Mrs. Harding to let her stay. Even if that meant begging on her hands and knees.

The door opened, and the footman greeted her. "I'm sorry, is Mrs. Harding expecting you?"

Violet paused and forced herself to meet the man's gaze. "I am Violet Edwards. I m-met with the headmistress last week, and sh-she told me to r-return. I've b-b-brought my belongings, and I intend to start l-lessons."

The footman's gaze held doubt. "Mrs. Harding has no students at this time."

"B-because *I* am her s-student," Violet argued. Her cheeks were turning crimson, but she forced herself to stand taller. "May I come in?"

He paused a moment as if considering a refusal. But since her coach had already gone, he relented. "Very well. I will see if she is receiving." He opened the door wider, and she followed him inside. Then he led her to a small drawing room she had not seen the last time she was here. "If you'll just wait here."

Violet chose a chair, and she overheard him speaking to another servant, ordering him to bring her trunk inside. Her nerves deepened, and she clenched her gloved hands together. She had made it this far, but what would happen now? Would Mrs. Harding agree to take her as a pupil? Where could she go if the matron refused? Her fears multiplied, intensifying as time went on. It was nearly a quarter of an hour before Mrs. Harding finally entered.

Violet stood from her chair, forcing herself to look at the woman and brave a smile she didn't feel. Slowly, she took a breath, forcing back the stammer. "Good evening."

Although the words were slow, she was proud of herself for

not stuttering. Mrs. Harding motioned for her to sit down. "Why are you here, Miss Edwards?"

"I've…" She forced herself to slow down again, and she never took her gaze from the widow. "…come to s-start lessons."

"Have you? I don't believe I've formally offered you a place as a student. You were given a task to complete first." The woman's voice was cool, reminding Violet that she'd arrived on the doorstep with no warning at all. She was all but trespassing.

Violet's first instinct was to lower her gaze and her shoulders, but she sensed that Mrs. Harding would not approve. "Y-you asked me to attend a b-ball." Her stutter returned with a vengeance, and she said, "I did what you told me to do. I observed the popular l-ladies and saw w-what they were d-doing. They were s-smiling at the m-men. F-f-flirting."

"I am glad you noticed. But Miss Edwards, just because I gave you a task does not mean I've accepted you as a student." Mrs. Harding's warning was clear enough.

Violet pulled out her reticule and laid a stack of guineas on a side table. "I can p-pay."

"This isn't about money," the widow argued. "What you're asking me to do is a monumental transformation." She gentled her tone and added, "I know you want to find a husband. And though you may not have found one yet, there *are* men who do not mind a stutter."

"I've run out of t-time. M-my m-mother is sending me away to Bedfordshire," Violet said. "S-she wants m-me to be a c-companion to m-my g-g-grandmother."

"Oh, I see."

"N-no, you d-don't. My g-grandmother b-believes that she can b-beat the stutter out of m-me. I c-cannot go." The tears rose up in her eyes, and she struggled to maintain her composure. "I-I-I just c-can't."

Mrs. Harding reached out and took her hand. With that kindness, Violet's defenses crumbled. She let the tears fall, though she tried to hold back the ragged sobs. "I've n-n-nowhere else to g-go.

P-p-please."

The widow offered her a handkerchief. Violet took it, but it felt as if her life had been upended. "I w-will do anything you ask."

Mrs. Harding let her cry, and after the tears had drained from her, Violet felt utter exhaustion. "I'll give you a place to sleep tonight, and we will talk in the morning. For now, you may remain here."

She was grateful for any kindness at all. After she dried her tears, she took a deep breath and calmed herself. Mrs. Harding rang for a servant, and when the maid arrived, she ordered, "Take Miss Edwards to one of the bedchambers. She will be staying with us tonight." To Violet, she asked, "Have you eaten?"

She nodded. "A f-few hours ago."

"All right." To the maid, she added, "Lucy, have Cook prepare some chamomile tea and biscuits, and bring them up after you have prepared a room."

"Yes, Ma'am." Lucy bobbed a curtsy and then waited for Violet expectantly. She rose from her chair with the handkerchief clenched in her palm.

Just before she followed the maid, she paused at the doorway. She kept her words slow, trying desperately not to stutter. "Th-thank you, Mrs. Harding."

As she departed the drawing room, she took note of the house. There was an air of peace here, the servants quietly performing their duties. She followed Lucy and noticed that the house was far larger than she'd imagined. Though it seemed like an ordinary townhouse, there were many rooms. She glimpsed a music room on one floor and a ballroom on another. The staircase continued up another flight and the maid brought her to a small bedroom that overlooked the street.

"I'll just light a fire, Miss," Lucy said. Within a few minutes, the room had a cozy warmth, and Violet went to stand before it.

For the first time, she felt as if she could breathe again. If she did everything Mrs. Harding demanded, she fully believed she could become someone else.

And perhaps one day, she would have a husband and family of her own.

Chapter Three

RACHEL WAS BUSY scribbling a list when Cedric arrived at the house. She hadn't expected him for hours, but his presence was welcome. "You're early. There's tea in the pot over there." She waved in the general direction of her half-eaten breakfast.

She'd awakened at six, unable to sleep any longer. She needed to plan out Violet's lessons and decide what materials were required and when. Yet, no matter how many lists she made, the tasks kept mounting higher.

Cedric came up behind her to read over her shoulder. "I thought Miss Edwards wasn't returning until tomorrow. I'm still making arrangements with Scarsdale."

Rachel set her pen down. "She stayed here last night. Apparently, her mother was planning to send her off to Bedfordshire to be a companion to her grandmother—a woman who believes that beatings will cure Miss Edwards's stutter."

"Ouch," he remarked. "So, we're her last resort, then."

"We are. But I'm still not certain we can help her. She doesn't seem to understand the magnitude of it all." Rachel turned to her list, wondering where to even start. Although she understood what the young woman wanted, this was not a situation where she could be encouraging or gentle. She needed this woman to find her anger, to be enraged at the sort of life she had. Only then would she have the courage to transform herself.

"Where will you start?" he asked.

"It will take the longest time to help her control the stutter," she admitted. "I've written a letter to a few people who might be able to assist. But I need her to understand that this will be the most difficult challenge she's ever had. She's going to cry. A lot. And it will not be easy."

Though Rachel knew what was needed to succeed, she hated hurting anyone at all. But then, she could help no one by being kind. It went against her nature to cause anyone pain, but she'd learned for herself the power of anguish. Suffering could be used as motivation because it would cause someone to fight back.

She set down her pen and regarded Cedric. "Miss Edwards will have to be broken before we can rebuild her into the woman she wants to be. Until she will never again slouch her shoulders or look at the ground. She will have to be enraged and find her power from that."

"The way you did," he said softly.

His words struck her deep, and a hollow ache caught her in the stomach. Absently, she rubbed her arm, the one her husband had broken during one of his drunken rants. "Yes." After a time, she added, "I know this will work, Cedric. But it doesn't mean I'll like doing it." With a halfhearted sigh, she said, "I'm sure she believes this is about wearing pretty dresses and walking around with a book on her head."

He reached out and touched her hand, offering silent comfort. "She needs Scarsdale to make her angry. He's perfect for this task. But I'll need money to tempt him. His father's gambling is bringing his family into ruin. I spoke with him earlier, but he's reluctant."

She hadn't been able to decipher very much about the earl, except that he flirted a great deal. But if anyone could coax a reluctant gentleman into doing his bidding, it was Cedric. "Use your ruthless side if you must."

That did evoke an answering smile. "I don't have a ruthless

side, and we both know it."

Rachel wasn't so certain. "If we're going to transform Miss Edwards into a confident debutante who can win any man she desires, we'll need to use every means possible. Are you certain Scarsdale can help her?"

"I cannot say. But I have another person in mind who would be a great deal of use, if you mean to break Miss Edwards down. I spoke with her a few days ago at the ball. She may be exactly what Miss Edwards needs." He shared his thoughts, and Rachel privately agreed that it would indeed be helpful.

"See to it," she ordered. "Tomorrow, if possible. But again, why do you think Scarsdale is the right person for her lessons about men?"

"She's furious with him. He said he had no interest in ever dancing with her."

Her hope faded, for he sounded like entirely the wrong sort of man. "Cedric, that sounds cruel."

But he only smiled. "What Miss Edwards didn't hear was that the others only asked him to dance with her as part of a wager. They wanted him to humiliate her, and he refused."

Her opinion of him improved slightly. "Well, I suppose that's better."

Cedric folded his arms across his chest. "I would never choose the wrong sort of man. I do know what you're looking for and why."

Rachel didn't miss the wistfulness in his voice. And though many didn't understand Cedric's preferences, she silently hoped that he would find the happiness he wanted. "See to it that Scarsdale comes here every morning. And he must be discreet. There can be nothing to threaten her reputation."

"You're going to take her as a student, then?"

"I am." *Heaven help her.* "I will give her one day to settle in and that will give us time to make the necessary arrangements. We begin tomorrow."

"WHAT ARE WE going to do, Damian?" His sister Melanie sat across from him at the breakfast table. "The debts are getting worse." She passed him a stack of letters. "I took these from mother's escritoire."

He glanced over the letters. All were overdue bills. One from the grocer, another from the shoemaker, and as he glanced through them, the amounts ranged from three pounds to twenty. None had been paid for months.

"I don't think the servants have received wages either," she confessed. "I overheard Mary talking about finding another position." His sister grew somber. "Should I...try to find work as a governess?"

"No." Damian took the stack of bills. "I will speak to the merchants and see what can be done." Although the simplest solution was for him to wed a wealthy young woman, that would take time.

His mind drifted back to the offer Cedric Gregor had made. One hundred pounds was indeed a generous offer, but why had the man suggested so much? It sounded entirely suspicious. And what role did Miss Edwards play in all this?

"We have to stop him," Melanie said. "I've tried talking to Father, but—"

"He's not going to change his ways," Damian answered. But neither did he want his family to face the humiliation of poverty. Reason wouldn't work with the marquess. The longer he stayed in London, the worse Jonas behaved.

"I think he and Mother should go north, to Scarsdale," he suggested. At least the marquess couldn't spend quite as much money there. "The air might do him some good. And Mother, too," he suggested.

"How will you talk him into it?" Melanie asked. "He won't go."

"I'll lie to him," Damian answered. "I'll tell him that I had a letter from a distant cousin about inheriting money. He'll go to claim it."

"And when the money isn't there?"

"It would still give us a fortnight," he reasoned. "Perhaps even a month if I can get Mother to join in the ruse."

Melanie paced across the room, wondering aloud, "If we can manage it, that will give us a little time to begin paying the bills. I have some things I could sell."

"Some of the paintings could go," he suggested. But inwardly, he was considering Cedric Gregor's offer. He wanted to know more about it, to fully understand what role they wanted him to play and how it related to Miss Edwards. The man had mentioned helping her, though Damian couldn't imagine how.

He reached into his waistcoat pocket, tracing the folded dance card. He should have tossed it days ago. He had no idea why he'd kept it. Perhaps because it represented a young woman's hopes.

Why was he even thinking of helping Miss Edwards? She was the very opposite of the woman he needed. He'd already decided that Lady Persephone was his strongest prospect. Her dowry could solve all his problems. And if she was a stubborn, spoiled woman, what of it? He could manage her well enough, despite her tantrums, if they lived separate lives. The last thing he should do was intertwine himself with another woman who barely had a penny to her name. Yet, he couldn't stop thinking of Mr. Gregor's offer.

Melanie was talking of what else could be sold, and her face held nothing but worry. "Mother thought I should have new gowns this year, but I really should send them back."

He forced himself to pay more attention. "Keep the gowns, Melanie. I'll find a way to pay the modiste."

It would take several months for his shipping investment to pay off, but in the meantime, there were ways to tighten the household accounts. He would look into his father's debts and talk to the debtors. Even if he paid small amounts in the beginning, it might help.

One hundred pounds would help more, his brain reminded him.

Why was he even considering this? He had the courtesy title of earl, and his family would be appalled if he entered into an arrangement like this. He knew nothing about Miss Edwards or Mr. Gregor. The man could be lying to him or hoping to entangle him in scandal of some sort.

But what if he *was* telling the truth? Whatever they wanted, they were willing to pay handsomely. He ought to pay a call and find out what it was. If nothing else, he could gather information. But no one could know. Discretion was everything.

Damian took out a piece of paper from the escritoire and began to scribble a hasty note for Mr. Gregor. It was too soon to make a decision; at least, not until he spoke with the man and fully understand what he wanted. But if Gregor agreed to pay off some of the bills—Damian would consider it.

"Damian, there's something else I need to tell you," Melanie continued. "Mother is...acting as if nothing is wrong. When I tell her we have no money, she behaves as if everything is fine. She's talking about my Season next year, but I know it can't happen."

"She doesn't want to face the truth," he said softly. And he didn't want to be the one to shatter the dream Clara was living in.

"But our time is running out. She can't go on like this."

"No," Damian agreed. "I'll try to talk to her." But now, it often felt that he had become the parent while the marquess and marchioness had become the children.

He didn't know how he was going to fix this, but if that meant humbling himself and finding work, he would do all that was necessary.

"Regan will return home from school soon," Melanie continued. "Should we make arrangements for her not to go back?"

"Not yet. It's better if she doesn't know about this." He didn't want their twelve-year-old sister to be aware of their financial troubles. "I'll take care of it."

"I want to help you," Melanie insisted. "Just tell me how."

"Help me convince our parents to leave for Scarsdale," he insisted. "I just need time, that's all."

"All right." She came closer to the desk. "What are you writing?"

"A letter to one of the merchants with a promise to pay them soon," he lied. Quickly, he folded the note to Mr. Gregor and sealed it with a bit of wax.

Melanie eyed him as if she didn't quite believe him. "Damian, what are you planning?"

"I'm planning to get us out of trouble," he said easily. "And with any luck, you'll be able to have that Season next spring."

"You don't have to marry Lady Persephone," his sister said quietly. "She's a terrible person."

"She's a duke's daughter and is the wealthiest heiress," he remarked. "I'll manage."

"She's arrogant and mean," Melanie countered. "I don't want her for a sister."

He stood from the writing desk. "You don't have to see her often. I'm the one who will encounter her the most. And women like her usually only want attention and money to spend."

"I don't like it. You deserve someone who will love you, Damian."

"Love is a myth," he countered. "Enjoy your fairy stories, Melanie, but don't imagine that they're real." He could never imagine falling in love with a young lady, much less Persephone. His best hope was that they could find a way to live together peacefully. That would be enough for him.

"Perhaps not," she hedged, "but if you can find a way to avoid marrying Persephone, that would be best."

"Then whom should I marry?" He was amused by the idea of her picking out a wife for him.

"Someone kind, who takes care of you. Someone you want to take care of," she offered.

Strangely, the image of Miss Edwards flashed into his mind

again. Her brown eyes had held anguish, and he'd wanted nothing more than to ease her pain. He closed his eyes, forcing the image back.

"Someone with a large dowry," he continued.

"That should be last on your list." Melanie took his arm, and they left the room. "But if you wed for money, you'll be miserable. That much I know."

"I may be miserable," he acceded, "But you will benefit from it. So, if my family is cared for, that's all that matters."

His sister squeezed his arm. "Find someone else, Damian."

He only smiled. But strangely enough, when he tried to think of another woman, the only face he could envision was that of Miss Edwards.

"ALL RIGHT, LET me look at you."

Violet stood tall, keeping her gaze upon Mrs. Harding. The widow walked a slow circle around her, and she stopped often to write notes.

"W-what should I d-do first?" she asked.

Mrs. Harding finished writing and then took out a clean sheet of paper. She passed it to Violet. "I want you to write down the sort of husband you want but can never have."

She blinked a moment. Now why would she want to do that? At her frown, Mrs. Harding continued. "You aren't going to be the same woman after this. You might as well choose something different."

Violet picked up her pen and dipped it in the inkwell. As she started to write, she grew amused. Of course, this would never happen. Men never even noticed her. But she wrote:

1. Handsome
2. Kind
3. An earl or a duke

4. Someone who adores me

"Why are you smiling?" Mrs. Harding asked.

"B-because, as you said, it will n-never happen." As she set her quill down, the image of Lord Scarsdale came to mind. He was most definitely handsome and an earl by courtesy title, but kind and adoring? Hardly. Yet, her idiotic imagination made her daydream of dancing with him. She thought of those deep green eyes burning into hers while his palm rested against her spine. The very thought sent a thrill beneath her skin.

"You may be right," Mrs. Harding said. "But for now, I've arranged for your first lesson. The dancing master will teach you how to move with grace."

She flushed, as if the headmistress had suspected her forbidden thoughts. Instead, she locked them away and faced the woman. "All right." Dancing *was* something she secretly loved, even though she rarely had an opportunity for a partner. Today would be a good day, Violet decided. She would enjoy the dancing, and she would master the steps. At least now she was doing *something* to improve herself. She was not trapped in a coach on the way to Bedfordshire where she would face daily beatings.

"I have another young woman who will be joining you in the lesson," Mrs. Harding said.

It surprised Violet at first, but then she supposed it made sense. This was a school for spinsters, and there were other ladies who wanted to transform themselves.

"Come into the ballroom. They are waiting for you to join them."

Violet followed Mrs. Harding, and the matron held the door open for her. "You will both learn from Mr. Brown. I will return for you in an hour for the next lesson."

"You're not staying?"

"I *do* have other responsibilities," Mrs. Harding remarked. "Now go inside, and perhaps you might learn something."

Violet took a step inside the ballroom. The other young woman was standing with her back to the door, and she wore a light blue gown. When she turned around, Violet bit back a groan of horror. For it was Lady Ashleigh.

Why was the young woman here? Violet could not believe her eyes. Ashleigh could wed any gentleman she wanted. What was happening?

"Hello, Miss Edwards," Ashleigh greeted her. She had a slight smirk on her face. "Or should I c-call you V-violet?"

The flare of rage caught her off guard, but she knew if she opened her mouth, the stutter would return. Instead, she held her tongue and glared at the young woman. *I'm not going to give her the satisfaction.*

Mr. Brown acknowledged her with a nod. "Good afternoon, Miss Edwards. I was just telling Lady Ashleigh that I will be teaching you both a country dance. Now face one another with your shoulders back. Chin up."

Ashleigh was still smirking at her. "Do you even know how to dance? I've never seen you with a partner at the balls."

Ignore her, Violet thought. Instead, she straightened her shoulders and pretended as if Ashleigh didn't exist.

"Now take each other's hands," the dancing master continued.

Violet froze at that. She had no desire to take Ashleigh's hand. But Ashleigh grabbed hers, pretending as if it didn't matter. It was awkward and awful, having to promenade with a young woman who hated her.

Why was this happening? Or, at the very least, why couldn't she have a gentleman partner? Not Lord Scarsdale, of course, but someone kind.

After learning a few more steps, Mr. Brown began to play the pianoforte. Ashleigh moved with a natural ease that revealed she'd been dancing for most of her life. Violet stiffened by comparison, and though she knew she took the right steps, her enemy's presence had stolen the joy from the lesson.

"W-w-why are you here?" Ashleigh taunted. "I suppose you didn't have a choice, did you? No man would want to m-marry s-someone like y-you. You're the worst of all the s-s-s-spinsters."

Rage gathered up inside her, along with tears. Violet was fighting to control them, but why did this horrible young woman have to be here? Why didn't Mr. Brown tutor Lady Ashleigh in her own home? She frowned, feeling like there was something quite wrong about this situation. It made no sense at all for Ashleigh to be here.

But then, an even worse thought occurred to her. What if Ashleigh told someone about this lesson? Her family might find out where she was in hiding.

"Go ahead and cry," Ashleigh taunted. "I know you want to." She took Violet's hand and gripped it hard as they moved through the dance steps.

A wayward tear *did* escape, though Violet tried to hold it back. And then, all her emotions came spilling out. She couldn't stop herself from crying, not only because of this hateful person, but because she was truly out of other options. She didn't have anywhere else to go. If she failed at this, she would be trapped with her grandmother for the rest of her life. Her tears were not because of Ashleigh's taunting—it was because the woman's words were true.

No one wanted to marry her. They believed her stutter would be passed on to any children, so the men ignored her. And, although Violet enjoyed dancing, she had only ever danced with her brother and a few men that her mother had somehow arranged. Which, of course, didn't count.

When they reached the end of the line, Ashleigh stuck out her foot at the last second. Violet couldn't stop herself in time, and she hit the floor hard.

"Oops," Ashleigh said. "I guess I took the wrong step." She held out her hand, but Violet didn't take it. Instead, she swiped at her tears and stood up. The dancing master made no mention of her fall, nor did he ask if she was all right. Instead, he continued on with the lesson as if nothing had happened.

It only got worse from there. Ashleigh continued teasing her, making fun of her stutter until Violet retreated inwardly. She stopped listening to the young woman and blocked her out. Even so, she took missteps and fumbled with the movements.

When the hour was over, she had never been more grateful. Ashleigh eyed her on the way out and said, "I think you're wasting your time, Violet. And your money. This will never work."

Violet said nothing at all. She followed them out to the hallway, feeling as if she'd undergone a round of fisticuffs. But she'd never risen to Ashleigh's bait, so at least she could be proud of that. She'd barely spoken at all.

After she was alone, she was about to return to the stairs when Mrs. Harding suddenly emerged. "Shall we discuss your first lesson?"

Violet had no desire to do so, but since she had no choice, she nodded. "All right."

The matron led her back into the sitting room and closed the door behind her. Then she motioned for Violet to sit down, and she chose the seat across from her. "How did you think the lesson went?"

Violet shrugged. "I knew parts of the dance, but others were new to me. I did the best I could."

Mrs. Harding's expression remained calm. "So, you thought the dancing was your lesson?"

At that, Violet faltered. If the dancing wasn't the lesson, then what was it? For a moment, she thought about it, and then clarity dawned on her. "It w-was Lady Ashleigh, wasn't it?" Mrs. Harding had done this on purpose. Somehow, she had convinced Ashleigh to come here and taunt her. But why would she do something like this? It made no sense at all.

The widow nodded. "And how did you respond to her?"

She paused, wondering what the woman meant by that. "I d-didn't let her teasing b-bother me."

"You cried," Mrs. Harding responded. "I saw the entire lesson from the adjoining room. The door was cracked, so you probably didn't notice."

A wave of uncertain emotions washed over her. For a moment, she didn't know what to say. She couldn't understand why Mrs. Harding had set her up to be mocked in such a way.

"But I-I didn't answer h-her."

"You failed badly," the widow said. "Just as I expected you would." She sighed and folded her hands. "I was hoping things would be different."

Her cheeks flared with embarrassment. "I b-b-barely spoke to her."

"You let her run over you, and you never once stood up for yourself. Why did you never respond? Why did you allow her to say such things to you?"

"Because sh-she would only have t-taunted me more. I didn't w-want that." Her emotions started rising higher, and she felt accusing eyes upon her.

"You're going to face girls even more vicious than Ashleigh. You will have to be stronger than that, and you cannot let them get away with it."

Violet didn't know what to say. The thought of talking back to one of the cruel girls was horrifying.

"You've let others run over you your entire life, haven't you?" Mrs. Harding mused. "Do you think Lady Ashleigh or Lady Persephone would allow anyone to do that? Do you think if another girl tried to be cruel, they would let it stand?"

"They're t-terrible girls," she muttered.

"But they are strong. And they get what they want." She stood from her chair. "I'm not saying you have to be rude or cruel. But if you continue to let others step all over you, you'll have to get used to being in the mud."

"I don't...know how to d-defend myself," Violet confessed. It was the truth. Never in her life had she dared to talk back to anyone. Not that her words would have been any sort of weapon.

Every time she felt fear, her stutter grew even worse.

"Keep it short," Mrs. Harding advised. "Learn to use your eyes, and your body language. A great deal can be said without many words."

She waited for the widow to tell her more, and when she said nothing else, Violet asked, "And w-what if they m-make fun of me?"

"Oh, they will. Be assured of it. That is why you will practice here. And you will fail, again and again. Until one day you stop caring whether you fail."

Violet's spirits plummeted at the thought. Mrs. Harding had likely read her thoughts, for the matron reminded her, "You chose to come here. You asked me to teach you how to get the man you want. But the truth is, until you decide you're worth having, no man will want you."

The widow walked to the door. "There are things you must learn that I cannot teach you. All I can do is give you the opportunity to practice."

"So, she's coming back," Violet said.

"Among others," Mrs. Harding agreed.

"What if she tells my mother where I am?" Violet asked. "I need to remain here in secret."

"Oh, Lady Ashleigh and I have an arrangement. She will tell no one, rest assured." Mrs. Harding turned the doorknob and looked back. "If you decide this is too difficult for you to endure, you can give up any time you like. But if you are willing to fail, you might learn something."

Chapter Four

THE NEXT AFTERNOON, the earl waited in the public house until he saw Cedric Gregor approach. The man had a slight smile on his face, as if he knew Damian's choices were limited.

"Scarsdale," he greeted him with a nod. "I'll admit, I was glad to receive your note."

"I haven't agreed to anything," Damian reminded the man. "I only wanted more information."

"Of course, of course," Cedric agreed. "I suppose you're wondering about our mutual acquaintance, Miss Edwards. And how, exactly, we want your help."

He was indeed wondering what connection the gentleman had to Miss Edwards. It seemed strange, somehow. Could he be her relative? And what did Cedric mean by "we"?

"I'd heard that Miss Edwards had left town." There were vague rumors that she had gone to be a companion to her grandmother.

"In a manner of speaking," Cedric agreed. "She left her parents' house to attend our school."

A school? This wasn't what he'd expected. Damian waited for the man to continue, but when Cedric said nothing else, he asked, "Why did you approach me? And why did you offer such an ungodly sum?"

Gregor regarded him for a time as if deciding whether to tell him the truth. Then he said, "I overheard you apologizing to Miss Edwards at Lady Shelby's ball. No one else would have done such a thing."

"It was manners, nothing more."

The man was stalling, but Damian remained patient, steepling his hands. Eventually the man would have to admit his reasons.

And finally, he did. "Miss Edwards is in need of a husband."

Damian gaped, but before he could say a word, Gregor continued, "Not you, of course. I'm well aware of your circumstances. And your father's . . . excesses. Which is why I thought you might be willing to help her."

His tension abated somewhat, though he still didn't understand what the man wanted from him. "Are you asking me to play matchmaker?" He couldn't think of anyone less suited to such a thing.

"No, not at all. Miss Edwards, as you might have guessed, has few options when it comes to marriage. She wishes to change that, and we have agreed to help her. But she will never gain a husband while she remains a stuttering, shy wallflower."

"I still don't know what you want from me."

"Let me put it to you this way," Gregor continued. "If she wishes to wed, she will have to learn how to talk to a gentleman. She needs to be more at ease."

"Then let her choose a gentleman whom she might actually wed."

"That's not what we want at all," the man responded. "We want someone she would never wed in her wildest dreams. Someone she doesn't like."

At that, Damian was slightly taken aback. Essentially, they had chosen him because Miss Edwards despised him. And he wasn't certain how to feel about that.

True, he'd insulted her without intending to. And she hadn't accepted his apology at all. But he wasn't accustomed to being disliked by anyone. Flirting with women was usually one of his greatest skills.

Damian narrowed his gaze. "What precisely are you expecting me to do?"

"Have a conversation with her so she can make mistakes. We want her to stutter as much as possible until she gets angry enough to start fighting back."

He was starting to understand what they were doing. "You want me to be the target of her anger."

"Exactly so. Her stutter grows worse when she's nervous or upset. You should provoke her, let her lash out at you. She should be able to say anything to you with no repercussions."

It was a strange sort of proposition, one he'd never imagined. "And what do you want me to say to her?"

Mr. Gregor raised his cup in a mock salute. "I don't care what you do or say. So long as she can hold a conversation with a man after you're through with her. Even better if her stuttering improves."

"For how long?" he asked.

"At least one week," Gregor answered. "Every day for an hour." When Damian gave no answer, the man continued "I want you there in the morning." He described a tailor shop within walking distance of where a coach would be waiting. "No one can know about this, or it will compromise her reputation."

And his own, Damian thought. He didn't want to risk being trapped into marriage with Miss Edwards. He took a moment to question the wisdom of this. It was a reckless risk to be entangled with her. The wisest thing to do was refuse. And yet, the bills were looming over them.

"One hundred pounds for a week?" he mused.

"One hundred pounds for a month," Gregor countered. "If you help her every day during that time."

That wasn't nearly worth it for the sum. "A fortnight," he bargained, "with the option for a greater amount if she succeeds."

Gregor extended his hand, and he shook it. "By the end of the fortnight, I'll wager that you'll *want* to stay longer."

He stood from his chair and passed Damian a scrap of paper with an address written on it. "You'll start tomorrow."

"I haven't made a decision," he hedged, uncertain if he wanted to start this soon. Especially when he didn't know if the man would keep his word.

"She needs a great deal of help," Gregor responded. Then he reached into his pocket and pulled out a bank note that had already been written for ten pounds with Damian's name on it. "We have to start as soon as possible."

It seemed the man had already predicted he would say yes. Though this wasn't how Damian had planned to earn more money, he was willing to entertain the possibility. And at least it was something discreet. "If I do help Miss Edwards, it will be for a trial period. I won't agree to another fortnight until after that." He paused a moment and then asked, "Does she know about this?"

Gregor shook his head. "She'll be horrified when she finds out."

"Good." And with that, Damian pocketed the bank note and departed.

"WE'RE GOING TO try something new today," Mrs. Harding said. "You need to learn how to be more commanding in your presence."

Not Ashleigh again, Violet thought to herself.

The matron signaled to a servant, and to her surprise, Violet saw a young dog on a lead. She couldn't stop her smile, for she had never owned a dog before.

"Oh, he's b-beautiful," she breathed, kneeling down to pet the dog. He was a mixed breed, colored brown with splotches of white on his face and torso. His tail wagged with enthusiasm, and he rolled to his back so she could rub his belly.

"He's untrained and needs a firm hand," Mrs. Harding explained. "You may keep him, as long as you can get him to obey you."

Now this was a task she was going to enjoy. She already loved the idea of owning her own dog. Violet stood, and the puppy instantly jumped up on her, putting his paws on her skirts.

"No. Down," she ordered. Of course, the dog ignored her and scampered in wild circles.

"He has not been fed this morning yet," Mrs. Harding said. "I suggest you use his breakfast as a training tool. When he obeys you, reward him with food. But only one piece at a time," she cautioned.

The servant handed over a dish of meat scraps, and Violet took it. Instantly, the dog began running in circles, panting with joy.

"I'll leave you to it," Mrs. Harding said. "But take him to your room. Train him there. In three days, if he is starting to obey, you may keep him. If not, he will go." From the woman's firm tone, Violet believed her.

"I w-will," she promised.

"You must practice being in command," she insisted. "Only reward him with food when he is being good. Oh, and there's one more thing."

Violet gently pushed the dog's paws aside and waited. Mrs. Harding added, "You will have a caller later this morning. A gentleman caller."

Her complexion whitened, for she wasn't at all ready for that. "D-don't you think it's too soon?"

"I think you are going to need a great deal of practice before you're ready to venture back into the ballroom," Mrs. Harding said. "We may as well start immediately."

A sense of anxiety welled up inside Violet, and her nerves tightened. A moment later, the headmistress turned back. "You needn't be afraid. I chose someone who has no interest in you. This is about practicing, not attempting to win his affections."

Though she supposed the words should have put her at ease, it only reminded her of how no one wanted her. This wasn't going to go well. She didn't know the first thing about talking to a gentleman. "What am I supposed to say to him?"

"He will have a list of lessons, but I will leave the conversation up to him. Your task is to be in command and not turn into a wallflower. Step outside of your shadows and be yourself," Mrs. Harding said softly. "Your *true* self."

"And what if he doesn't like who I am?" *What if no one does?* Violet thought to herself. She was too accustomed to not talking. The idea of spending time with a strange gentleman was, quite frankly, an awful prospect.

The dog began jumping up again, pawing at her, but Violet pushed him aside. If she could barely control a dog, how could she ever succeed in gaining a husband?

Or perhaps that was the point. She couldn't.

"As I said before, I don't expect him to like you," Mrs. Harding replied. "That's not what this is about."

"Then what is it about? I don't understand what you want from me. I'm not ready to have a gentleman caller."

"You're not ready for any of it," the matron responded frankly. "But you came to me, and you begged for my help. You're just upset because I'm forcing you to face your fears."

The woman was right, but Violet admitted, "I didn't expect it to be like this."

"I told you it wouldn't be easy," Mrs. Harding said. "If you want to leave, just say the word."

Her spirits dimmed at the thought. No, she didn't want to leave. But she hadn't expected her lessons to be about facing those who wanted to hurt her. She'd mistakenly believed that the School for Spinsters was about fixing her stutter and her appearance so men would be interested.

Instead, it was about breaking her down and making her worst nightmares happen. She felt emotionally bruised, and the thought of a gentleman caller made her dread the day even more.

As a distraction, she turned her attention back to the dog. He continued circling her and licked her palm when she bent down.

"I've nowhere else to go," Violet admitted at last. "I suppose you might as well do your worst if you think it will help me."

Mrs. Harding straightened. "I do want to help you, Miss Edwards. But more than that, I want you to find out who you truly are. After that, you shouldn't care what anyone else thinks."

Violet picked up the fallen lead to take the dog with her. "I'm going to t-take him into the g-garden instead and work on his training there," she said. "Send word to me when the caller has arrived."

"I would prefer if you—"

But Violet continued to walk away. If Mrs. Harding wanted her to learn to be assertive, she might as well begin now.

And when she risked a glance behind her, she saw the matron smile.

Damian had been given a single instruction from Mr. Gregor while he waited in the conservatory. *Argue with her.*

He still wasn't certain he should even be here. He'd gathered from a servant that Mrs. Harding's school was actually the infamous School for Spinsters. The headmistress Mrs. Harding was helping Miss Edwards to improve herself.

But why did they want him to antagonize the lady? What was the reason for arguing or making her angry?

Abruptly, he heard the skittering of paws approaching, along with, "Rupert, heel!"

The dog ran to him, his tail wagging with joy, and he planted his paws on Damian, licking his hands. Immediately, Damian stood and commanded, "Down."

The dog ignored him at first, but then he repeated in a stern tone, "Down."

With that, the animal sat. He seemed to be considering

whether to bolt, but Damian lifted his hand in a silent command to stay.

"I'm s-so s-sorry," he heard Miss Edwards say.

But when he turned around, she appeared mortified. "Oh, no. Not you."

"The very same," he said. "Did you miss me?" He couldn't resist the urge to tease her.

"Not at all," she answered. With a sigh, she muttered to herself, "Of course. It w-would be you. Who better to torment me?"

Damian gave a light bow. Her expression held frustration, but her brown eyes gleamed with annoyance. She was wearing a light blue day dress and her brown hair was caught in an updo. There was nothing unusual about her appearance, except for a single daisy that she'd tucked behind her ear. Something about the incongruous flower made him wonder more about her.

"So, you've come to study at the infamous School for Spinsters, I see."

"Don't make f-fun of me," she warned. "I have my reasons."

So did he. Financial reasons that he wasn't inclined to discuss with her. He pulled out a chair and gestured for her to sit. "Very well, then. Shall we begin?"

"Begin what?" She sat down, eyeing him with wariness.

"I have been given orders to argue with you," he said. "For an hour at least." He chose a chair and sat across from her. "What shall we argue about?"

She stared at him in disbelief as if she couldn't believe what he was saying. Her consternation heightened when he pulled his chair closer. "I know," Damian decided. "Let's discuss the sort of gentleman you want for a husband. I can argue with you about your choices. Tell me what you're looking for."

"I am *not* d-discussing that with you."

"Excellent. See, we're arguing already." He smiled at her and realized he was enjoying this lesson. In a way, it was liberating being able to say exactly what he wanted to without restricting his conversation. There were no games, no rules, save one.

Provoke her into arguing.

Miss Edwards bit her lip, and her cheeks held a flush. But instead of engaging in the argument, she glared at him. Her scolding expression brightened her features, and as he waited for her reply, he noticed that she did have a lovely face. Her brown eyes held hints of gold and hazel, and her pursed lips only drew his attention to them. Her upper lip was slightly larger, and the pinkish tint contrasted against her pale skin.

For a moment, he wondered what was going on inside her head. He leaned back in the chair and crossed his hands behind his head. "Well, go on, then. Which gentleman do you want to marry? Are you hoping to wed some boring knight or a baronet?" he ventured.

She let out a sigh. "You're going to k-keep asking, aren't you?"

"Of course." He saw no reason to deny it. "Why wouldn't I? It's a fascinating conversation, and one that lends itself to a great deal of arguing."

She studied her gown, smoothing out an invisible wrinkle. "I don't want boring, but I also don't have m-much of a choice."

"That's not entirely true," he remarked. "There are some men who will pursue anyone in skirts. Especially those who do not have an heir and are nearly eighty."

"I don't want a man old enough to be my grandfather," she said. "Teeth *are* a requirement."

He did laugh out loud at that. "And what of walking? Does it matter if he has a cane?"

She glanced at the ceiling as if appealing to the saints for patience. "No." Then she frowned and shook her head. "Yes. That is, I-I would want him to be at least mildly attractive."

"So, you don't want to close your eyes during your wedding night."

"We are *not* speaking of w-wedding nights," she said. "Or anything else of that nature."

He'd meant only to tease her, but somehow, he suspected

that Miss Edwards had indeed daydreamed about her fictional wedding night. It made him wonder if there was any passion beneath her soured expression.

"Then what sort of man *do* you want?"

"Someone kind," she admitted, softening her voice. "Someone who doesn't care if I s-stutter." She reached down to pet the dog. The animal turned his head to lick her palm, and she rewarded him by rubbing his ears.

"I don't think all men would care about your stutter," he said truthfully.

She let out a snort of disbelief. "Of course, they do."

He wondered if she'd noticed that her stutter had diminished during their conversation. "Actually, I think it's your shyness. You don't talk to anyone. You don't even look at anyone."

She did look at him then, and in her eyes, he saw the heartache. "That's not true. I *have* tried to t-talk to men. They turn their backs on me."

He didn't know what to say to that, so he tried to turn the conversation in a different direction. "Well, one thing is clear. You definitely don't want a man like me," he said lightly. "I'm the very opposite of kind."

"True," she agreed. "And what's w-worse is that you tease."

"I do." He saw no reason to deny it. "There's no need to be serious. I have a reputation of a notorious rake to maintain." The words sounded hollow, even as he spoke them. The truth was, his days of enjoying vices were over. He had no right to drink, gamble, or enjoy women when his family's livelihood was crumbling.

But Miss Edwards surprised him when she leaned forward and demanded, "Tell me, why *do* women l-like you?"

He nearly laughed at the question and then realized she was asking a genuine question. "I suppose it's because they enjoy my company. Some find me handsome, though to be honest, I'm only average." He thought a little longer and decided to provoke her once again. "It might be because I'm rather good at kissing."

Her eyes widened for a moment before she shook her head. "I don't believe you."

"Well, it's a little early for a demonstration. We really don't know each other that well."

He winked at her, and she rolled her eyes. "Could your vanity be any w-worse, Lord Scarsdale? Do you think every woman wants to kiss you? Much less m-marry you."

"Why? Doesn't every woman want a husband who can kiss her until she swoons?" Although he was still teasing, he admitted to himself that he *was* curious about kissing Miss Edwards. How would she respond to a kiss? Would she panic and pull away? Or would she surrender, giving herself over to the moment? He had a feeling that she had a hidden, sensual side.

"Kissing doesn't make you swoon." Despite her denial, her cheeks held a flush. "N-no man could do that."

"I could," he argued. *Depending on where he kissed her.* But though he was tempted to say it, he refrained from embarrassing her further. "Suffice it to say that, given enough time for thorough kissing, I believe that I *could* make a woman swoon." Especially if the kisses were in more intimate places.

At her look of disbelief, he acknowledged, "Well, it's not as if you'd want me to *show* you what I mean. You'll have to take my word for it." He studied her closer, noting the soft flush of her cheeks. "Have you ever been kissed?"

"Of course, I've been k-kissed."

Her flush deepened, and he said, "On the lips?" She looked away, and he had his answer. "Unless you were kissed on the lips by a man, it doesn't count."

She shrugged. "I think you're only boasting."

"You asked me why women liked me. I answered your question, that's all."

She crossed her arms and regarded him. "Why are you really here, Lord Scarsdale? Was this part of the wager you mentioned the other night?"

He hadn't thought she would draw that conclusion, but it

made sense. "No, not at all." He regarded her and added, "Would you believe that I want to help you?"

She shook her head. "N-not in a thousand years."

Damian had no intention of telling her the truth, that he was completely out of funds, and they had offered to pay him so he could reduce some of his father's debts. Instead, he answered, "I have my reasons."

He was beginning to understand what Mrs. Harding and Mr. Gregor were trying to do for this young woman. Miss Edwards was held back by her timid demeanor, and she needed to be more commanding. Arguing with him forced her to speak her mind. And the more she challenged him, the less conspicuous her stutter became.

The dog rolled to his back, exposing his stomach. Miss Edwards knelt to pet him, and the animal wiggled with delight.

"Is this your dog?" he inquired.

"N-not yet, but he will be. I am training Rupert." She stopped petting him, and the dog rolled over and jumped up with his paws on her shoulders. He licked her face, and Miss Edwards started to laugh.

It was the first time he'd heard her laugh, and the unfettered happiness lit up her face. Her brown eyes gleamed with warmth, and her smile transformed her. A wayward lock of hair fell against her cheek, and she tucked it behind the daisy. For a moment, he wondered whether her hair was as soft as he thought. What would it look like around her shoulders?

A better question—what would *she* look like after she'd been thoroughly kissed with a man's hands running through that hair? He forced the thought away, for it would never happen.

"Training, hmm?" He glanced at the dog who was still trying to jump on her.

She pushed him down and defended the dog. "I've only just started t-today," she said. "Rupert doesn't know anything."

"I think he knows more than that," Damian predicted. "He knows you'll let him do whatever he wants."

"That's not true." She put his paws down and picked up the leather lead. "S-sometimes he obeys me."

This time, she withdrew a dried piece of meat as a distraction. Before she could offer it, Damian cautioned, "Make him wait for it." She slid a glance at him and then turned back to the dog. When he tried to jump up, she pulled back the treat.

"No," she said quietly. It took some time, but after he gave her his full attention while seated, she rewarded him with the meat. The dog wolfed it down and danced in a circle, his tail wagging madly.

"Have you ever owned a dog?" he asked. She shook her head, which was what he'd already guessed. "I've had dogs my entire life. And while they can be good companions, you must show him who is master. He cannot obey some of the time. He must obey *all* of the time."

"He's l-learning," she said.

"And he can learn," Damian agreed, "but you must be firm with him." To demonstrate, he lifted his hand and caught the dog's attention. Immediately, Rupert froze. Damian held the dog's gaze for several seconds before he rewarded him by rubbing his ears.

"Now you try," he said. "Take your hand like this." He reached for her gloved hand, and she flinched the moment he touched her.

Then he realized what he'd done. "I'm sorry, Miss Edwards. I should have asked you first."

She relaxed at that, and he decided to be frank with her. "If it makes you feel any better, I wasn't trying to make you uncomfortable."

"Because I am the very l-last person you'd ever want to dance w-with," she said, repeating the words he'd used against her on the night of Lady Shelby's ball. "Yes, I know." Her words held the edge of resentment.

So, they were going to be honest with one another. It was as good a start as any. "As I said before, I don't believe in humiliating women in public. That was what they wanted me to do, and I refused."

"B-because dancing with me would be t-too embarrassing."

"No, that wasn't the reason."

"But it is," she insisted. "Everyone w-would wonder why an earl like you would d-dance with someone like me. And they would laugh."

He paused a moment, trying to think of what to say in response to that. "I don't know if they would pay much heed to it."

She gave a wan smile. "I've been t-teased all my life, my lord. I'm used to it." Her stoic acceptance bothered him, for it seemed that she'd already given up.

"Then why are you here?" he asked. "If you are used to being tormented by the *ton*, then why would you attend this school? What do you hope to accomplish?"

Her cheeks reddened at the accusation. "I want to change myself. I would l-like to believe that I can be something more than I am."

Her words sobered him. And while he wanted to reassure her that she could indeed change herself into whatever she wanted, he couldn't make that promise.

For he hadn't been able to do that either.

Chapter Five

V IOLET SAW THE sudden shift on the earl's face, as if he didn't believe it was possible for her to change. And though he was probably right, she had to do something. Nothing she'd done so far had attracted any man's notice.

"Has there ever been anyone you wanted to marry?"

She shook her head. Out of nowhere, a sudden rise of loneliness caught her, and unwanted tears filled her eyes. The last thing she needed was to cry in front of this man. He knew nothing about her, and this would only make him believe she was even more pathetic.

"Did I hurt your feelings?"

His voice was entirely too kind, which made her even more frustrated with herself.

"N-no."

"Then why are you crying?"

"I'm not crying," she insisted. "There's no r-reason to cry."

Only that no man has ever wanted you, her heart mocked. *Why would you be sad?*

He handed her a handkerchief, but she waved it away and swiped at her eyes with her gloved hands. "I'm f-fine." To change the subject she asked, "Why *are* you h-here, Lord Scarsdale? I'm certain you have p-places to be."

His expression tightened, and he shrugged. "Perhaps I shouldn't have come. But I was intrigued by the idea, I'll admit. Does your family know you're here?"

"No. And you won't tell them, either." She sent him her sternest glare, though beneath it was her own fear that he could completely undermine her plans.

"And what if I do?" The wicked look returned to his eyes, making her wonder if he was trying to provoke her.

"Don't you dare." She straightened in her chair, though truthfully, what could she do except warn him? She was entirely at the mercy of his discretion, which frustrated her to no end.

"I could." He leaned back, a lazy smile on his face. "Is there a reason why you're in hiding?"

Though she suspected he was teasing, she leaned closer. "My f-future depends on these lessons. You will not take that from me."

He rested his wrists on his knees and leaned closer to her. "I rather like you this way, Miss Edwards. You're far more interesting when you're angry." He reached out and slid his thumb down the edge of her jaw. The unexpected touch shocked her, and her skin warmed beneath it.

"I'm serious," she said, pushing his hand away. "My mother w-was trying to send me away to be a companion to my g-grandmother. She believes that if I am b-beaten each day, my s-stutter will go away."

At that, he sobered. "So, you ran away."

She shrugged. "Not exactly. But I am very s-serious about these l-lessons."

For a long moment, he studied her, and she didn't look away. "I have my own reasons why I agreed to help you. But I promise that I will tell no one that you are here."

His green eyes held a solemnity, and she believed him. They came from opposite worlds—every woman wanted him while no man wanted her. He was the handsome nobleman, and she was the ordinary girl with the stutter. But despite everything, she

there was ⌐
would he agree to help ⌐
Harding or Mr. Gregor.

"What is it you want to learn the most?" he asked softly.

She blinked a moment. "I need to l-learn how to stand up for myself. It was a-awful the other night at Lady Shelby's ball." Persephone had unsheathed her claws that night, and Violet had been utterly unprepared for it.

He inclined his head to acknowledge her words. "What would you have done differently?"

"I-I don't even know." She gave a helpless shrug. "They h-hate me."

"That's not true," he countered. "You don't exist to them."

The words were harsh, but he was right. She didn't exist to the ladies, nor anyone else for that matter. She had become invisible to the *ton*. But how could she even begin to make her presence known?

"When I go b-back, they'll only tease me m-more," she predicted. Ladies like Persephone and Ashleigh had no qualms about teasing others. They enjoyed the power over her, of lifting themselves up while putting her down.

"Probably." The earl shrugged as if he fully expected it. "The only way to avoid that is to be seen with someone important.

how hard I try," she admitted. There were days when she could speak several sentences without stuttering and others when it seemed that every other word was a battle.

"Maybe not. But you let it control you. I suppose you believe that if you didn't have a stutter, everything would be better."

"I don't know. But it c-couldn't be worse." She reached down to pet the dog, drawing comfort from his presence. Rupert turned to lick her hand, then wagged his tail and put his paws back up on her skirts. This time, she gave him a disapproving look as she pushed his paws away. "No," she ordered.

The dog appeared contrite and sat a moment before lowering his head. She felt badly for scolding him and reached down to rub his stomach.

"Do you want my help?" he asked in all seriousness. "Or is this uncomfortable for you?"

She glanced back at him, wary of whatever it was he meant to suggest. "That depends."

"I *could* truly help you," he said. "If you're willing to listen to my advice."

"You don't understand," she argued. "You're not a w-woman. You don't know how cruel they can be." To him, young women

like Persephone and Ashleigh were feminine and lovely crea-
tures...whereas Violet had only ever known them as her
tormenters.

"I know what Mrs. Harding wants you to do. And if you can
succeed, it will make a difference. Not only toward finding a
husband, but more about finding your own confidence."

"And you think you can t-teach me?" she asked. Now he was
the one with overconfidence. She knew her limitations, and he
could never understand.

"I know I can."

"How?" He spoke of finding confidence as if it were choosing
a new dress to wear. She'd endured over twenty years of her own
failures. Did he believe he could simply snap his fingers and
change everything about her?

"When you walk into a room, you need to draw attention to
yourself."

"I do that already w-without even trying," she remarked drily.
"Every time I open my mouth, I draw unwanted attention."

He tilted his head to the side, studying her. "Come with me
to the door. I'm going to show you what I mean."

She leaned back in her chair in silent defiance. "Do you honestly believe that the w-way I w-walk into the room will make a
difference?" She already knew it would do nothing at all.

"It could. But it's also the way you command the room."

She already knew she would be a complete failure. She had
no title, no wealth—what right did she have to behave that way?

"Just try," he commanded, studying her. "I want to watch
you."

At that, she faltered a moment, but he didn't take his gaze
from her. He watched her as if she were a lady whose attention
he craved. And Violet noticed his deep green eyes, the strong line
of his jaw. She couldn't stop her blush, but she did stand from the
chair. Her nerves heightened with every second he watched her.
"Stop staring at me." She walked toward the door, taking her
gaze from him. Why was she even doing this? What good would

it accomplish?

"You'll need to get used to men staring at you if you can overcome your fear." His words only made her nerves worse, for he almost sounded as if he were attracted to her.

"I will always b-be afraid," she admitted. "That will n-never change." But he kept his gaze on her, and it rattled her feelings.

"Pretend you're not afraid, even though you are," he urged.

Violet raised her chin, deciding that it was best to get it over with. She stared back at the earl as she walked. For a moment, she pretended to be someone else, a woman of worth. She kept her posture straight and walked with confidence she didn't feel.

But when he smiled at her, it made her question why he was here again. Though he said he had his reasons, she couldn't help but wonder if he *had* agreed to a wager of some kind. Was this part of an elaborate joke? The thought made her withdraw into herself. By the time she reached his side, her shoulders had fallen, and her gaze was upon the floor.

"You started out well, and then you turned into a wallflower again," he remarked.

"I *am* a w-wallflower," she snapped. This would never work. She didn't know why she'd played along with his game.

"Well, stop being one. This time, walk into the room and stare at me as if you want to murder me."

"That won't be difficult." She turned around and went back to the door. This time, she glared at him and strode across the room. "Better?"

"Indeed," he pronounced. "But you really do look like you're planning to kill me."

Violet did smile at that and tamped back an unexpected rise of laughter.

"Should I be afraid of you?" he ventured. "Are you truly contemplating murder?"

"I might be." Once more, she turned and went to the door. She strode across the room with purpose. Although some of her anger was gone, she did manage to imitate the sort of walk Lady

Persephone might assume.

"Could you walk like that in a ballroom filled with people?" he asked. "Especially with Lady Persephone and Lady Ashleigh taunting you."

Her expression faded as she imagined it. "P-probably not." Those women knew how to get under her skin, to make her feel like a nobody.

"Why? Because you're afraid of them?"

He really wasn't mincing words, was he? But to be truthful, she didn't even know if she could set aside her fears and confront the women. "I don't like them," she answered. "They make m-me feel small."

"You don't have to like them. But you will need to confront them. Put them in their place if they are rude."

"It's impossible. They're h-horrible."

"Then you might as well give up now. Pack your bags for your grandmother's house."

She straightened and glared at him. "So I can empty her chamber pots and endure daily b-beatings for my stutter?"

He shrugged. "Only if you let them. Which, given how you tend to let others run all over you, it isn't surprising that they'll succeed."

His words cut her down in a way she'd never imagined. For someone trying to help her, all he was doing was making her angry. And she'd had her fill of it.

Violet reached for the dog's lead. "I think we're finished here."

He walked to the door and then turned back. "Until next time, Miss Edwards."

And with that, he left.

"IT's GOING WELL, isn't it?" Cedric Gregor paused at the doorway. "Admit it. I was right about Scarsdale."

"You weren't wrong," Rachel answered. She had overheard bits and pieces of their conversation, and the earl had most certainly challenged Miss Edwards. And best of all, the young woman hadn't backed down. It was progress indeed.

"I've been thinking," Cedric continued. "It's been three years now. Don't you think—"

"I'm not ready." She knew he was wanting to play matchmaker for her. "Put the thought from your mind."

"Not all men are like your husband," Cedric said gently. "I could find a gentleman who is kindhearted. You needn't even remarry. You could have a sordid affair." His voice held teasing as he approached her desk. "You *are* a widow after all. You can do as you please."

"If I intend to remain headmistress of the school, an affair is the last thing I need." The very thought of a man touching her again was terrifying. It had taken an entire year to realize that she was free of her husband, that Anthony wasn't coming back. She had resigned herself to the fact that she would never remarry or have a man in her life again.

"A friendship then," Cedric suggested. "One day, you may grow bored of this school. You might want a companion."

"Then I shall have a cat," she said, raising her chin to look at him. "If you are the one who wants a companion, by all means seek out your own affair."

His face turned wary. "Rachel, you know how dangerous that is."

"But you have been *my* companion for the past year. People likely believe that we are together. You do escort me to many of the balls."

"People know that we are not together," Cedric said softly. "But I do want you to be happy, Rachel. You've given me a home, employment I adore, and I am content with it."

"So am I," she insisted. But from the gleam in his eyes, she wasn't so certain he was going to let this go. "Cedric, do not try to play matchmaker with me. Swear that you won't."

"I cannot swear that I won't look," he hedged. "I wouldn't be who I am if I didn't look among the gentlemen of London." He grinned and sat down in a chair, leaning upon her desk. "But I know you're lonely. I see it when you think I'm not watching."

He was right in that. At night, she sometimes dreamed of what it would be like to know love or passion. It was hard to indulge in matchmaking when she had never experienced it herself.

"I promise I won't do anything until you're ready," he said. "But when you are..."

She only smiled. "Eternity is a long time, Cedric."

VIOLET DIDN'T LIKE the earl. Not at all. Though she'd known Mrs. Harding would use an unconventional means of helping her, she'd never imagined they would ask Lord Scarsdale to become her torturer. Or worse, that he'd accept their offer. She still didn't understand why.

Violet picked at her breakfast food, wondering whether he truly intended to come back. He'd been teasing in his demeanor and honest that he didn't think she'd succeed. It made her angry. No, she wasn't a confident young woman. The idea of walking across a ballroom with all eyes on her was nothing short of terrifying. But somehow, she would have to set her fears aside to become someone else.

Mrs. Harding entered the dining room and cleared her throat. Before she could speak, Violet asked, "Is Scarsdale returning today?"

The woman's expression never changed. "I have brought Mr. and Mrs. Pettiford to meet with you. They await you in the music room."

It wasn't an answer to her question, but she supposed it was the woman's way of telling her not to ask. Violet stood from the breakfast table and thanked the footman who cleared away her dishes. She followed Mrs. Harding to the music room where she found an older, bearded man waiting for her. A woman sat at the pianoforte, presumably his wife.

"Miss Edwards, let me introduce you to Mr. Pettiford," Mrs. Harding explained. "He is an excellent singing instructor. His wife Mrs. Pettiford will be accompanying you."

Singing? The very thought was ridiculous. She couldn't sing.

"I-I'm not…that is, I can't s-sing."

"Everyone can sing," Mr. Pettiford answered. "But in your circumstances, it will be especially beneficial."

"W-why?" She didn't understand his reasons for being here. A sudden horror washed over her. Mrs. Harding did not intend for her to perform at a musicale, did she? Although it was something ladies did often, the last thing Violet wanted was to be the center of attention.

"You cannot stutter when you sing," Mrs. Harding said. "It is physically impossible." Violet continued to stare, feeling dumbfounded. Before she could think of any answer, the headmistress continued. "In order for you to begin diminishing your stutter—it will not go away entirely—you will spend the next three days singing. If you need to communicate at all, you must do so by singing."

It took an effort to keep her mouth closed. "S-singing? All day?"

"All day," Mr. Pettiford agreed. "You won't be going out in public, so while you might feel foolish, only the household will hear you."

"I have already told them what to expect," Mrs. Harding said. "They are not to obey any of your requests unless you sing for them."

"But I . . . don't know any s-songs," Violet protested.

Mr. Pettiford laughed heartily. "But that will be the fun of it. You may choose any tune you like and set whatever words you want to say to music. Though it might seem ridiculous, you'll spend three days in liberation from your stutter."

Violet couldn't even imagine it. And yet, the idea of even a few hours without being held prisoner by her voice was intriguing. Then she thought of having to sing, and her face flushed with embarrassment.

"I think it's time we begin," Mr. Pettiford said. Mrs. Harding excused herself and closed the door. The singing instructor turned to his wife and said, "My dear, let us begin with scales. I think we'll start in E major."

It took a moment to match her voice to the notes, but he had her sing a series of vowel sounds. To her surprise, her voice flowed easily over the notes.

"Don't be shy, Miss Edwards," Mr. Pettiford urged. "Put more air behind your notes and sing louder. You do have a lovely voice. Share it with us."

She did, and it was like listening to a stranger. Never in her life had she heard her voice without a stutter, and it *did* feel as if she were someone else. To her surprise, her voice didn't sound as terrible as she imagined. It wasn't bad at all.

During the next hour, Mr. Pettiford took her through the scales. Then he gave her a piece of sheet music. "This song has many words and phrases that might give you trouble when you speak. But they shouldn't be a problem when you sing."

She glanced at the song and saw that it was filled with words that began with L, F, and W. Her immediate thought was to suppress a groan. But as he taught her the song, it was strange to realize that she could not stutter the words. They flowed from her voice easily, and when it was over, she felt the urge to cry. She'd never known what it was like not to stutter.

"Very good, Miss Edwards," Mr. Pettiford praised her. "My wife and I shall return in another three days to see your progress. And remember. You may only sing until we return. It is the best way to grow accustomed to the feeling."

She managed a nod and was about to thank them when she realized she had to sing the words. "Thank you, Mr. and Mrs. Pettiford," she sang.

His smile broadened. "You're very welcome."

Just as the singing instructor and his wife departed, Lord Scarsdale entered the music room. Oh, no. She as going to have to sing in front of the earl. How horrifying. She'd hoped he wouldn't return for a few days—or better, she'd hoped he would give up and not return at all. The last thing she wanted was for him to tease her again. And he would, as soon as she opened her mouth.

He glanced at the Pettifords and asked, "Lessons, I suppose? I thought I heard singing."

She nodded. *Don't ask me to talk.*

Mrs. Harding saved her from answering when she returned and said to the earl, "Miss Edwards is to have another dancing lesson next. I would like you to join her as her partner." To Violet, she said, "Please show Lord Scarsdale to the ballroom upstairs."

When Violet gave no response, Mrs. Harding waited. "Did you hear me, Miss Edwards?"

She nodded again. The matron's gaze sharpened, and she said, "Well, you can't remain silent forever. Remember the rules. Three days."

"Three days for what?" the earl asked.

At that, Mrs. Harding retreated from the room with a sly smile. Humiliation washed over her, but Violet forced herself to sing. She chose the tune of Amazing Grace and sang, "I have to sing for three days. I am not allowed to speak."

Lord Scarsdale started laughing. "Whatever for?"

"I cannot stutter when I sing," she continued, keeping the tune of the hymn.

"That's brilliant," he answered, still laughing. His green eyes warmed with amusement, though she didn't find it funny at all. "Do I get to sing with you?"

"You needn't make fun of me," she sang. This time, she changed her tune to a darker hymn.

"I would never make fun of you," he sang back in a deep

baritone. "But you have to admit, this is rather entertaining. And your voice is quite good."

She glared at him and sang, "Don't make fun of me. This was not my idea."

"No," he sang, "but I think your dancing master will think we've both gone daft. It will be great fun."

"You needn't sing," she insisted.

"Oh, I wouldn't miss out on this opportunity. Can you imagine how he will respond?" he sang.

At that, there came a soft knock at the ballroom. The dancing master, Mr. Brown, entered the room and greeted them.

"Good morning, Miss Edwards." Then he greeted the earl. "My lord, I am Elias Brown. I believe Mrs. Harding said you are Lord Scarsdale."

"Indeed, I am," he sang heartily.

The dancing master blinked in surprise. "Well...I suppose we should begin."

"Miss Edwards, will you do me the honor?" Scarsdale sang again. His green eyes held humor, and when she looked into his face, she felt herself being drawn in. There was warmth in his expression, of a man having a good time. She didn't quite know what to think of that. Yesterday, he'd provoked her and argued until she was glad he'd gone. Why had he come back?

"If you wish," she sang back. She was about to explain to Mr. Brown what was going on, but Scarsdale interrupted.

"We are having a wager, Mr. Brown," he sang loudly. "Miss Edwards claims that she can sing for the next two hours without stopping. I think I can outlast her."

"Er...if you say so," the dancing instructor answered. "Mrs. Harding asked me to teach you the waltz today, Miss Edwards."

"I have waltzed before," she sang quietly.

"So have I," Scarsdale answered. He held out his hands, and sang, "Miss Edwards, I think we should hum or sing the music to a waltz. That will help us keep the tempo."

"What song did you have in mind?"

"Not a hymn," he sang. "But perhaps one of the waltzes. We could set our own lyrics to it."

She moved closer and he took her hand in his. For a moment, she was dimly aware of Mr. Brown giving them instructions on how to stand and how to move their feet.

"Don't worry about your feet," he sang softly. "Just look at me."

She obeyed, and his green eyes looked into hers. Her face flushed, and she didn't know what to say or do. Never had a man as handsome as Lord Scarsdale held her hand.

"Don't forget, we don't like each other," he reminded her. His voice was deep, and she found herself caught up in this man.

"No, we don't," she sang back. "You would much rather be dancing with Lady Persephone."

She was dimly aware of Mr. Brown taking out a violin and playing a flowing tune while Scarsdale began the waltz, taking command. He was an excellent dancer, and she enjoyed moving with him.

"You're good at dancing," he complimented her. "Actually, you're quite good at many things. The singing was a surprise I never imagined."

But when he held her waist, her heartbeat quickened. She wanted to lower her gaze from his eyes, but she forced herself to meet them. For a moment, she memorized his features, the careless lock of longer blond hair across his forehead, longer than most men wore it. His face held strong lines, a jaw that revealed a stubborn nature that matched her own.

And that mouth. She found it fascinating, for he did talk too much. And yet, there was a sensuous tilt to it, as if he kissed women often. What would it be like to kiss a notorious rake? She couldn't help but wonder.

"You're staring at me," he sang lightly. "Why is that?"

"I'm trying to decide what to think of you," she sang softly. It was the truth, but she wondered if it made him uncomfortable.

In answer, his hand pressed against her spine in a silent warning. Heat burned through her skin, for never had a man touched her like this. It was both innocent and entirely wicked. She knew that a man like Scarsdale had enjoyed many women. They adored him, and she knew it was his sinful ways.

He spun her in a circle and his hand moved higher, just above her waist. Then his thumb edged her ribcage, gently stroking. Violet imagined those hands rising higher and wondered what he would do next. She was wearing a high-waisted morning gown with short stays, and now, his hand was just beneath her breasts. Her nipples tightened beneath her chemise at the thought of his hand cupping her against the silk.

"You already know what to think of me," he whispered. Those eyes had gone heated, his mouth a dangerous offer of more. Violet wondered what it would feel like to have his hot mouth against her throat, and she inhaled sharply.

Abruptly, the music stopped, and Mr. Brown came closer. "Forgive me, my lord, but I do believe there should be more distance between you and Miss Edwards. The waltz is already a scandalous dance, and we would not want idle tongues to wag when you dance in public."

"Of course not, Mr. Brown," he sang. But his eyes suggested something else entirely.

Lord Scarsdale increased the distance but took Violet on another turn around the room. "Have you ever waltzed with a man before, Miss Edwards?"

"Only with my brother," she sang softly. "And never at a ball."

Even though Scarsdale's hand was back at her waist with a respectable distance between them, she found herself slipping beneath his spell. He was an experienced dancer, and for a moment, she lost herself in the waltz, pretending he was a suitor. The dance was exactly what she'd imagined it would be, and she closed her eyes as she spun in his arms.

When the song came to an end, she opened her eyes and saw that Scarsdale's expression had turned stony. Something had made him angry, and she couldn't tell what it was.

At first, she thought of apologizing. But then she stopped herself. She'd done nothing wrong at all. "What is it?" she sang softly.

"We are not courting," he said in a dark whisper. "There is nothing between us, so don't imagine there is."

"I know there's not." A flash of anger kindled inside her. And though she felt ridiculous, she sang quietly, "That's why you're here. Because there will never, ever be anything between us. You're safe."

He stepped away from her and shook his head. "I don't believe you. This was a mistake."

Mr. Brown cleared his throat and inquired, "Is something the matter, Lord Scarsdale? Shall I reteach the steps to you both?"

In an instant, the earl masked his anger. With a sheepish grin, he admitted. "She won the wager and sang longer than I did." To Violet, he added, "Congratulations, Miss Edwards." He gave a sweeping bow, and then departed the ballroom without saying farewell.

It left her cold that he had abandoned her so easily. What did he mean, this was a mistake? It had never been real. The dancing, the singing—all of it. Why would he suddenly leave? He knew there was nothing between them. Had he given up already?

And although she'd always known it was a possibility, she still couldn't suppress the unexpected hurt feelings.

Chapter Six

DAMIAN SUSPECTED HE was, quite possibly, the greatest fool who ever lived. He'd accepted Cedric Gregor's offer in return for having funds to pay some of the bills. It had been a business transaction, nothing more. They had chosen him because Miss Edwards didn't like him.

The problem was, he'd misread the entire situation. He'd mistakenly believed that she was a wallflower who was too shy and reserved to get past her fear. Instead, he'd found a woman who was determined to change her fate.

She had a lovely voice, and she danced with a natural grace he'd never imagined. But it was that look in her eyes that had utterly stopped him. Her brown eyes had studied him with interest. He'd seen that look on many women's faces before; it was nothing new.

But what unraveled him was his own response. He'd wanted to touch her, to slide his hands over her skin. When she'd closed her eyes during the dance, she'd looked exactly like a woman in the throes of lovemaking.

No, Miss Edwards was far more than a wallflower. She was dangerous because she'd awakened something within him. He'd let down his shields, being entirely himself. And if he returned to see her again, he suspected he would like her even more.

He had to marry an heiress. That was an undeniable fact. If he explored his unexpected response to Miss Edwards, it would only lead to trouble. He might break her heart without meaning to.

He stared at the sealed letter on the desk, forcing himself back to the present moment. It would be far better if he abandoned the idea of helping her. Miss Edwards didn't need to imagine things that would never be…and he didn't need to wonder about the fascinating woman behind the stuttering wallflower. It was time to stop daydreaming and start changing his own fate.

The marquess entered the study and greeted him. "Is something the matter? You wanted to see me?"

Damian handed his father the letter he'd invented about the false inheritance. "This arrived for you today."

"Another one, eh?" The marquess only tossed it onto a stack of bills. Damian had already sorted them from the most urgent to those that could wait. The payment he'd received for his time during the past two days would settle the first few.

"I'm not so certain that one *is* a bill," he said, picking it up as if to examine it. "You may want to open it."

"They're all bills."

When Jonas ignored it again, Damian reached for the letter. "It's from your Aunt Petronilla's solicitor. Didn't she die a month ago?" He feigned ignorance, hoping his father wouldn't remember that Petronilla had died three years ago.

Although his father would learn the truth soon enough, it was better that he remembered almost nothing about her. Damian had deliberately chosen a relative his father wouldn't know very well.

"Don't be foolish. I have no Aunt Petronilla."

Even better. Some of the tension relaxed from Damian's shoulders. "Wasn't she your uncle's second wife?" He behaved with false innocence, although he knew perfectly well who she was.

"Well…er…perhaps." Jonas was sorting through another

stack of papers on the desk.

"If she died...is there a chance she could have left you an inheritance?" Damian mused aloud. He needed his father to understand the implications. "There could be money involved."

His father stilled at that. The mention of wealth had indeed captured his attention. "Give me that." He opened the letter and skimmed the contents. A moment later, his rigid expression transformed into a smile. "Well. It seems you're right. Apparently, Aunt Petronilla thought well of me." His face brightened. "Who would've thought? I don't even remember her."

"What does the letter say?" Damian feigned interest in the contents.

His father straightened. "Her solicitor says that there will be a reading of the will within a fortnight, and it's important that I be present." Jonas smiled, as if imagining the forthcoming wealth.

"It must be a great deal of money if he wants you to travel," Damian predicted. He supposed he ought to feel guilty for the elaborate lie, but all he felt was nothing. His father had created this mountain of debt. And if a single letter would give Damian time to fix their difficulties, so be it.

"I'll have to go north. The estate isn't far from Scarsdale from what he said." The marquess puffed out his chest, his tone filled with self-importance.

"That's convenient," Damian remarked. "You'll be able to stay in our own house." Far away from London and out of trouble.

"Indeed." Jonas reread the letter and tapped it on the desk. "I'm very glad you made me open this. When I think of the opportunity I could have missed..." He shook his head in wonderment.

"What about Mother?" Damian inquired. "Will she stay behind?"

"Oh, no," Jonas responded. "Apparently, Aunt Petronilla mentioned her as well. She might as well go with me." He smiled, staring off at the bookcase. "This could change our fortune."

"When will you leave?"

"What's that?" He broke free of the reverie. "Oh. Well, I'll have to order the servants to pack our belongings. I imagine we'll leave by tomorrow. It's quite a journey to Scarsdale, so we'll need enough time to travel. Clara hasn't been feeling well as of late. This might cheer her up." With a jovial laugh, he added, "This calls for a celebration!" He rang for a servant.

"Champagne, perhaps?" Damian suggested.

"Most certainly. And I may go and play cards tonight. With a new inheritance and luck, I could be back on my feet by the end of the month."

Not if Damian had anything to do with it. "Champagne first," he said lightly. "We'll drink to your new fortune."

And he intended to get his father so foxed, the man would be unable to walk out the door, much less play cards. Jonas clapped him on the back. "An excellent idea."

A moment later, his sister entered the room. "Well, the pair of you seem happy."

"A possible inheritance from my Aunt Petronilla," Jonas beamed. "Your mother and I will be traveling north in the morning. We'll stay at Scarsdale until the will reading."

Melanie caught Damian's eye with a knowing look. "That's wonderful news, Father. I do hope you've inherited a great sum."

He shrugged. "One never knows. But it could change everything, my dear."

"You must write and tell me everything," she insisted. "I will be eager to hear all about it."

The marquess sighed. "It will be a month at least until our return. There will be many details, of course. I presume the pair of you will be well enough without us?"

"Of course." Damian kept the smile pasted on his face until the champagne arrived. He poured a generous portion for his father and only a small glass for himself. "Are you attending the Hawthorne ball tonight, Melanie? Do you want me to escort you?"

"I would be glad of it," his sister answered. "Father, I know you'll need time to make the travel arrangements, so you needn't accompany us."

Jonas raised his glass in a toast and then took a long drink of the champagne. "Yes, yes, of course. But if Clara wishes to go, I might join you there tonight."

Over the next hour, Damian allowed his father to prattle on about his predictions of an inheritance that didn't exist while steadily refilling the man's glass. Jonas's mood remained jovial, even as his words grew slurred. Damian quietly ordered the servants to begin packing.

But as his plan started to come together, his mind drifted back to the waltz he'd shared with Miss Edwards earlier. The singing had been a moment of humor for both of them, and he'd enjoyed dancing with her. Until the moment when he'd caught himself falling beneath her spell. Something about that moment had seized his senses, making him fully conscious of her soft smile and gentle beauty. During the dance while he'd rested his gloved hand upon her back, she had stared into his eyes. Her brown eyes had warmed, and he'd found himself staring at her full lips. She truly did have a beautiful face, even if she rarely looked anyone in the eyes.

He'd grown so accustomed to her invisibility that he'd never stopped to truly see her. Beneath her façade of awkwardness, she'd caught his interest. If he had moved a little closer, he could have tasted those lips. He wondered whether Miss Edwards would be timid and blushing if he kissed her. Likely, she'd strike him with her fan.

But...what if she kissed him back? Was there more beneath the shyness? Was she a woman of hidden passions who might kiss him with enthusiasm? He didn't imagine he'd ever find out. A woman like Miss Edwards would never participate in a dalliance. No, she would likely kiss a man for the first time on her wedding night, if such a night ever happened.

You shouldn't go back, his conscience warned. He already knew the consequences. And yet, this was a temporary means of paying certain bills, he told himself. It didn't mean anything. He would distance himself, and after it was over, they would go their separate ways.

He couldn't deny her bravery, for she'd risked everything to change her fate. He was trying to do the same thing to help his family.

When his drunken father stood and nearly fell flat on his face, Damian caught him. "You may want to rest for a little while, Father." He kept a firm grip on the marquess and helped him lay down on the settee.

"A good idea," Jonas answered. "I'll just rest a moment and then join you both at the ball. Ask your mother if..." His words broke off when he passed out.

It hardly mattered whether the marquess slept here or up-stairs, but at least he would not be gambling tonight.

And then Damian had a month to try to resurrect his family's fortunes and keep his father out of debt. God only knew if he could succeed.

"IT'S TIME FOR new gowns," Mrs. Harding told Violet. "I've brought in a modiste so you can tell her what styles you wish to wear. A hair stylist will also pay a call."

Violet tried to behave as if she were delighted by the idea and followed the matron down the hallway. Though she felt foolish, she sang, "It sounds wonderful."

It was a lie. All of yesterday, she'd thought about the earl and wondered if he would change his mind and return. Which was a ridiculous notion. He'd practically accused her of imagining there could be any sort of attraction between them.

The very thought was impossible. Why had he believed such a thing? Oh, Scarsdale was handsome enough. She'd have to be blind not to notice that. And she had enjoyed his gaze upon hers during the dance—how could she not? But she was practical and understood that there would never be anything between them.

But like a splinter, his reminder irritated her, digging beneath her skin until she wished she could pry the thought from her brain. He wasn't coming back, and that was that.

Why then, was she so disappointed? She didn't like him, and he didn't like her. For goodness's sake, the man would smile and flirt with anyone in a skirt. She let her mind wander and realized that her melancholy was because the earl represented hope. All her life, she'd dreamed of having a man look at her the way he had during that fleeting moment.

As she passed the sitting room, her dog Rupert stood and followed her, his paws clicking against the wooden floor. She had taken the earl's advice and had continued training Rupert by rewarding his good behavior. She kept his daily meals of dried meat in a small pouch, and instead of feeding him all at once, she parceled out the food during the day according to how well he listened. During the past two days, the dog's behavior had steadily improved until now, Mrs. Harding had promised Violet could keep him.

"You need to stay," she sang to the dog when they reached the stairs. He promptly sat and stared at her. She gave him a piece of food, which he wolfed down. "I'll be back, and you can have more."

She followed the headmistress up the stairs to another small sitting room where the modiste was waiting. "Good afternoon. I am Yvette," the woman greeted her. The modiste motioned for her to come forward. "May I take your measurements, Miss?"

Violet felt uncomfortable singing, so she simply nodded. Mrs. Harding didn't seem pleased by this, but the modiste hardly noticed. The woman measured her and wrote down the numbers, and Violet glanced at the fabrics the woman had laid out.

There was a garish shade of orange that reminded her of a pumpkin. Another length of silk was a sickly yellow color. And the last color was one she couldn't quite describe, but it seemed to be a cross between green and brown. None of these would suit her at all. For a moment, Violet wondered what she should do. Though she didn't want to seem ungrateful, she couldn't imagine wearing a gown made from any of these colors.

"Do you see anything you like?" the modiste asked, her voice cheerful.

Violet glanced back at Mrs. Harding, whose face remained stoic. The matron hardly ever smiled.

"I..." she began. With a deep breath, she forced herself to speak slowly, and she tried to use the same technique in singing as she did in speaking. "I'm afraid not."

The modiste appeared disappointed. "These are the latest colors. Very popular among the *ton*."

"They d-don't." Violet coughed to hide her stutter. Then more slowly, she said, "They don't suit me."

"I really think you should reconsider, Miss...?"

"Edwards," Violet finished. "And n-no, I'm not wrong." She straightened and slowed her speech. "Do you have...blue...or rose?"

"Miss Edwards, I don't believe you followed the instructions Mr. and Mrs. Pettiford gave you," Mrs. Harding warned. "Remember what they asked you to do."

The singing again. The thought of singing in front of the modiste was embarrassing, and quite frankly, she didn't want to. Then again, she was here to learn. Mrs. Harding had given her a place to stay, and she shouldn't be ungrateful.

Violet was about to apologize when suddenly she stopped. The entire point of these lessons was to transform her into a woman of confidence. Never in her life had she stood up for what *she* wanted. And she didn't want to sing.

"Miss Edwards?" Mrs. Harding prompted. "You need to sing your words to get rid of your stutter."

But the stutter would never truly go away. The singing had helped, and certainly there was no stuttering when she did sing.

But even if she sang for days, it wouldn't eliminate the stutter entirely. Why should she feel foolish if she didn't want to?

It was as if a door had suddenly swung open. She'd grown so accustomed to doing what everyone else wanted her to do, she'd lost sight of what *she* wanted.

"No, I d-didn't forget their instructions." She smiled at the matron. "I...would prefer to speak. I will sing later...if I w-wish."

Violet thought she detected a hint of an answering smile from Mrs. Harding, and it gave her courage. She turned back to the modiste, who appeared confused by their conversation. But Violet saw no reason to explain.

She glanced again at the fabrics and, truthfully, the thought of wearing dresses made from these materials was horrifying. She simply couldn't do it.

Why should she choose colors she despised? There was no reason for it. Why not simply refuse? "If y-you do not have any other colors, I've no wish to waste your time any longer," she said. "Thank you for coming."

The modiste exchanged another look with Mrs. Harding. "Well, I might have another fabric you might like. Let me see."

She picked up another bundle, and while she was looking, Violet turned back to the headmistress. "Is Lord Scarsdale returning today? F-for another lesson."

Mrs. Harding shrugged. "I've sent word to him to join us for luncheon. Whether or not he joins us?" She let her voice trail off.

A sudden surge of anticipation filled her, though Violet knew better than to imagine he would come. Lord Scarsdale didn't want someone like her—it was pointless to imagine otherwise.

But when the modiste began setting out lovely colors of deep blue and a white muslin with purple ribbon, Violet decided that she *wanted* to change who she was. And although it would take time and she would probably fail miserably, she needed the earl to return. With him, it was safe to practice. She could say whatever she wanted to say and behave however she liked.

She turned back to Mrs. Harding and asked quietly, "Please

ask him. I do w-want to see him again."

DAMIAN SHOULDN'T HAVE come. It was a mistake, and he knew it…but the practical side of him realized that this was a faster way to pay off the debts. It only required an hour of his time.

Before his parents had left on their journey north, he'd learned of a few more expenses his father had incurred, to include a new horse that they didn't need. His father's spending habits were a nightmare, but Damian realized that wasting hours in the study trying to unravel all the expenses was less useful than spending an hour with Miss Edwards when he would actually be earning money.

Earls weren't supposed to work. It was not at all the way he'd been raised. But selling off their family belongings would attract notice. It was likely that their family name was already the subject of gossip, and it infuriated him that his father had dug them into such a graveyard of financial ruin.

And so, he'd changed his mind about Miss Edwards's lessons. As long as he made it clear that he had no intention of courting her—that this was a means of paying off debts and nothing more—then he ought to be able to help her in some small way.

He knocked on the door and a footman opened it. "Good day, my lord. Mrs. Harding wishes to speak with you first."

He followed the servant and didn't have to wait before Mrs. Harding met him in the hallway and motioned for him to enter the drawing room.

"I thought we could have a word before you see Miss Edwards," she began. "If you'll just close the door."

He did and then chose a seat across from her. The headmistress regarded him for a long moment and then nodded her head as if she approved of something. He couldn't tell what it was.

"You've been very helpful to Miss Edwards," she began, sliding a letter toward him. He realized it was list of bills that were now paid. "As a bonus, these have been taken care of."

Though it galled him that he'd had to resort to these measures, he said, "Thank you." He'd never imagined that Mrs. Harding would offer more than the agreed-upon payment.

She folded her hands in her lap and said, "Although you've only come twice, I've noticed a change in Miss Edwards. She has been making good progress, and I would like to know if you are interested in helping her for a longer period of time?"

He hesitated, for he had only a month before his father's return. "Mrs. Harding, we both know I shouldn't even be here. I am trying to repair the financial debts my father has caused, but this is a risk to both of us."

"I am aware of that," she said. "But I do not think it will take as much time as you believe it will. And Miss Edwards is ready to begin the next phase of her lessons."

"What do you mean?" He sensed that there was more to this than dancing or singing.

Mrs. Harding pursed her lips. "When she reenters society, it is our hope that men will be interested in her. I'm certain you know that there will be unwelcome suitors, as well as those she may desire."

He waited, not certain where she was going with this. "You want me to teach her how to defend herself?"

"In a manner of speaking." She paused and steepled her fingers. "You are known around town as a notorious rake. And we both know you have no interest in Miss Edwards."

"Correct on both counts." But he had an uncertain thought about what she wanted. "I'm not going to try to seduce her."

"Of course not," she reassured him. And yet, he saw the calculating look in her eyes. "But she has no experience with men. If one sincerely wanted to court her, I suspect she would be too afraid of him. I want you to help her practice."

She slid another paper toward him. "And because this involves more…personal contact, I have increased your fees."

He was starting to wonder how she could afford it. "What,

precisely, are you asking me to do, Mrs. Harding?" Her insinuation was making him uncomfortable.

"Nothing you don't want to do," she answered. "I had initially hoped you could join Miss Edwards for luncheon, for I've been wanting to test her table manners. But instead, we will make it into a light supper instead."

"I cannot stay longer than an hour or two," he reminded her. "I have made promises to my sister to act as her escort tonight."

"Of course," she demurred. She slid a piece of paper toward him and said, "This is the first lesson for you. I want to see how Miss Edwards responds."

He read the list and his sense of uncertainty grew. It was indeed crossing the line, and he wasn't certain he should.

But when she passed a bank note toward him, his guilt increased. The amount would solve a great many of his problems in a short period of time. "And if it makes her uncomfortable?"

"Both of you are free to refuse," she said. "But, of course, this is only for today. If you return in the morning, there will be more."

He was beginning to feel as if a snare were encircling him, drawing even closer. Though Mrs. Harding behaved as if this were nothing more than tutoring, he sensed she was setting him up. And he didn't like that feeling at all.

"I will see her today," he agreed, pocketing the bank note. "And then I will determine whether I will return or not."

Chapter Seven

VIOLET WALKED INTO the dining room and was startled to see Mrs. Harding and Lord Scarsdale already waiting. Though she'd wanted him to come, it surprised her that he'd agreed. Had he changed his mind about helping her? Especially after what had happened the last time, she'd thought he had given up on the idea.

Her heart gave a leap, though she scolded herself for it. "Good evening," she sang.

At that, a faint smile creased his mouth. And although there was nothing between them, she couldn't deny her own attraction. Scarsdale was a gorgeous man whose dark blond hair and green eyes made him appear like a Roman god. If he turned his charm toward a woman, he could easily provoke a powerful attraction. She'd felt it herself while they were dancing. Likely he'd noticed, which was why he'd pushed her away so quickly. A faint blush rose in her cheeks at the memory.

"I'll leave you to the next lesson," Mrs. Harding said. "A footman will remain near the door as a chaperone."

Scarsdale inclined his head, and when they were alone, he asked, "So what lessons have you had since I was here last?"

"Not too many. A modiste came to measure me for new clothes."

He gave a nod, and she sensed a silent judgment for her gray gown. Her mother had chosen the fabric because it was sensible, and although Violet didn't like it, she had few clothes of her own.

"You needn't sing if you don't want to," he offered.

"I don't want to stutter tonight," she responded. "And though it may make me sound silly, I would prefer to say what I wish."

The footman came and served the spring soup of leeks and potatoes. He ladled a helping for her and another for the earl.

"I'm surprised you returned," she admitted. She continued to sing, even though she felt foolish. "Why did you?"

He tasted the soup and then admitted, "It was rude of me to leave like that. I apologize."

She tried the soup and waited for him to elaborate. When he didn't, she prompted, "Did I do something wrong?"

He thought a moment before answering. "To be perfectly honest, no. But the look on your face when we were dancing…I didn't want you to get the wrong idea. There will be nothing more between us aside from friendship."

Was that what he'd believed? She'd simply enjoyed the dancing. "I never had any illusions about us, my lord. I know I'm not what you want." Violet tasted her own soup and found it to be creamy and delicious. She savored the flavor for a moment before she sang, "If that's why you left, rest assured, I don't expect anything from you. Quite frankly, I'm not certain why you came tonight. This is a risk toward your reputation, and it's hardly worth it."

He didn't answer but toyed with the soup. It appeared that he was distracted, and she offered, "If you don't want to be here, you don't have to stay."

"I have a short amount of time before my father returns to London," he said. "I'll make the most of the free time I have remaining."

She studied him, sensing once again that he hadn't been entirely truthful with her. "Why *are* you here, Lord Scarsdale? This wasn't your choice, I'm sure of it."

When he didn't answer, she prompted again, "Was it that wager again? Did Lady Persephone force you into this? Was your plan to pretend to be my friend and then embarrass me at a ball?"

His expression tightened. "I told you, there's no wager."

"That doesn't mean I believe you." She pushed her soup aside, noting the guilt on his face. "I'm not stupid, my lord. I know you aren't helping me out of the goodness of your heart."

If he even had one, she thought. The more she considered it, the more she was convinced that this was a ruse of some kind. But why would he play along?

Money, she decided. This had something to do with money.

"Did she offer to wed you if you pretended to help me?" Violet guessed. "Was that it?"

"I'm not going to answer your questions," he said. "I have my reasons, and that's enough."

But she wasn't going to abandon this. Softly, she sang, "You're being paid to be here, aren't you?"

He said nothing, which was answer enough. And though it was humiliating, she shouldn't be surprised. The earl would never volunteer his time without a good reason. And in this instance, he was being compensated. She should have known.

Violet sighed and gathered what was left of her self-esteem. "So, what is our lesson this evening, my lord? Something to do with food?"

"Not exactly." He set down his soup spoon and said, "It's difficult to explain."

He appeared uncomfortable, and she wondered if it was something to do with dancing again. Instead, he changed the subject and asked, "What do you enjoy in your spare time, Miss Edwards?"

"I love to read." She could spend hours curled up with a good book by the fire. "Sometimes at the end of the day, I'll come down to the library before bed and choose a new book."

His expression turned interested, and he said, "Will you show me the library here?"

"After we finish eating," she promised. The footman brought over the fish course, and they both ate before she realized that the library must have something to do with the lesson. He ate, but his mind seemed to be elsewhere.

"Do you want to go to the library now?" she offered. She couldn't understand why he seemed so distracted. It was as if he were having an inner battle with himself.

He set down his fork and napkin. "Yes. We can return to dinner afterwards."

"And then you'll tell me what my lesson is?" Or show her, depending on whether the library had anything to do with it.

"Of course," he promised. "This won't take long."

She sent him a suspicious look. "What exactly are you planning to do?"

"Look at books," he said. "I want you to show me some of your favorites." His voice had deepened, and the words washed over her like an invisible caress. Violet set down her fork, not knowing what any of this was about. But he was starting to make her nervous.

"All right, then." She stood from her chair. "Follow me."

He did, but when he joined her side, his hand was close to hers. She hadn't put her gloves on, and the slight bump of his bare fingers against hers was a shock. She could almost imagine him taking her hand, his warm palm enclosing hers. And it seemed as if her body had awakened from slumber. She grew aware of his physical form, and goosebumps rose up over her skin for no reason whatsoever.

What are you doing, Scarsdale? Every defense she possessed became an invisible brick wall between them. She pulled back her hand and put distance between them. Then she opened the library door and led him inside.

He closed the door behind him, and she hesitated. "Perhaps you should leave it open. Mrs. Harding said there would be a chaperone, but I don't see the footman."

"We won't be here long," he promised. "Show me your favorite books."

She wondered what on earth this was about, but she went over to the shelf beside the window. With her fingertips, she traced the leather volumes, searching for one while he stood nearby. His presence was unnerving, though he hadn't done anything at all except stand close by. "If I were to choose a book to read before bed tonight, it would be this one. It's an adventure story." She pulled out a copy of *Gulliver's Travels*.

He reached out to take it from her, and their fingers brushed again. She felt a searing heat and an uncertain awareness of his body. For a moment, she imagined what it would be like if he pressed her back against the bookcase and leaned in to steal a kiss. Violet risked a look at him and saw that he wasn't staring at the book at all. He was looking at her.

And he wasn't eyeing her like a friend. He was staring at her as if he wanted to toss the book aside and claim her mouth.

You've gone daft. He doesn't want to kiss you. Violet bit her lip, trying to force back the image. But she couldn't take her eyes away from the earl.

"Shall I read it to you?" he offered.

He could read a ledger on farming techniques, and she would be captivated by his voice. "I-if you want." She stopped singing, unable to keep it up any longer. "We could return to the dining room and f-finish our meal."

Scarsdale set down the book and said, "It's a little cold in here. I'm going to light the hearth."

"Y-you don't need to do that. W-we won't be here long."

But he ignored her and prepared the fire, nonetheless. Violet was caught up by the sight of his muscled arms flexing while he bent low. She sat down, trying to understand why her brain seemed to have left her. They were friends, that was all. Why then, was she staring at his body, wondering what he looked like with no clothing on?

Stop it, she warned herself. But her wayward mind painted the picture of how she'd come downstairs in her nightdress last night to read. She had curled up with the book, resting her head against the settee until she'd nearly fallen asleep. For a moment, she imagined Scarsdale finding her in her nightdress and laying her back, kissing her thoroughly.

Dear Lord, her brain had disappeared entirely.

The earl finished with the fire, and a small blaze burned on the hearth. "That's better." He took the book from her.

"W-why are we here?" she blurted out. Surely this could have nothing to do with the lesson. She couldn't understand the purpose. Scarsdale was up to something, but she couldn't guess what it was.

"Because I, too, like to read." He picked up the book and opened to the first page of the story. He cleared his throat and began reading, *"My father had a small estate in Nottinghamshire. I was the third of five sons."*

Against her good judgment, she curled up on one side of the settee while he remained on the other. His baritone voice held her spellbound, and she listened intently to the familiar story. He continued reading, but as he did, he glanced up at her on occasion and caught her gaze with his.

Oh, the man could read. She could listen to his voice for hours, and she smiled as she got caught up in the tale. He read to her, and during the story, he adjusted his position until his knee was touching hers.

She lost sight of the story then. Instead, she was conscious of the heat of his body. She found herself drawing closer to him without really knowing why. Then he closed more of the distance until their shoulders were almost touching. Violet memorized his features, the line of his face and the sensual mouth that read to her. She saw the way his muscles strained against the linen shirt he wore beneath his jacket. His trousers covered powerful thighs, and she wondered whether his legs were as strong as they appeared.

"Miss Edwards?" he interrupted, setting the book aside. "About the lesson...?"

"Yes?" She almost didn't recognize her own voice.

This time, he rested his hands on either side of her, trapping her against the settee. His gaze fixed upon her with an unspoken hunger that she didn't understand. "Do you know what the lesson was about?"

She didn't know and, frankly, she didn't care. "No."

Her fingers itched to touch him, but more than that, she wanted to kiss this man. She knew nothing would ever come of it, but she would have a memory to last. What would he do if she reached up to his face? Would he berate her and walk away?

She knew it was a terrible idea. And yet, she couldn't stop herself. She reached up to his cheek and pressed her palm against it. Slowly, she drew it down his jaw, and he caught her hand in his. "You're failing miserably, Miss Edwards."

"At what?" Her whisper was barely audible, but she'd loved the feeling of his rough face against her fingertips. She could feel the slight rise of beard stubble.

"Avoiding men who are trying to seduce you," he answered.

So that was why he'd brought her to the library alone. Her cheeks burned with embarrassment, and true, she'd utterly failed at keeping him at a safe distance. The problem was that she liked Scarsdale. She liked his humor, and when he'd read to her just now, she'd been enthralled by his voice.

"That's not what you're doing." She knew well enough that she was perfectly safe from him. "You don't want me. You said so yourself on the day we waltzed."

He said nothing, and her heart trembled at his silence. She'd been expecting him to agree. Instead, he kept his hands in place on either side of her. His eyes burned into her as if she were the only woman in the world. No man had ever looked at her like that. And though it was probably just an act, she couldn't deny how much she craved the attention.

His mouth hovered above hers, and she knew he was waiting for her to push him away, to defend herself. And though she ought to do just that, another part of her wanted more. She wanted her first kiss from a man like him—to experience just a taste of the life she would never have.

"Push me away, Miss Edwards," he demanded. "Do it or face the consequences."

His words shocked her, but in a way that tempted her even more. What sort of consequences did he mean?

A wicked side of her wanted to call his bluff, to see what he would do. An impulse sparked within her, to seize something she'd never had before—a man's interest.

"This means nothing," she said, reaching up to his face again. "I know you're going to w-wed someone else."

But she pulled him close and stole her first kiss.

AT THE FIRST touch of her mouth, Damian lost himself. He'd known this was dangerous, and he'd fully expected Miss Edwards to shove him away. But when her lips touched his with an innocent offering, the darker side of him took over. She wanted to be kissed, did she? So be it.

"What are you doing?" he demanded against her mouth.

"Accepting the consequences," she answered, kissing him again. The sweetness of her mouth took him apart, making him crave even more.

"This means nothing," he repeated against her mouth. He coaxed her mouth to open to him, and he slid his tongue inside. She jolted at the contact, but then she drew her hands into his hair, welcoming him.

My God, Violet Edwards had a sensual side. She yielded to him, inviting him in, and when she kissed him back, it was as if she'd touched a hot poker to his body, setting him on fire. Her hands explored his face, tracing a path down his jaw. She gave several smaller kisses, learning the shape of his mouth.

His brain was roaring at him to stop, but he didn't want to. Not yet. If she thought she could turn his lesson against him and make him want more than friendship, she was wrong.

He was torn between wanting to frighten her off...and wanting to teach her what she yearned to know. Why had she kissed him? She'd insisted that it meant nothing, but how could it not?

No, he needed her to understand what she'd done. She needed to be afraid, to shove him back and be horrified by the storm she'd conjured. If she wanted to be kissed, then by God, he wasn't going to give her genteel, soft kisses. He was going to plunder her mouth and show her what a mistake she'd made.

He pressed her back against the settee, giving her nowhere to go. This time, he kissed her hard, gripping her hair while his tongue slid against hers. He wanted her to know that he wasn't safe. He had seduced many women, all of them willing. And if she thought she could command him, she was wrong.

But then she slid her own tongue against his, tasting him. She gave a soft moan and met his passion with her own. Gently, she swirled her tongue in his mouth, and his body went rigid. Her hands moved to the back of his neck, and her fingertips caressed his skin in silent invitation.

It was as if she'd stored up her own hunger over twenty years and released it upon him. He'd kissed dozens of women, but none like this.

Her hands gently massaged his nape, slipping beneath his jacket. Damian couldn't stop the unexpected surge of desire. His shaft was aching for release, and she shifted beneath him until he was cradled against her thighs. With every kiss, instead of growing frightened, she returned the passion. And it set him on fire.

He wanted to unlace her gown and bare more skin. He wanted to remove the layers, exposing her breasts to discover what color her nipples were. He wanted to take the soft point in his mouth to torment her in the way she was maddening him right now.

Violet Edwards was more than he'd ever imagined, and he tore his jacket and cravat off, loosening his shirt. He took her hands and moved them beneath the linen, feeling the cool touch against his burning skin.

Stop this, his brain warned. *Or you'll regret it.*

But how could he regret the way she was touching him? Her hands moved over every inch of his back, sliding up until she reached his shoulders. She was memorizing him, he realized. And in turn, he wanted her naked body atop his, to feel every curve, every bit of softness. Then he wanted to slide his aching length deep inside, thrusting until she arched her back and came apart within.

She's innocent. And she doesn't know what you're doing. He knew that, but every time he tried to stop, she seemed to draw him closer.

"Was I supposed to resist you?" she whispered.

"You were," he answered against her lips. "This wasn't part of the lesson."

"What if I want it to be?" She moved against him, and he felt as if she'd tilted the world sideways. The slight pressure of her body on his was making him dangerously hard.

"Miss Edwards," he spoke against her mouth. "You're not ready for this."

"I know." Her voice was a whisper. "It's only a dream that won't ever come true."

He didn't know what she meant by that, but it struck him that she was...nearly seducing *him*. She truly thought this was a dream of sorts? That she could indulge in a stolen moment with no consequences?

Her wistful sadness made him realize that he was doing the same thing—allowing himself to be caught up in a forbidden tryst. He had responsibilities to his family, and he couldn't give in to desire. He reversed their positions and pulled her to sit beside him. Her hair was falling down, and she buried her face in her hands.

Whether she knew it or not, Violet Edwards was made for seduction. When she lowered her hands, her face held a pained expression, of a woman who had discovered what it was to surrender to a man…and had liked it.

"You've never been kissed before today, have you?"

She shook her head. "I only wanted to know what it was like." Her expression turned sad. "I'm sorry. I shouldn't have kissed you."

"No. You shouldn't have." He tried to keep his tone even, but his body was still raging with need. He wanted to lay her back down on the settee, raise her skirts, and pleasure her until she screamed.

Now where had this come from? He'd never imagined Miss Edwards could be so fiery and reckless. He turned to look at her—truly look at her. She'd behaved like a dying woman released from an invisible prison, one who had only hours to live. And she'd seized exactly what she'd wanted.

He didn't know what to think of their arrangement anymore. How could he possibly pay another call, knowing what it was to taste her sweet lips against his?

Footsteps approached, and he ordered. "Hit me on the face. Hard."

"I—I couldn't. No."

"They're going to know otherwise," he ordered softly. "Do it, Violet."

She raised her hand, appearing horrified, before the door opened, and she struck him. His cheek burned from the force, but at least she'd done it.

"Good," he said loudly. "If a man ever tries to corner you, hit him just like that. Use your hand, your fan—whatever you have."

Her expression grew stricken, her cheeks burning. "I think you should go."

He agreed with her and bowed his head. "Until next time, Miss Edwards."

VIOLET COULDN'T BELIEVE she'd kissed the earl. Whatever had possessed her to do such a thing? She barely knew him, and he likely believed she was throwing herself at him.

She suppressed a groan, wondering what on earth would happen now. She'd behaved like a desperate spinster, and she was ashamed of herself. Never in her life had she believed a kiss could affect her so strongly. It was as if she'd become a different person.

Now she was starting to understand how a woman could fall into seduction, surrendering to a man. She'd acted like a lovesick fool.

She didn't love the earl, not at all. But why had he kissed her back? She'd expected him to push her away. He couldn't be...attracted to her, could he? No, never. And yet, the hunger of desire had consumed her as he'd devoured her lips.

"Are you all right?" Mr. Gregor asked. "You can leave the library, you know."

"I know." But she couldn't quite bring herself to walk through the door.

"Did he hurt you? If so, I'll make certain the earl doesn't come back."

Her cheeks burned, but she shook her head. "No. He didn't hurt m-me." Not outwardly, at least. But inwardly, she felt as if he'd awakened a dormant part of her. Now that she'd kissed him, how could she ever forget that?

"At the end of this week, we have decided to test your skills. You will attend a masquerade ball."

What? She wasn't at all ready for that. It had been barely a week of lessons. Although she was making progress toward rebuilding her confidence, she didn't know if she could don the identity of someone else, even with a mask.

"I can't," she blurted out. "It's too soon."

"You can," he said gently. "This is a chance for you to be someone else. No one will know who you are. We'll leave before the unmasking."

"They'll know e-exactly who I am as s-soon as I speak," she argued.

"You have made good progress," he offered in an encouraging voice. "There are ways to disguise it. I believe you can do it."

She heard the sincerity in his voice, but she couldn't quite imagine attending a ball. At least, not this soon.

"You will have the opportunity to try a different identity," he repeated. "And isn't that what you want? To become a more confident woman?"

It was, but she didn't feel ready at all. "This would be a d-disaster."

"To be truthful, I don't think Mrs. Harding will give you a choice. We need to see whether you can apply your lessons to the outside world. If you can, she will allow you to stay another fortnight and continue."

Were they seriously threatening her chance to stay here? "I've paid my tuition," she pointed out. Was he implying that they would ask her to leave if she showed no improvement?

"And this is part of your lessons," he said gently. "If you do not wish to go, and you would prefer to return home, that can be arranged."

"No." The last thing she wanted was to face her mother again. "But why would you think I could do this? I will be discovered, and then it's all over."

He shook his head and shrugged. "You need to find your courage, Miss Edwards. It will do you no good to remain here in hiding. The only way to become someone else is to try it."

She couldn't imagine it, but perhaps she could delay it. "Can't we wait a little longer?" she begged. "At least another week. Please."

"No, Mrs. Harding wants you to attend this masquerade ball. The Duke and Duchess of Westerford are hosting it."

She closed her eyes. Then this was a ball for Lady Persephone. Her stomach clenched at the very idea of attending. Not only would she have to face the woman who had made her life a misery, but she would have to watch the earl court her. "I'm sorry, no. I'm not ready."

But Mr. Gregor wasn't listening. "You will wear one of your new gowns, and Mrs. Harding will help you prepare. Both of us will be there to observe. Then we can see whether you've made enough progress to continue the lessons."

Violet tried a different tack. "My mother believes I am in Bedfordshire with my grandmother. What if she is there and discovers me?"

"Don't remove your mask," he warned. "As long as you behave with confidence, she will have no idea it's you."

He wasn't listening at all. "But I don't have an invitation," she protested. "Lady Persephone would never want me there." She couldn't imagine showing up at a duke's ball uninvited. And the moment Persephone learned of her identity, the young woman wouldn't hesitate to humiliate her and have her thrown out.

"But I *do* have an invitation," Mr. Gregor countered. "And I told them I would be bringing my niece. The duchess was glad to allow it."

"This isn't a g-good idea."

"Neither is hiding away," he said. "You're starting to stand up for yourself, which is the most important thing. The singing has helped reduce your stutter."

But it wasn't gone, Violet thought. It would never be gone. She was starting to find ways to smooth out her speech, slowing it down, and choosing words that gave her less difficulty. Yet, she knew if she grew nervous, the stutter would return in full force. And the thought of conversing with strangers—even while wearing a mask—was horrifying.

"I don't want to go," she said quietly.

"I'm sure you don't," he answered. "But you will have a few more lessons with Lord Scarsdale beforehand. And then you will attend."

Her face burned hotter at the thought of more lessons with the earl. "I don't know," she murmured.

"The only thing holding you back right now is fear," Mr. Gregor answered. "It's time you faced it."

Chapter Eight

DAMIAN RODE BACK in the hackney, wondering what in God's name he'd done. He'd meant only to show Violet the dangers of being alone with a man. But when she'd kissed him, the touch of her lips on his had ignited his senses. He'd never imagined that an innocent kiss, a gentle yielding, could evoke such fire. For she was forbidden to him.

Leave her alone, he warned himself. She'd kissed him because she'd wanted to. He had tasted her loneliness, and it had echoed his own. Strange, how he'd flirted with countless women, but it had never meant anything at all. In spite of the teasing, he'd known that the women didn't love him. They were interested in his title, nothing more.

Now, he had to pretend to be someone he wasn't, someone rakish, a man who got what he wanted, even if it was nowhere close to the truth. Resentment swelled up within him, for he knew his choices were limited. He had to marry Lady Persephone or at least someone wealthy. He had no right to flirt with someone like Miss Edwards, for she wouldn't understand that it wasn't real.

And God help him, he didn't deserve a nice woman. Not after everything he'd done.

Damian leaned back, his body jostling to the rhythm of the

horses' hooves. It reminded him of the first time his father had meant to take him riding. He closed his eyes, every detail as vivid as it had been fifteen years ago...along with the familiar guilt. He'd been so young then, so naïve.

As a child, Damian had had an overactive imagination. He'd read stories late at night until the candle burned low. And when his lessons were done, he played with Melanie, though she was hardly more than four years old. She'd been the princess while he was the valiant knight. He'd even used his grandfather's letter opener, pretending it was a dagger.

"I am going on a quest, Melanie. There could be dragons," he'd warned her. "You must stay in the tower, and when I return, I will bring you the treasure."

His sister had beamed at him. "I want cake, too."

"The most delicious cake I can find," he'd promised. Then he'd bowed low and tucked the letter opener inside his waistcoat. "I hope I do not die." The words were somber and dramatic, as he'd meant them to be.

Melanie appeared alarmed, as if she meant to cry. "Don't die, Damian."

"I will do my best," he vowed. When he turned around, he saw a box on the far side of the room, just larger than his hand. He was fairly certain it was his mother's sewing box, for the top of the box was made of silk, embroidered with colorful thread while the sides were inlaid with mother of pearl. The box was perfect for his imaginary quest.

"I shall take this enchanted box," he told Melanie as he picked it up and tucked it inside his waistcoat, "and inside it, I will bring back the heart of the evil dragon."

His sister laughed and reminded him, "But I still want cake."

"And cake," Damian said as he departed the room.

Melanie's nursemaid came inside, smiling as he bowed to her. Today was going to be a good day, Damian decided. He walked outside, down the large stairs, to the gravel driveway. Then he overheard his father giving orders to the groom to saddle his horse.

"May I come with you, Father?" he'd pleaded. "I'm a good rider. I've been practicing every day." And it would be perfect for his imaginary quest. While his father rode with him across the estate, Damian could imagine his journey to find the dragon.

He was eager to show the marquess what he'd learned. If he could keep up with his father while riding, he was certain he could gain Jonas's approval.

"Have you then?" His father had smiled. "Well, then, let's see what you've learned." He gave the order for the groom to saddle a pony.

Damian suppressed a wince, for he really wanted to ride one of the larger horses. "I can ride one of the mares," he insisted. "Even Starlight." The mare was one of his father's prized brood mares, and though he'd only walked around the grounds on her back, he wasn't lying.

His father appeared amused by him, and finally, he gave a shrug. "If you think you can manage."

"My lord, I would advise against it," the groom said. "The mare is in season."

The marquess shrugged. "I don't think it will bother my gelding at all. And if Damian is as good of a rider as he says he is…"

That was all it took to straighten his shoulders. In his mind, he envisioned riding his noble steed across a barren landscape, searching for the dragon.

"What do you have there in your waistcoat?" his father asked.

"It's a treasure box," Damian said.

Jonas's amusement was evident with his eyes. "I thought it was your mother's sewing box."

"It is." Damian was fairly certain it contained thimbles or thread for embroidery. "I'm going to capture the dragon treasure while we're riding and bring it back to Melanie in this box."

"Oh, indeed. You must be a brave lad if you're going to face a dragon."

Damian was glad his father didn't mock him. Of course, he knew that dragons weren't real. But it was fun to pretend.

They rode across the field, the sun shining. Damian let his imagination wander, and when they neared the river, he imagined it was a vast ocean with sea monsters. His father quickened his pace toward the bridge, and Damian followed.

Strange how his life could fall apart in a matter of seconds.

He barely remembered what happened. One moment, he was following his father. The next, the mare had thrown him off her back and into the river. He'd been so startled, he'd inhaled water and had sunk down into the freezing depths. He struggled to kick to the surface, but his coat and shoes weighed him down.

His father had pulled him out of the water, and Damian choked, gagging at the water he'd swallowed. He staggered to his knees, too frightened to realize how he'd nearly drowned.

"You're all right," Jonas said, gripping him tightly. "Breathe, boy."

He coughed some more, leaning over. And then he realized the box and letter opener were gone.

"Mother's box," he managed. "It's in the river. With grandfather's letter opener."

His father held him tightly and said, "It doesn't matter. All that matters is that you're safe." It almost sounded as if his father were about to cry, but men didn't cry, did they? Still, his father kept stroking Damian's hair, as if he'd been frightened.

"I'm going to take you home now." He lifted Damian onto his own mount and swung up behind him. Then he took the reins of the gelding and the mare, leading them home.

It was only later that night that he'd learned the terrible truth. His mother had put her favorite necklace into that box—the diamond and emerald necklace that she'd worn on her wedding day. And now, they were lost forever in the river because of his foolish imaginings.

Damian stared outside the coach, feeling the familiar sting of shame. They'd never found the jewels, even though his father had personally gone to search the river along with dozens of servants.

After that terrible day, he'd set aside his imaginings and had put away his books. He'd gone away to school and had done everything he could to atone for the loss. Which meant becoming the son they wanted him to be. He'd been careful for so many years...until his father started gambling away their fortunes.

After that, he stopped caring about anything. What did it matter if he made the right choices or behaved in the right way? It changed nothing. His mother hardly noticed him, nor did she care.

And so, he'd rebelled against all of them, doing whatever he wanted. He'd drunk too much brandy, enjoyed women, and had attended balls and soirees until he'd stumbled home for the night.

Yet, during the past few years of debauchery, he'd become someone he didn't know anymore. He was empty inside, a shell of a man.

When Violet had kissed him, something changed. He couldn't say what it was. But somehow, it made him imagine what it would be like to be that knight he'd once wanted to be. Someone noble and good, fighting for what was right. The look in her eyes had held astonishment and wonder, and in turn, something had stirred within him. He'd wanted to kiss her again, to be closer to Violet.

She was already fighting to transform herself into a different woman, someone brave and worthy of admiration.

A dull ache caught in his heart, for he only wished he could do the same.

VIOLET HAD SPENT nearly every day practicing her singing and her speech with the Pettifords. She was starting to get more accustomed to speaking, though the stutter never entirely went away. Even so, she found herself singing quite often, mostly to herself, because it was nice not to stutter.

But today, her nerves were strained to the breaking point. Mrs. Harding had informed her that Lord Scarsdale was returning for another lesson.

"What sort of lesson?" she'd asked the matron.

"Cards," she answered. "We'll play a game with Lord Scarsdale after luncheon. Violet, do you play whist?"

"I do, yes."

"Good." She smiled and offered, "You will be his partner when he arrives. Send word to me, and I will meet you both in the sitting room."

For the past hour, she'd been practically pacing, wondering whether he would come. And when he finally did, she felt her cheeks burning with humiliation.

You kissed him, she reminded herself. *He never wanted that from you. It's a wonder he returned at all.*

"Good afternoon, Miss Edwards." He kept his tone even. "I understand we are to be partners in a game of whist?"

She nodded. "We are, yes."

He eyed the door a moment and said, "Where is the dog?"

"He's outside."

"Good. We'll go out and join him so we can talk for a few moments before our game of whist." He didn't give her a chance to argue but simply opened the door wider and waited for her to accompany him.

"The door to the garden is o-on the opposite side of the house," she said. He led her there, and then they continued down a small staircase. He opened the door for her, and she stepped outside into the sunlight. Rupert was napping in the grass when they walked toward him.

"We've always been frank with one another, haven't we?" he began. "I can tell I've made you uncomfortable, and I know it's because of the kiss in the library."

She let out a heavy sigh. "You're right."

"It wasn't that terrible, was it?" He eyed her warily, and she resisted a smile. No, the kiss had been wonderful. It had made her dream of things she could never have.

"No, but I made an idiot out of myself," she confessed. "It was my f-fault for kissing you, and I take the blame for it. I know you're going to m-marry someone else, and it was stupid and impulsive of me."

Rupert trotted over to see them and nudged her hand with his head. Scarsdale leaned down to pet the dog. "It wasn't stupid. Surprising, yes. But not stupid."

"I didn't like hitting you afterwards." Though she'd understood why he'd demanded it of her, it had bothered her to strike him. It had been a day of firsts.

"That was part of the lesson. You didn't have a choice." He turned back to her and asked, "Why did you kiss me?"

Could he embarrass her any more than this? When she didn't answer, he prompted again, "Be honest. If it helps, we can argue about it."

But she couldn't truly find the words. How could she explain that it had been a reckless act of yearning? "You're n-not going to let this go, are you?"

He pulled his pocket watch from his waistcoat. "We have plenty of time."

"Time to embarrass me?" she shot back. But he truly was a stubborn man. For some reason, he wanted to know the truth.

Then he added, "The lesson was about defending yourself against an eager suitor."

"And I failed it," she admitted. "I know."

"What if it happens again with someone else? What if a man tries to steal a kiss or worse, compromise you?" His gaze grew sober. "I might not be there to protect you."

She grew motionless at his words. Did he truly feel as if she were his responsibility? She forced herself to look at him, and when she stared into his eyes, she saw a flare of unexpected heat. He reached out and traced his thumb along her jaw, as if memorizing her. For a moment, she couldn't move, wondering if he was going to kiss her again. She wanted to slip her hands beneath his jacket, feeling the strong muscles of his back beneath her hands. She wished she could explore his skin, running her mouth along it.

Though it terrified her in every way, she lifted her gaze to his. "I kissed you because...for a moment, I wanted to know w-what it was like to kiss someone far above me. Someone I'll never have."

Heaven only knew what provoked her to speak the truth. He likely saw her as pitiful. But instead, he never took his eyes off her.

"There's something about you that drives me to madness," he said roughly. In that aching moment, she longed to feel his mouth on hers once again. And the way he was looking at her, she suspected he felt the same. It was a heady sensation, one she hardly knew how to manage.

"We should have a wager, Miss Edwards," he said. "With our card game. We'll make it more interesting."

"Wh-what do you mean?" The touch of his hand on her cheek evoked a heat throughout her body. Her mind warned that this was a wicked wager, one to which she should not agree.

"We're not going to be partners in cards," he said. "We'll have a competition. Whoever loses has to pay the winner a forfeit."

Her eyes widened at his proposition. For what could he possibly want from her? She couldn't imagine it.

"What sort of forfeit do you want?" she asked.

His wicked smile made her imagine being in a room alone with him, kissing him until her knees went weak. The rush of anticipation filled her, and she pictured laying back on a chaise longue with his body atop hers. The thought made her suppress a shiver.

"If you lose, I want you to spend an afternoon with me," he answered. He didn't elaborate, and her overactive imagination conjured the idea of letting this man thoroughly seduce her.

He doesn't want that from you, her brain warned. But her heart ignored the warning, rejoicing in the prospect.

"And if I win?"

"Then I am yours to command," he answered. "You may do what you wish with me." His voice held a hoarse tone, and she wondered if he sensed her desire.

In this wager, she realized she would win, no matter the outcome. Either he wanted her to spend time with him—or she could ask him to do whatever she wanted.

She took a deep breath and covered his hand with her own. "If I win, then I will ask for a future favor. You will do as I ask, no matter what it is."

His slow smile unraveled her senses. And then, without asking permission, he leaned in and stole another kiss. His mouth was warm against hers, and the sensation reminded her of this man's power over her.

"You're going to lose at cards," he remarked. "I'm very good."

Violet only smiled.

IT WAS NOTHING short of war. Instead of being Violet's partner, Damian had become her opponent, despite Mrs. Harding's protests. He studied his cards, noting the way Violet was smiling beside him. She had already taken several tricks, and she was well on the way to winning this game. He'd never imagined she had such a ruthless streak within her. The secret smile on her face suggested that she was enjoying herself.

Although he was partners with Cedric Gregor and she was paired with Rachel Harding, the game was clearly between the two of them. Damian needed to distract her, to force her into a wrong move.

He threw away a ten of hearts, which she trumped with a queen. He suspected she had higher cards in her hand, but she kept them out of view. Beneath the table, he moved his knee to touch hers. Though he kept his view on the game, he was aware of how she'd tensed.

Mrs. Harding threw away a low card and Mr. Gregor trumped both of them. "Excellent," Damian said.

But Violet was not to be outdone. She swiftly took the next two tricks, and in between her turns, she took his hand in hers and held it firmly in a silent warning not to distract her. Damian ignored her and gently stroked her palm with his thumb. He didn't miss the slight tensing in her shoulders in response.

"Miss Edwards will be attending the Duke and Duchess of Westerford's masquerade ball on Saturday," Mrs. Harding said. "Will you be there?"

He gave a nod and led off with the king of spades. "I've accepted her invitation." It truly wasn't a question, for the ball was hosted by Persephone's parents.

"Good. I have another task for you. You're going to ensure that Miss Edwards does not revert into becoming a wallflower."

At that, Miss Edwards cleared her throat. "I'm still h-here, you know. You needn't talk about me as if I am invisible."

He bumped her knee beneath the table once again. "She will not retreat. I'll see to it."

"Good. Because I want Miss Edwards to speak with Lady Persephone." Mrs. Harding laid down a trump card and took the trick.

Damian wasn't so certain that was a good idea, though he understood what Mrs. Harding was implying. Violet did need to face her greatest fears. But Persephone would do everything possible to sabotage Miss Edwards's opportunities. "I won't allow Lady Persephone to cause any trouble. I promise you that."

"Good. But Lord Scarsdale, I would advise you to be cautious," Mrs. Harding said. "While you are to be commended for helping Miss Edwards develop her confidence, do not do so if it means sacrificing your own future."

The warning was not lost on him. "I've no intention of that," he said. "And I have every faith Miss Edwards will find a suitable husband." He took the next trick, and then led off with an ace. There was a flicker of distress on her face that had nothing to do with cards, and he felt the answering echo in his chest. But he knew Mrs. Harding's caution held merit. Somehow, he'd fallen into a trap of his own making.

He liked Violet, but it went far beyond her beauty. It was the softness of her smile when she rubbed her dog's ears. It was the wicked gleam in her eyes when she trumped his best card and her unspoken triumph. Or the way she'd waltzed with him on the day they'd spent singing together. Most of all, it was the way she'd awakened him with her kiss.

He'd known it was wrong, but that night in the library, he'd recognized her loneliness as a mirror to his own. The kisses had only made him want her more. He enjoyed spending time with her, and she kept surprising him at every turn.

"I think we can all agree that you have been very helpful to Miss Edwards, Lord Scarsdale. But it is probably best that our agreement should end after that ball," Mrs. Harding continued.

Damian didn't argue with Mrs. Harding, for she was right, and they all knew it. He wished he didn't have to accept any money at all for helping Violet. But then, he didn't have a choice. Instead, he gave a nod and led off with a king.

Only to be suddenly destroyed when Violet played an ace. Within moments, she took command of the game, pulling all remaining tricks. He'd never seen it coming. She could easily have taken his king earlier, but she had held off, waiting for the right moment. And now he'd lost.

She smiled at him, and he couldn't help but be proud of her. She had lured them into complacency and then won the game with no mercy.

"It's unfortunate that you aren't allowed to play cards at White's," he remarked. "You could win a fortune."

Violet gathered the cards into a stack. "I believe I won our w-wager, Lord Scarsdale."

"So, you did." He kept his face impassive, not wanting to explain what she'd won.

But Mrs. Harding asked anyway. "And what did you wager?"

Violet straightened and said, "A future favor. Perhaps I'll force him to take me to Gunter's to enjoy ices. Or perhaps he'll have to dance a w-waltz with me at the ball before we say our farewells."

The lie slipped easily from her lips, but he realized he wouldn't mind any of those activities with her.

He didn't know how it had happened, but he didn't want their time together to end. Somehow, Violet Edwards had captured his interest. Her courage and determination went beyond that of any woman he'd ever known.

If she were his wife right now, he would toss the cards aside and take her upstairs. He imagined unbuttoning her gown and baring her skin to his mouth. Her expression faltered when she saw his stare, and she stood from the table. "It was a good game, Lord Scarsdale. I will walk you out."

He excused himself from the table and thanked the others for the game. In the hallway, she walked alongside him toward the front door. With every step, he sensed her slipping further away. And he stopped near the staircase, wanting to extend their time together. He wanted to somehow tell her that he didn't want it to end this way.

"Is something wrong?" she asked.

He eyed her for a moment and said quietly, "There was a book I wanted to borrow. From the library."

Her face went scarlet, and she glanced downward. He didn't have to say another word, but she led him down another corridor until they reached the room.

The moment they entered the library, he closed the door behind them and turned the key in the lock. She stared at him, and in her eyes, he saw the same hunger he felt. Within seconds, he pressed her back against the shelves, kissing her hard.

She melted into him, and their tongues mingled. He kissed

her so fiercely, he wanted nothing more than to tear the gown from her body and claim her. He couldn't grasp why he felt this way, but it had become an intrinsic need to touch her.

"Why are you kissing me?" she murmured against his mouth.

"Because I want to." The words came out more gruffly than he'd intended. "And I'm not finished yet." He kissed her with all the pent-up desire roaring within him. Her arms came around his neck, and when her tongue slid against his, he groaned.

"I won the game, Lord Scarsdale," she reminded him. "You are . . . mine to command."

And if that wasn't the most arousing sentence he'd ever heard, he didn't know what was. He moved his mouth to her throat, kissing the soft skin between her neck and shoulders. "What do you want from me?" He had the sudden image of being alone with this woman, of using his hands and mouth to pleasure her.

She kissed him back, and he drew her hips to his, needing the softness of her body. His body had gone rigid, and he imagined loosening her stays, revealing the breasts he ached to touch. Although he'd had women before, there was something about the way she kissed him that made him feel like he wanted to be a better man. And he didn't want to let her go.

Violet chose her words carefully. "I will tell you on the night of the masquerade ball. I will ask my favor, and you will grant it to me."

"All right," he murmured against her lips before he captured them again. She met his desire with the force of her own need, and when her hands moved beneath his coat upon his shirt, he ached for her.

"When we're at the ball, you're g-going to remember every time you kissed me." Her voice held a sudden heaviness as she drew her mouth away from his. "When you dance w-with Persephone, you'll remember dancing with me."

She kissed him, and he took her face between his hands, savoring her touch. Her fingertips splayed upon his back beneath his shirt, and his breathing remained unsteady. Somehow, she had found a way past his defenses, and every word she spoke was true. He wanted this woman in a way he'd never wanted anyone else.

"Violet," he murmured, using her name for the first time. "I—"

"Don't say it." She put her fingertip against his lips. "I already know what you're thinking. I don't w-want apologies or excuses." Then she brought her mouth to his and kissed him softly. "I will claim my favor from you, and after that…" Her words trailed off, and he felt the silent sting.

When he looked into her eyes, he saw the unspoken pain. Deep inside, he felt the echo of loneliness and regret.

Violet touched his cheek with a wistful smile. "And perhaps you won't forget me when you marry someone else."

Chapter Nine

V IOLET STARED INTO the mirror, haunted by the insecurities
that kept emerging. How could she attend a ball Persephone's father was hosting? Masquerade or not, she wasn't ready.
Her stutter, though it continued to improve each day, would
never completely disappear. And when she stared at her brown
hair and brown eyes, she felt like a wren trying to masquerade as
a peacock.

Then, too, there was the favor she'd won from the earl. She
didn't yet know what she would ask of him. For that matter, she
might not even speak with him until later tonight. He would
likely be at Persephone's side, along with her other suitors.

A knock sounded at the door, and she called out, "Come in,"
expecting Lucy to help her get dressed. Instead, she saw Mrs.
Harding.

The matron came inside and glanced at Violet in her dressing
gown. "How are you feeling about tonight?" Her voice held quiet
sympathy.

"I'm afraid," Violet admitted. "I have a new gown that the
modiste made for me. And Lucy said she would find a simple
black mask."

Mrs. Harding sat down on a small stool beside the window.
"Oh, I think we can do better than that. I have one of the finest

hair stylists in London waiting downstairs. I also commissioned the modiste to make a true gown and mask for you. Tonight, you *will* be noticed. And if I have anything to do with it, every eligible gentleman in London will be fascinated by you."

The thought was both dizzying and exhilarating. Violet let out her breath. "I don't know w-what to say."

"If I give you that chance to be one of the most beautiful ladies at the ball, will you take it?" she asked. "Are you strong enough not to be a wallflower? Especially if Scarsdale is there."

Violet hesitated. Although her instinct was to say no, she wasn't ready, she thought again of the earl's second kiss in the library. Her cheeks flushed at the memory, along with the painful realization that she was losing her heart to the man.

Mrs. Harding studied her and said, "Have you...developed feelings for the earl?"

Violet closed her eyes. "I know he has to marry an heiress. It doesn't matter whether I feel anything or not."

"Oh, it matters a great deal." The matron stood from her stool. "Do you remember when I asked you to make a list of qualities you wanted in a suitor? A man you thought you'd never have?" Violet nodded, though she'd thought nothing of it at the time. Mrs. Harding continued, "Do you think it's any accident that we chose the Earl of Scarsdale for you?"

At that, Violet blinked. "He was meant to help me."

"True, but we also thought he might make a good husband for you."

A startled laugh broke from her throat. "How could you ever imagine that would happen? It's impossible."

"Is it?" She gave a serene smile. "Don't you think there's a reason we allowed you to be alone with him in the library?"

Violet winced. "I didn't mean—that is—w-we—"

The matron waved her hand. "That's neither here nor there. The reason I bring it up is because it's clear to the rest of us that the earl likes you. You like him. If he asked you to marry him, would you agree?"

Violet stared at the woman in disbelief. Never in her life had she even considered the possibility. *But what if?* her heart urged.

"It's a yes or no question," the matron said. "Ignore the reasons why."

Violet took a deep breath. "Yes. I would marry him."

Mrs. Harding studied her. "Then you must fight for the man you want. Ignore what he thinks he wants or thinks he must do. If you want to marry Scarsdale, then seize the opportunity we've given you. It's time to arm yourself for battle." She rang for a servant.

For a moment, it was as if an invisible door had opened, one Violet had never imagined she could step through. All her life, she'd been accustomed to being the pitiful wallflower, too afraid to speak to any man at all.

But she wasn't afraid of Lord Scarsdale. He challenged her to speak her mind, and when he'd kissed her, she'd felt the evidence of his desire.

Was it even possible to win his heart? She didn't know if she had the courage to reach for such an impossible dream. But if she never tried, failure was inevitable.

When a knock sounded at the door, Mrs. Harding walked over and opened it. Three women entered the room: one with a comb and scissors, while Lucy and another maid carried a large box.

"Show her the gown," Mrs. Harding ordered. "And the mask."

Lucy opened the box, revealing a high-waisted gown of deep emerald green. It appeared to have numerous silk leaves sewn all over it, and the short sleeves were a darker green. The maid pulled it out to lay it upon the bed, and Violet had never seen anything more breathtaking. There was a matching lace fan and a black mask embroidered with tiny green leaves. "It's beautiful," she said.

"You will be Eve tonight," Mrs. Harding said. With a sidelong smile, she added, "You could even bring an apple with you if anyone wants to understand your costume. The only question is whether you can tempt your Adam—the earl, that is—to learn what he truly wants."

"I don't have the dowry he needs," Violet admitted. "Even if I do want him." But her heart pounded at the thought of Scarsdale choosing her instead of Persephone. She *did* want to fight for him. When she imagined marriage, it would be wonderful to spend her nights in his arms or to see his face at the breakfast table each morning. He was worth fighting for, even if it was an impossible battle.

"Convince Lord Scarsdale that he is intelligent enough to find another way," Mrs. Harding said. She reached for Violet's hair and undid the ribbon tying it back. "You're going to be the most beautiful woman in London tonight, when we're finished with you. If the earl is half the man I think he is, Scarsdale is fully capable of saving his family from financial ruin by himself."

DAMIAN STOOD AMID the ballroom guests and, for a moment, it seemed as if he were standing in the queen's antechamber, awaiting an audience from Lady Persephone. He was fully aware that she was playing all her suitors—offering just a touch of encouragement but never making promises. In some ways, he deserved this, for he'd behaved in the same manner toward many young ladies in the past.

Even so, he was starting to wonder if Persephone would ever agree to marry anyone. Perhaps it might be in his best interests to consider other heiresses. But then she made her entrance, dressed in a ballgown of white silk. It was designed to resemble a swan, trimmed with feathers and a mask adorned in the same manner. Four gentlemen surrounded her, and she laughed, fanning herself with a lacy white fan.

Damian started to cross the room, keeping a smile on his face that he didn't feel. He knew what he had to do, and it was better if he set aside his reluctance and focused on the future for his family.

But Violet was right. He couldn't stop thinking about the hours they'd shared together. With her, he could be completely himself and say whatever he wanted to say. The only way he could tolerate a marriage with Persephone was if they lived on separate estates.

Even if he chose a different heiress to wed, he suspected she could never compare to Violet. And as he walked toward the duke's daughter, he wondered if there was another way out.

There was a slight murmur of voices while another young lady entered. Damian glanced at the door and his breath caught. She wore a gown of deep green, adorned with leaves and embroidery, and the fabric had a slight sheen to it. Her brown hair was caught up in a fashionable updo, while more leaves were intertwined amid the strands. Her black mask was tied behind her face, and around her throat she wore an unusual emerald necklace shaped like a serpent. In one hand she carried an apple.

"If that's Eve, I'll be her Adam," he heard a gentleman remark beside him. "Who *is* that?"

But Damian knew exactly who it was—Violet Edwards. He'd never seen her look more beautiful, and the effect utterly struck him down. Was this the same woman he'd kissed in the library? The same one who had destroyed him in whist and waltzed with him while singing?

He knew he was staring, but he didn't care. Violet kept her shoulders back, her posture erect as she walked inside with Cedric Gregor, who had not bothered to wear a mask. Behind her was Mrs. Harding, who had also revealed her face.

But he would have known Violet anywhere, even if she had arrived without an escort. Her smile was serene, and he wasn't the only gentleman who started to approach.

Damian glanced at Lady Persephone, but she was already preoccupied with her other suitors. She was frowning at Violet, but she wasn't about to leave the company of her worshippers.

He pushed his way past a few gentlemen and greeted her. "Good evening." He suspected Violet would not appreciate him giving her away. In a low voice, he asked, "What are you calling yourself tonight?"

"Lady Eve," she answered. "If I must give a name, that is. It's a masquerade, so I will try to remain anonymous."

"You look stunning," he told her. "It's good to see you again." With a nod to Mr. Gregor, he offered Violet his arm. "Would you care to dance?"

"Perhaps a l-little later," she answered, then bit her lip with frustration. "Not just yet."

He could tell that she was trying to gather her courage, and he wanted her to know that he would be her ally tonight. "Save a dance for me, then."

"I w-will." She closed her eyes lightly and sighed. "Why do I keep doing that?"

Her stammer was likely her greatest fear, understandably so. "If you accidentally stutter when you are speaking with someone, cough instead," he suggested. "No one will notice."

She gave a nod to his advice. Even so, he could tell how pale she was. "Don't be afraid of them. You can do this." Before she could answer, he added, "If you need a rescue, tuck your fan beneath your left arm. I'll come to you."

His offer seemed to ease some of her tension. "Thank you, Lord Scarsdale."

He bowed. "Don't forget about that dance. We did practice the waltz earlier. I'll claim that one, if I may." Her cheeks flushed at the memory of their dancing, and he recalled resting his hands upon her waist. Which led his mind to remember their stolen moment in the library and how her soft lips had felt against his. He forced the thought away, for it would do neither of them any good. Then he inclined his head and murmured, "Good luck."

"I'll need it."

He could hear the raw nerves in her voice, and he wanted to boost her courage. "Just pretend that the gentlemen are me," he offered. "You can be angry with them all you like." And with that, he turned and walked away.

He had to remember his purpose here—to win an heiress. When he glanced at the new debutantes, all wearing white or pastel colors, all masked, he thought of Melanie again. She ought to be here. And if he didn't do what he must, she would never have that opportunity.

He steeled himself and went toward Persephone. Along the way, he saw Lady Ashleigh walking past him. Her light red hair gave her identity away.

"Lady Ashleigh," he greeted her.

She stopped and turned to him. "Lord Scarsdale."

He gave a slight smile. "It's not much of a masquerade, if we can tell who people are so easily, is it?"

She touched her hair. "I didn't feel like dyeing my hair or wearing a wig." With a shrug, she said, "Persephone would never stand for it." She paused a moment and said, "I suppose you intend to join her line of suitors."

"I suppose I must. Since it would not be good manners to toss them all outside, much as I might want to."

Lady Ashleigh's expression softened. "You're a better man than she deserves, Scarsdale." Before he could answer, she raised a gloved hand. "And that doesn't mean I'm asking you to court me instead. I know full well the sort of woman you need to wed."

It was a curious thing to say from another heiress, so he probed a little deeper. "Is there a gentleman who has already caught your eye?"

She shook her head. "Were it possible, I wouldn't marry at all. It's not what I want. But women don't seem to have a choice. We do what we are told when we are told to do it."

The conversation had taken a turn he hadn't expected. She was speaking as if she were a trapped woman. "Is everything all right, Lady Ashleigh?"

She stiffened. "Never mind. Forget I said anything at all." She gestured toward Persephone. "I would bid you good luck, but you'll need more than that." Just as she was about to depart, she jolted at the sight of an older woman. "Mrs. Harding," she greeted her in a stiff voice. The matron smiled and inclined her head as the young woman departed.

Once Damian was alone with her, Mrs. Harding said, "You're doing very well with Miss Edwards, I must tell you. She has made tremendous progress with your help and with the help of Lady Ashleigh."

"Lady Ashleigh?" He turned to face her. "What does she have to do with this?"

"I hired her as well," Mrs. Harding said. "She was in need of funds, so we sent her a letter and gave her an opportunity. All she had to do was behave like an exceedingly rude young lady. Which she did in a manner that accomplished the exact reaction from Miss Edwards that we wanted."

He frowned at that, not understanding it at all. "Lady Ashleigh is an exceptionally wealthy young woman. Why would she ever need money?"

The matron shrugged. "Not every woman is in command of her family's wealth. I saw an opportunity and made use of her."

Idly, he wondered if Lady Ashleigh was in a similar situation to his own, one where she had little control over her life. He had no time to wonder about it any further when Persephone waved for him to come and join her. "Will you excuse me, Mrs. Harding?"

"Of course."

But as he went to join the woman who held the power to transform his own future, he couldn't help but risk a glance back at Miss Edwards, hoping she would be all right.

VIOLET'S APPREHENSIONS DEEPENED with every moment. Mr. Gregor offered her his arm. "I am going to introduce you to the duke and duchess. If they ask for your name, it will be Eve Smith, my niece." Then his voice hardened. "Don't turn coward now. This is the true test of what you can do now."

Violet swallowed, feeling as if her entire body were encased in ice. She couldn't quite catch her breath, but she forced herself to follow Mr. Gregor.

The man smiled broadly as he crossed through the room. Then he brought her directly to Lady Persephone's mother, the Duchess of Westerford. "Your Grace." He inclined his head and said, "I was delighted that you allowed me to bring my niece this evening. May I present her to you?" He winked and added, "I could give you her name, but perhaps that should wait until later?"

Violet lowered her head when the duchess took her gloved hand. "It's a pleasure to meet you, my dear. Have you met my daughter Persephone?"

Yes, and she's a terrible person, Violet thought. But of course, the fictional Miss Smith had never met the young woman. *Answer slowly*, she warned herself. She took a deep breath and said, "No, Your Grace."

When there was no trace of a stutter, she barely held back her smile.

"Then I shall have to introduce you," the duchess said. "I am certain you will become friends."

I am very certain we won't, Violet thought.

"Of course," she answered. "Thank you...for allowing m-m—" She coughed and cleared her throat to disguise the stutter. "...me to attend your...ball," she finished.

"You are quite welcome," the duchess said with a smile.

Violet took a deep breath and returned the smile, grateful that she'd managed to hide her misstep with the cough.

Mr. Gregor led her across the room, and she passed by another gentleman she hadn't seen before. His dark blond hair was unfashionably long, tied back in a queue, and his beard was long, nearly to his chest. He reminded her of a fairytale character who had been imprisoned for a hundred years. His clothing appeared as if it had been crumpled into a heap, and it was ill-fitting.

"That's Mr. Cameron Neill," Cedric remarked. "I'm surprised the duke and duchess invited the gentleman. Most people don't."

Violet wasn't surprised. But when she risked a glance at him, she saw a reflection of herself in the man. Certainly, he appeared worse than a beggar from a physical standpoint. But more than that, he was clearly an outsider who had no idea what to do in a ballroom. He remained by the wall alone. *I know what that feels like*, she thought.

The dancing began, and to her shock, a friend of Mr. Gregor's asked her to be his partner. She took her place in the line, and it struck her that this was the first time in years that she'd been asked to dance.

Although it might be because Mr. Gregor had told the man to ask her, she didn't care. As she changed partners, Violet couldn't help but smile. She was having fun. She spun and danced the quadrille, even laughing at one moment.

Until the earl became her partner for a brief moment. Then she grew conscious of the touch of his hands, the look in his eyes.

Time for battle, she told herself. But when she glanced back again, she saw him looking at Persephone in the same way.

A sudden spark of jealousy flared up, even though she knew it was unfair. He had chosen the woman he wanted to marry, and it wasn't her.

Then do something about it.

The unspoken words reminded her that she was behaving like a coward. If she wanted the earl, then she needed to set aside her fears and fight.

The dance ended, and her partner led her back. "May I offer you a glass of lemonade?" he asked when they reached Mr. Gregor's side.

"That would be wonderful," she said. "Thank you."

He bowed and went toward the refreshments.

"You're doing well," Mr. Gregor complimented her. "Now, for the true test."

Violet wasn't certain what he meant, but he offered his arm again. "Shouldn't I wait until the...gentleman returns with my l-lemonade?"

"Oh, he'll find you," Cedric replied. "Though you may wish it were something stronger." He led her through the crowd of people to face Lady Persephone. The moment Violet saw the young woman, all her old fears came roaring back. The humiliation, the tears...the sickening feeling in her stomach.

Mr. Gregor nodded in greeting to the young woman. "Lady Persephone, may I introduce you to my niece, Miss Smith, who has recently come to town?"

"Now how did you ever recognize me?" the young woman teased.

"Such beauty cannot go on disguised," Cedric said in his most charming voice. And of course, Lady Persephone fell neatly into his trap.

It took an effort for Violet to maintain her smile. But it was clear that he was playing into the young woman's vanity.

"Why didn't you wear a mask, Mr. Gregor?" Persephone teased.

"At my age, sometimes my eyesight is not what it once was. Better to leave the mystery for younger guests," he answered, giving a bow. "I'll leave you two to get acquainted."

Persephone smiled again and then turned to Violet. "Why, hello. I'm surprised that there is someone left in London whom I haven't met."

Violet answered slowly. "I'm...pleased to know you, Lady Persephone. Everything ...is lovely."

"Of course, it is. We spent weeks planning it all." The woman paused a moment and eyed her. "Are you certain we haven't met before? You do seem familiar."

The sickening twist in her stomach tightened, but Violet lied, "I arrived in...town only a few days ago."

"So, tell me about yourself," Persephone said. "I want to know everything."

The very thought of having to hold a full conversation with her most dreaded enemy was impossible. But Violet steeled herself and laughed. "My life is v—" She coughed lightly when she felt the stutter returning. "Very dull. Tell me about yours."

Persephone beamed, and Violet felt a sense of relief when the young woman began talking. "Well, I have dozens of suitors. It's the *choosing* of a husband that I find nearly impossible. They are all handsome, of course. And rich. They all have titles. How will I ever pick one?"

She paused and waited until Violet realized she was going to have to talk again. "P-p—" She coughed again to disguise her stutter and then changed her words. "The one whom you love."

"Hmm," Persephone mused, "except that I don't love any of them. They're all the same."

At that, Lord Scarsdale came over to join them. He ignored Violet and turned his full attention to the lady. "You look beautiful, as always, Lady Persephone."

Although she knew he could not acknowledge her, Violet felt a slight twinge of uncertainty. She reminded herself that they were both playing a role. He shouldn't have even recognized her.

Persephone smiled as if Scarsdale had paid her proper homage. "I was wondering when you would come to see me."

"I had to push my way past an army of suitors to reach your side," he teased. "Dozens at least."

The lady all but preened at his words. Did she even realize that the earl was only saying what she wanted to hear? Or did she not care?

"Have you met Mr. Gregor's niece?" Persephone asked Lord Scarsdale. To Violet, she added, "I'm sorry, but you didn't tell me your name."

"Later," Violet promised, though she had no intention of giving it.

Scarsdale turned to her but let no emotions show upon his face. "I met her only briefly."

Likely he'd admitted it in case Persephone had witnessed

them talking. But it hurt to see an invisible shield on his face. Even so, Violet glimpsed a warning in his green eyes.

"Would you care to dance, Lady Persephone?" he asked.

"Not yet. But you should dance with this young lady for now. That is, unless someone else has claimed this one?"

Violet shook her head.

"Shall we?" the earl asked, offering his arm. She took it, and when they reached the dance floor, he said in a low voice, "She's watching us. We have to behave like strangers."

Violet doubted that Lady Persephone was watching at all. More likely, the woman was enjoying the compliments from the suitors surrounding her.

The warmth of his palm against her spine was more soothing than she'd imagined, and she savored the forbidden touch. "Are you e-enjoying yourself tonight, Lord Scarsdale?" She spoke freely, not even bothering to disguise her stutter around him. No one could hear their conversation anyway amid the music.

The earl's expression grew guarded. He looked as if he wanted to say something but couldn't find the words. At last, he simply said, "I am now. And I'm glad you seem to be causing a stir among the gentlemen. Have you chosen a suitor yet?" he teased.

You, she thought, but didn't say it. Scarsdale spun her in a circle, but even so, she could feel the distance growing between them. This time, she stared into his eyes and said, "There is a man who caught my interest. But I don't know if he sees me in the same w-way."

A flash of an unnamed emotion crossed his face. "I'm glad for you." His hand slid against her waist, and her skin tightened, imagining there were no boundaries between them.

"I meant what I said when I told you how lovely you look tonight. I don't think you'll have any trouble catching a man's eye."

"Perhaps," she remarked.

But his gaze never faltered. "I'm proud of you, Miss Edwards.

You deserve to reap the rewards of your hard work. I am glad you've made such progress."

She inclined her head to acknowledge the compliment. "Thank you."

But when they continued dancing, he prompted, "So tell me the name of the gentleman who has caught your eye." He smiled, but she noted a protective tone in his voice.

"No." She smiled in return, enjoying the elusive conversation.

"I could help you," he offered.

"Possibly." But only if he returned her affections. Even so, she wasn't about to embarrass herself by revealing the truth. "I suspect he hardly notices me at all."

"Everyone in this room noticed you," he countered. "I should be grateful that you agreed to dance with me. Your dance card will undoubtedly be full tonight."

She didn't know how to answer that. Instead, she said, "While you will likely have to pay court to Lady Persephone." She paused and asked, "How can you consider m-marrying a woman like her?"

"Because I care about my family," he answered, keeping his face neutral. "And though you and I are friends, she can't know that."

"Friends." She did smile at that, though she wanted to be so much more. "After tonight, do you suppose our paths will ever cross again?"

There was a slight shift on his face, as if he hadn't expected her question. Then he met her gaze squarely. "I hope so. Though our arrangement may be somewhat...unusual, with you, I don't have to give you empty compliments or behave differently. It's rather nice to simply be myself."

This was dangerous territory, for she did like the man he was. Yes, he was caught in a trap of his father's debts, but the earl did seem to be a decent person. And no decent person ought to willingly marry Lady Persephone.

"M-may I be frank, Lord Scarsdale?"

"Aren't you always?"

"Don't m-marry a woman like Persephone," she warned. "Your life will be a m-misery. Choose someone else. Anyone."

"She is the solution to our family problems."

"She's playing with you. She knows you w-want her, but she doesn't c-care. I imagine if you showed interest in anyone else, she would try to snare you b-back again." Women like Persephone wanted to be worshipped and didn't particularly care by whom. The quantity of suitors mattered more to her.

"My father is fifty thousand pounds in debt," he countered. "What else can I do?"

She stilled at that. Although he'd mentioned his father's debts, she hadn't imagined it was that much. But even so, she regarded him with full honesty. "Don't you think your happiness is worth m-more than fifty thousand pounds?"

He held her gaze steady. "No. I don't." The dance ended, and she curtsied as he bowed. He escorted her back to Mr. Gregor, and then disappeared among the guests in the ballroom. It bothered her deeply that he was so willing to sacrifice himself. But she hadn't imagined that his father's debts were that staggering. The paltry amount Scarsdale was earning with her would hardly do more than pay the bills for food.

Mr. Gregor was staring at her, and at last, she demanded, "What is it?"

"I think I may have found a potential suitor for you," he said. "If you're willing to meet him."

For whatever reason, her heart started pounding. "Who?"

Mr. Gregor paused a moment. "I've been watching him for the past hour. He seems to be a kindly man, but many women have avoided him because of his appearance. I think you might be willing to look beyond it."

Violet was starting to feel uneasy about this. "Tell me."

He led her toward the terrace, and she saw a gentleman standing near the edge, looking out over the gardens. He was alone, and at first glance, she noticed his shabby appearance and longer hair. It was Mr. Cameron Neill, the gentleman Mr. Gregor had pointed out to her earlier.

"I'll introduce you," he offered.

"No, really, I—" Her words broke off when they drew closer.

"Good evening, Mr. Neill," he remarked. "I would like to introduce you to my niece."

"Forgive me, what did you say?" The man turned as if Mr. Gregor had interrupted his thoughts.

"I said I wanted to introduce you to my niece." He gestured toward Violet.

Mr. Neill frowned a moment, his glance resting upon Violet. "Is this about our earlier discussion?"

What earlier discussion? Violet wondered. Had Mr. Gregor already tried to arrange a match with this man? She was trying to look beyond his appearances. He did have nice blue eyes, but it was impossible to tell much about his face, for he wore his beard and mustache long, and his hair appeared unkempt. It almost seemed as if he'd been shipwrecked upon an island.

"No, not at all. I thought the two of you might become acquainted." Mr. Gregor smiled and then turned back to Violet. "Mr. Neill has been out of the country during the past few years. He has only recently returned." He paused and added, "I see Mrs. Harding over there. I'll leave the two of you to get acquainted, but we will be just there on the other side of the terrace."

In other words, they would chaperone from a distance. *No, don't leave,* she wanted to plead, but that would be terribly rude. She resigned herself to the fact that this might be part of their plans.

But she ventured a polite smile and extended her hand. For a moment, he didn't seem to know quite what to do. An unnamed emotion crossed over his face before he took her hand and pumped it firmly. "A pleasure to meet you, Miss—er, I didn't catch your name."

"It's a masquerade," Violet answered. "You're n-not supposed to know who I am."

At that, the man gave a genuine smile. "Just so. Though I suppose you already know my name."

"Just so," she repeated.

He laughed, and she realized that they were even more alike than she'd imagined. Both were wallflowers, and neither of them was socially adept. For a moment, she studied him, wondering if he might be a possibility for a husband. While his hair and beard were ridiculously long and his clothing unkempt, his eyes were kind.

Yet, he didn't make her heart beat faster the way Damian did. She didn't feel the rise of goosebumps on her skin when he smiled.

And so, she steeled herself and spoke slowly. "Are you enjoying yourself this e-evening, Mr. Neill?"

"It's not quite what I thought it would be," he admitted. "I wasn't expecting so many people." Then the conversation ended again. Violet waited to see if he would offer anything else, but the awkward silence stretched further.

At last, he said, "I hear that the Duke of Westerford has a magnificent library. Over a thousand books, I'm told. Have you seen it before?"

"No. This is the first time I've...been to a b-ball here," she confessed. She loathed the fact that her stutter had returned, but he didn't seem to mind.

He nodded. "I must admit, I am tempted to go and see the library for myself. Would you like to come along?"

Her last memory of a library involved being thoroughly kissed by the Earl of Scarsdale. His hot mouth had devoured hers, and she'd never forgotten the fierce desire he'd evoked. Her cheeks flushed at the vision, and she shook her head. "No, thank you, Mr. Neill. But I will wish you a good evening."

With that, she returned to the hallway. Mr. Gregor and Mrs. Harding were still on the far side of the terrace. She nodded to them and was about to return to the ballroom when she heard a woman's voice from behind her.

"Violet. I was hoping I might see you here."

When she saw Lady Ashleigh, everything within her froze. The young woman wore an ice blue gown, and her red hair was pulled into an updo with strands of pearls intertwined.

For a moment, Violet didn't speak, not wanting to reveal herself. But then Ashleigh continued, "Could we talk for a moment?"

She saw no choice but to give a nod. This was entirely unlike Ashleigh, and her instincts went on high alert. "What is it?"

Ashleigh beckoned for her to step away from the others. "I...don't know how to say this. But...I wanted to apologize for what happened during the dancing lesson. I was cruel. Mrs. Harding insisted that I behave like the most terrible person I could imagine. In return, I was paid."

Violet didn't know whether to believe her. "Why would y-you need money at all?" Lady Ashleigh was a renowned heiress. Her father, the Marquess of Rothfield, was one of the wealthiest peers, second only to the duke.

"You're not the only one seeking an escape," Ashleigh said. Her face had gone pale, and she glanced around. "I just wanted to tell you. I didn't like the way I behaved, but she told me to do it." Guilt seemed to cloud her features. "I don't suppose you believe me, but I thought you should know."

Violet grew somber, not really knowing how to respond. She didn't trust Lady Ashleigh, but it *was* possible that she was telling the truth. During that first lesson, she'd never imagined that she would be mocked and belittled. But she now knew the purpose of it—to make her angry and make her see how powerless she had become.

Though she knew Ashleigh wanted forgiveness, she couldn't yet give it. For all she knew, this was part of a wager—to make her believe there was remorse when it was only another ruse.

"You were c-cruel," she answered at last. "I never imagined you c-could be that terrible."

Ashleigh's expression fell. "I know."

"I don't know how anyone could be that awful f-for any reason." She met the woman's gaze with her own silent accusation.

"You wouldn't understand," Ashleigh said. "But I needed the money." Her face turned cool again. "Good luck this evening."

Violet could almost hear the unspoken words: *You'll need it.*

Chapter Ten

DAMIAN STOOD WAITING near Persephone, and with every moment he waited, he felt more foolish. He knew Violet was right. The duke's daughter was indeed playing him. Were she not a wealthy heiress, he wouldn't have considered marrying her. But he owed it to his family to wed an heiress.

He didn't want Melanie to wait another year before her debut. She deserved to find a husband who would adore her. Instead, she was trying to decide what else they could sell in the household.

And he, of course, was trying to sell himself to the duke's daughter. He decided to bring Persephone a glass of lemonade, and when he arrived at her side to offer it, she gave a false smile. "Aren't you a thoughtful gentleman, Scarsdale. But I'm not thirsty just now." She turned to another suitor, ignoring him.

He felt foolish holding the lemonade, and it made him realize that he was literally at the lady's beck and call. And she treated him no better than a servant. To be truthful, she probably thought of him in that way.

This couldn't go on. He'd been patient, allowing Persephone time to make her decision. But he'd had just about enough of her teasing.

He saw Violet standing at the edge of the ballroom, and he

crossed over to see her. She appeared shaken up, as if she'd seen a ghost. "Here." He handed her the lemonade. "What's wrong? You look upset."

"It's nothing," she admitted. "Lady Ashleigh recognized me, that's all." She took a sip of the lemonade. He sensed that there was more, but she wasn't going to admit it.

"Ashleigh won't tell anyone you're here," he promised. A subtle warning would likely take care of the problem.

"Thank you for the lemonade," Violet answered. She finished it in silence, studying him. "What about you? Is everything all right? Y-you seem upset as well."

"I am." His anger was on edge, mostly anger at himself. He'd believed he could coax an arrogant debutante into marrying him, when the truth was, she was simply enjoying the game. Persephone could have any man she wanted, and she knew it. And she was savoring the attention for as long as possible.

"Do you want to walk through the gardens?" he blurted out. "I need time to think. And I need someone who will be honest with me and tell me that my idea is idiotic. If I even think of an idea."

"I can do that," she said with a light smile. "But you can do nothing to compromise m-my reputation. It would hurt y-you, as well."

"Fortunately, no one even knows who you are. Now let's go somewhere we can talk." He offered his arm, and as they passed a servant, she gave him the empty glass.

They walked across the terrace, and he nodded to Mr. Gregor and Mrs. Harding as they continued down the stairs into the gardens.

"Now what's happened?" Violet asked.

"You were right," he confessed. "Persephone is playing all of us. And I have a feeling that she's enjoying it. She doesn't want to marry any of us—she just wants the attention." He led her along the gravel pathway toward a stone fountain. The water trickled from the mouths of dolphins with a mermaid as the centerpiece.

"You're not wrong," Violet agreed. "The question is, do you have the courage to do w-what you must?"

He paused in front of the fountain, not knowing the answer to that. He could see two possible options. One, force Persephone's hand and demand an answer. Or two, abandon the quest for Persephone's hand in marriage and choose another heiress. He already knew which option Violet preferred. "I worry that whatever I choose, it won't work."

"Perhaps not," she said. "But what you're doing now isn't w-working either."

He let out a slow breath, unable to deny it. It was infuriating, being led astray by a woman who cared nothing for any of her suitors. His pride stung at the realization. "Do you think I should stop courting her?"

She nodded. "I do. But not for the reasons you think." He tilted his head, curious as to what she meant by that. Then Violet continued, "It will make her furious. She b-believes she has you tied up in strings. T-tell her that you understand she does not wish to marry you, and that you now respect those wishes."

The more he thought of it, the more he realized Violet was right. It might provoke Persephone to want him back.

"She doesn't want to lose any of her suitors," Violet said. "And if you l-leave, others might follow."

"They won't," he said. "But you're right, it will get her attention if I stop courting her." Yet, he didn't know if it was worth the risk. Persephone had a vindictive streak and might spread false rumors to deter other heiresses from his courtship.

Damian walked with Violet along the outer perimeter of the garden and then started to guide her back toward the terrace. Changing the subject, he asked, "What did Lady Ashleigh say to you?"

"She offered an apology for her behavior," Violet answered, "and she probably wondered what I was doing here. But I worry that she might say something to Persephone. Or worse, my mother. I can't let anyone find me here."

"I'll find out for you," he asserted. "And I'll make sure Lady Ashleigh says nothing about you being here tonight." Though he didn't think the lady had any reason to do so, his protective instincts rose up.

They reached the terrace, and as he escorted her up the stairs, he saw Persephone standing by the doorway. There were three different gentlemen standing near her, but her attention was fixed solely upon him. Her lips tightened into a frown, and when he saw her, he gave a polite nod.

"Lord Scarsdale." She acknowledged him by lifting her chin. "Did you enjoy your walk in the gardens with Miss Smith?"

"I did," he agreed. "And are you enjoying your array of suitors?" Though he kept his tone light, to sound as if he were teasing her, he wasn't. Not really.

"I thought you would be among them," she sighed. "Or was I wrong to think that you've abandoned me?" She gave a long-suffering pout, making it clear that she expected his apology and adoration.

"Not abandoned," he said gently. But he didn't exactly want to behave like a sycophant, bowing to her every whim. He'd been shadowing her for months now, and Persephone had never accepted a proposal from any of her suitors.

Perhaps it was time to change things. Damian could feel Violet's silent encouragement, and he decided to take the leap of faith. "I have come to realize that perhaps you do not wish to marry a man like me. And so, it might be best if I leave you to your other suitors."

Her face whitened with anger before she masked it. "Now, Damian, don't be foolish. You know I adore you."

But her words rang false. He smiled and answered, "I will bid you a good evening, Lady Persephone." Then he offered his arm to Violet. She took it and accompanied him as they walked down the hall.

"Slow down," she whispered. "Wait just another moment, but do not g-give in."

He was about to ask what she meant, when he heard Lady Persephone calling out, "Scarsdale, really. Come back and talk with me awhile."

At first, his instinct was to obey, but Violet squeezed his elbow in warning. Instead, he turned back to Persephone and gave her a warm smile. The shock on her face was almost worth it.

Then he turned and walked away.

VIOLET LAUGHED IN the coach on the drive back to Harding House. "Did y-you see her face? She looked as if she wanted to murder me."

"You did nothing wrong."

"Oh, but I did. She could have set me on fire with her eyes. Mark my w-words. She will send word and ask you to pay a call on her. If you want her hand in marriage, she might offer it to you." She leaned back in the coach, imagining it.

Lord Scarsdale had offered to bring her home early, and although Mr. Gregor had initially joined them in the vehicle as a chaperone, he'd asked the coachman to drop him off at White's. Though it wasn't entirely proper to be alone with the earl, she hardly cared. It was only for a little longer.

Damian sat across from her, and his smile mirrored her own. "Thank you for your advice, Miss Edwards. I do believe you may be right. Lady Persephone wants what she doesn't have."

Violet had known the ruse would work, but at the same time, it bothered her. Lady Persephone cared about no one but herself. She would be incensed by the idea of losing a suitor and would do everything to bring Lord Scarsdale back to heel.

"Is something wrong?" he asked quietly.

"No. I'm just tired," she admitted. She untied her mask and set it on the seat beside her. Then she reached down and removed her shoes. It felt good to remove them, for they'd been pinching her toes.

Lord Scarsdale's expression shifted, but he said nothing. "I thought you did quite well at the ball. And except for Lady Ashleigh, no one guessed who you were."

"I don't trust her." She wouldn't put it past the woman to spread gossip all over London. And Violet still didn't understand what connection Lady Ashleigh had to the School for Spinsters. Why would she join in the dancing lessons? It made no sense at all.

"I agree that she is not to be trusted," he said, "but it hardly matters now. Even if she does tell people, they might not believe her."

That much was true. Violet sighed and stretched out her toes.

"Are you comfortable, Miss Edwards?" he asked. She detected a note of humor in his tone.

"Yes, very. Y-you should take off your own shoes. I imagine your f-feet hurt as much as mine."

He eyed her for a moment. Then before she could protest, he reached down to her stocking-covered foot.

"Scarsdale, what are you d-doing?" Her words broke off when he began to massage her aching soles. The gentle touch of his hands made her moan with gratitude. "Oh, that f-feels so good. Don't stop."

She closed her eyes, savoring the pressure of his thumb against her foot. It was so improper to let him touch her in this way. She knew that, and yet, she didn't want it to end. When in her lifetime would she ever have a handsome earl massaging her feet? It would never happen again.

Why not enjoy it? She kept her eyes closed while Scarsdale traced the outline of her heel, moving in soft circles.

And suddenly, she imagined that his hand was somewhere else. What if those clever hands went elsewhere? On her shoulders…kneading away the tension before descending lower.

He reached for the other foot, repeating the motion, and she let her mind wander. Only this time, she thought about how it would feel to have his thumbs grazing the edges of her breasts.

Perhaps he would even touch her nipples.

She let out a soft gasp at the image, and when his fingers circled her skin, she thought about him caressing her upon the erect tips. Without knowing why, she grew wet between her legs, and she shifted upon the seat.

I want him, she realized. *And he owes me a favor.* The thought was tantalizing, making her wonder if she dared to be so bold.

"Violet." His voice was husky, and she dared to look at him.

"What?" Her voice trembled in the whisper.

"This is what I imagined a marriage would be," he confessed. "Attending a ball with my wife. Perhaps rubbing her feet afterwards if she wanted me to."

"Every woman would want her husband t-to do that," she said with a quiet smile. "It's wonderful."

He knocked on the ceiling of the coach and ordered the coachman to continue driving around town. Then he set her foot down and reached for her hands. "Do you know what else I would want?"

She shook her head, unable to breathe. His eyes were riveted on her face, and God help her, he looked the way he had that day in the library. As if he wanted to capture her and kiss her until her knees went weak.

Her heartbeat quickened in her chest as she looked into his eyes. It was dark outside, and no one could see them. "Tell me."

"When we got home, I would take her up to our bedchamber and close the door." He reached up to her face and edged his thumb along her jaw. A thousand shivers washed over her, and her own yearning deepened.

"Then what?" She couldn't deny her curiosity or the longing rising within.

Instead of answering her question, he leaned in and stole a kiss. She kissed him back, resting her hands upon his chest. For a few minutes, he simply claimed several kisses, until she relaxed against him, enjoying it.

Although she ought to question why he was kissing her in the coach, she didn't want to. All her life, she'd been the forgotten wallflower, the woman no one wanted. But right now, she held his full attention. He *did* want her, and she savored the forbidden feelings.

"I would kiss my wife," he said against her lips. "And I would begin to undress her." His hands moved beneath her cloak to the back of her gown, and he rested his fingers upon the buttons.

"Show me," she whispered.

For a long moment, he didn't move. Perhaps it was hesitation or perhaps it was honor. But she knew their time together was drawing to an end. And if he had to sacrifice himself to that horrid woman, at least Violet could claim a few moments to herself first.

She had no intention of losing her innocence—but she did want to know more. And who better to teach her than a man who knew how to seduce a woman?

"You owe me a favor," she said quietly. "I want to collect it now."

His eyes grew hooded with desire. "Tell me what you want."

She was afraid to admit the truth, but this would likely be her only chance. It took all her courage to say, "I want you to touch me. The way a husband touches a wife."

Damian unfastened her cloak and let it fall before he began loosening the buttons. One by one, he freed them until he reached her stays. Her gown grew looser, and suddenly, she grew nervous, not knowing what he would do.

He seemed to sense her unease, and he began kissing her again as a distraction. Then he pulled her to sit on his lap with her back to him. He arranged her skirts until she could feel the hot ridge of his erection pressing against her bottom through his trousers. She knew very little about the sexual act, but his arousal only deepened her own.

Her mind tried again to talk her out of this, but her heart yearned to know more. It took only a few moments for him to lower her gown, trapping her arms in the sleeves as he bared her skin. Though he left her chemise in place, his hands moved to cup her breasts through the soft linen.

"If you were my wife, I would strip you naked until you could feel my hands upon you." He didn't touch her yet, and the anticipation only heightened her tension. He leaned in and kissed her throat while his hands rested upon her heavy breasts.

She was desperate for him to stroke and caress her bare skin. But he did nothing more than cup her, with the linen barrier between them, though she desperately wanted more.

"I would pleasure you until you couldn't stand." His tongue slid against her neck, and she dug her hands into the coach seat, wondering when he would move his hands.

"You're so lovely," he said, moving his hands slightly higher. Her nipples were tight, aching for him, but still, he didn't touch them. "But more than that, I like spending time with you. I enjoy our lessons and the way you speak your mind to me."

"Scarsdale, please," she begged.

His hands moved higher and, this time, she felt the heat of his palms against her nipples. She exhaled sharply, and he moved his hips against her. Only then did he caress the erect tips with his fingers. Sensations poured through her, and she let out a moan.

This was a moment forbidden to both of them. She reached back to touch his hair, savoring his wicked touch. With every stroke, she felt as if her body grew hotter, and between her legs, she craved him.

"I know this w-won't last," she whispered. "I know I'm not who you want. But..."

"Right now, you're exactly who I want," he contradicted. He lifted her up and drew her to face him. He moved her skirts aside until she was straddling him. And dear God, despite the barriers of fabric, she could feel the ridge of his manhood. She wanted to know more, and a wicked part of her wanted him to unfasten those trousers so she could feel him. The very sensation of his thick length against her drawers was so shocking, she felt her inhibitions starting to waver.

"If you were my husband," she whispered, "I would l-love

this. With you." Her arms came around his neck, and he claimed her mouth again, more intensely this time. His tongue threaded with hers, and he began to move against her. She could feel him, and it kindled her desire even hotter.

"But somehow, I don't think I'll ever have this with someone else," she confessed. "I don't know if anyone would even want to marry me."

"They will," he swore as he reached for her breast. He slid his hand beneath the chemise and touched her bare skin for the first time. She shuddered, gripping his hair as sensations poured through her. His thumb edged the puckered nipple, and she pressed her hips closer to him, wanting him closer. "I have no doubt of it, Violet."

But she wouldn't marry him. There was no chance of that.

"Men may be idiots, but they're not blind," he said, his mouth brushing against her lips while he tantalized her breasts and nipples. "You are a beautiful woman. And very desirable."

In his arms, she believed it. Their time together was running out, but she wanted to know more. Lord Scarsdale had awakened her to the restless yearning of desire.

"There's so much more I need to learn," she said, threading her hands through his hair. "I w-want you to teach me." To make it clear, she pulled his face down to hers and kissed him. She didn't care that this was utterly forward behavior or that the coach could stop at any moment. Right now, she surrendered to her own needs.

And when he cursed against her mouth and ravaged her lips, she drew his hands to her breasts so he would have no doubt what she wanted.

DAMIAN FELT THE softness of her curves, and her kiss drove him wild. He didn't know when everything had changed or why Violet was offering herself, but right now, he didn't care. Yes, it was reckless, and he knew better than to seduce an innocent. He wasn't about to claim her virginity in this coach. But there was far more he could show her. And by God, he could teach her how to find her own pleasure.

He moved to the edge of the seat, adjusting her green skirts as he turned her to face him. Then he unfastened the buttons of his trousers, freeing his erection. There was only the barest layer of linen between their bodies. He gripped her waist and moved against her, thrusting gently.

Violet let out a breath, gasping as their bodies met. But she pressed against him, and somehow her instinctive movements were exactly right. He rewarded her by seizing her hips and using his body to tantalize her. At the same time, he imagined sliding his manhood against the wet seam of her body.

"Scarsdale," she whispered. "I can hardly breathe."

She closed her eyes, lifting up against him, and he guided her in a rhythm of pressure and release. And God above, it felt good. "You want to know what it would be like to be seduced by a rake?"

Her lips were swollen, her hair falling down against her face, but she nodded. "Yes."

"There's not much time," he warned. "And I'm not going to claim you. But we could have...our own lesson."

He reached beneath her skirts. Against his palm, he felt the silk stockings, and he caressed them for a moment. He moved his hand higher to her knee, never taking his eyes from her face. Then he drew his palm upward between her thighs until he found the slit in her drawers.

"Look at me, Violet," he commanded. He touched her intimately, and she was already slick with desire. He moved his thumb against the bud of her sex, and she gave a cry of shock.

"Damian," she murmured. "I've n-never felt anything like that before."

If she were his lover, he would lift her skirts right now before he plunged deep. He had no doubt he could easily pleasure her.

She was so responsive, and he leaned forward, hovering his mouth above her breast. The anticipation was driving her wild, and even now, she squirmed against him, seeking her own release. But they had only just begun, and he wanted to draw it out as long as possible until their time ran out.

"Do you want me to stop?" he asked, stroking lazy circles against her swollen flesh. "Or do you want to learn more?"

Dazed, she whispered, "I know I should tell y-you to stop. But I keep imagining what it would feel like."

She moved her hands beneath his jacket and helped him take it off. Slowly, she slid her palms down his chest as if he were everything she'd ever dreamed of. Then she loosened his shirt and reached beneath it to touch his chest.

"You're so strong," she said. "I love touching y-you."

And God help him, he wanted her. He savored the way she moved her hands over his chest, resting upon his wildly beating heart. She touched him as if she had all the time in the world. There was no calculated motive, only her desire to learn every inch of his skin.

Never in his life had he wanted a woman more, and it stunned him.

He lowered his head to her breast and tasted her nipple for the first time. The moment he suckled her, he slid his finger deep inside her slick depths.

Her reaction was a throaty moan, and she glided her hand down his chest. His erection was straining against her skirts, and her palm accidentally bumped it.

He was beyond caring and drew her hand to curl around him. "Stroke me, Violet."

She obeyed, and he nearly lost it with her first squeeze. He showed her how to start a rhythm, and he slid a second finger inside her, mimicking the motion of her hand.

"Scarsdale," she whispered, "what are you doing to me?"

"Pleasuring you," he answered. "You're in command. If you want me to move faster, then you do the same. If you want me to slow down, I will."

In the darkness, he could no longer see her face, but she began to move her hand upon him in long, deep strokes. He did the same and lowered his mouth to taste the sweetness of her nipples.

"I've n-never felt anything like this before," she answered. "I don't know what to do."

THIS WICKED MAN was making her feel things she'd never imagined. He was using his mouth and tongue to torture her, and the pleasure was so blinding, Violet could hardly bear it. It was almost too much to endure.

She was treading on the edge of something she didn't understand. But she experimented with him, changing the pace and moving her hand faster. Although he was seducing her, she almost felt as if he'd given her that power.

Her breathing was unsteady as he entered and withdrew with his fingers. She felt a slight moisture at the head of him and then she stroked him with her thumb. Scarsdale let out a hiss, and she asked, "Did I hurt you?"

"Only if you stop." His own breathing was as unsteady as hers, and she clenched his fingers deep inside. She noticed that he grew harder as she moved her palm, and the pleasure was so strong, she arched to meet it. Her gasps held a rhythm of her own, and his touch was searing.

He lifted her skirts higher and pressed the thumb of one hand to her bud while he penetrated with his other fingers. She was straining hard, moving her fist against him until they were both on the edge.

"Let go, Violet," he demanded. "Surrender to what you feel."

She tried to obey, focusing on the white-hot pleasure that was burgeoning deep inside. And abruptly, she seized up, her body erupting with a hard release. A flood of pleasure crashed upon her, and she bucked against his hand, arching her back as it went on and on.

Violet was nearly crying out as her body trembled, and he took her hand and moved it against him. It took only seconds before she felt him shudder, and a warm wetness coated her hand. He crushed his mouth to hers to muffle his own shout as he lost control.

She was pliant against him, his fingers still buried deep within. Never had she known such a pleasure existed.

But instead of feeling joy, she wanted to break down into sobs. Not because she was embarrassed or felt regret. No, it was because this man was going to marry someone else. She would not be his wife, nor would she share his bed.

Lord Scarsdale had completely torn her life apart in a matter of minutes. The tears flooded her eyes, even as he held her gently and tried to help her with her clothing before he fastened his own.

Damian wasn't hers and never would be. He had no right to touch her in this way, and yet he'd given her a precious memory, one she would carry for always.

The coach drew to a stop, and Scarsdale kissed her softly. He enfolded the cloak around her, and she didn't bother to worry about her corset or her gown. If she held it closed, the cloak would hide everything.

For a moment, neither of them could speak. "I need to go," she whispered.

He opened the door to the coach and exited to help her down. But his hands lingered on her waist a little longer.

It took everything she had to turn away from him so he would not see her tears fall.

Chapter Eleven

"**Y**OU WANTED TO see me, Lady Persephone?" Damian was surprised to find the lady in the drawing room of her father's house, chaperoned by her maid instead of surrounded by suitors.

"Yes, I did." She smiled calmly. "I thought we could talk."

For a moment, she seemed like a different person. Gone was her usual flirtatious demeanor, and instead, she sat upon a gilded chair with an expectant look as if they were friends. Which, of course, they weren't. His suspicions tightened, and he wondered what she was up to.

She gestured for him to sit down. "Would you care for tea?"

Damian gave a noncommittal nod. It didn't matter what she poured in the cup, truthfully. But she demonstrated her ladylike skills in pouring out, and he stared at the steaming cup.

"I must admit, you hurt my feelings last night," she said in a soft voice.

"In what way?" He kept his tone neutral, fully expecting her games.

Persephone added sugar to her own cup of tea and stirred it. "When you said you no longer wished to court me." Her face fell, and she confessed, "I've been leading you on, haven't I? I made the mistake of believing you would wait as long as I wanted. But then you danced with *her*, didn't you?" She took a sip of her tea, her dismay evident. "Mr. Gregor's niece, whatever her name was."

She sent him a pointed look, but Damian ignored it. He wasn't about to reveal Violet's identity. Instead, he asked, "Why am I here, Lady Persephone? You've made it clear enough that you don't want me as a husband."

"That's not true at all." She blushed prettily and took another sip of tea. "And that is precisely why I asked you to come today. No pretenses. Only possibilities."

He didn't know what to say. And so, he simply took a sip of the tea he didn't want, as a means of avoiding an answer.

"I thought we could...get to know one another better," she suggested. "I have spoken to my father about us."

Damian felt a rise of unease. After last night, he'd abandoned all thoughts of marrying a woman like Lady Persephone. He'd never truly liked her as a person—but he'd been willing to tolerate her vanity for the sake of saving his family. And somehow, when he'd said he didn't want her, there had been an invisible release of a burden he hadn't known he was carrying. Then, too, it wasn't fair to Persephone. He'd been acting as badly as she had, pretending he wanted to marry her. It wasn't fair, and it wasn't right.

And then, he'd enjoyed Violet's company so much, he'd nearly seduced her. He'd been caught up by her innocent responses, from the way she'd kissed him to the way she'd trembled in his arms. There had been nothing but honesty and desire between them.

How could he possibly entertain the idea of marrying Persephone now? The very thought was abhorrent. He wanted Violet, not a frivolous debutante who couldn't decide which suitor to dance with.

Persephone was looking at him with expectancy, so he inquired, "What exactly did you say to your father?" he asked.

"I told him that you had asked for my hand in marriage. And

that the two of you should discuss it." She gave him a wide smile. "I must confess, it wasn't until you turned me down that I realized what I would lose, my lord. I have grown so accustomed to having you at my side, the thought of you not being there was...simply awful. I must apologize for my behavior." She gestured for him to take a sandwich, but he couldn't bring himself to eat. His stomach was churning, for he knew what he ought to say—and yet, he didn't want to wed this woman. Not when he preferred dancing with Violet, singing with her, and most of all, taking her into his arms.

Persephone waited for him to speak, but he had no idea what to say. At last, she prompted, "Will you not accept my apology?"

Oh. He gave a single nod.

"Thank you, my lord. I cannot tell you how glad I am that you will forgive me." She leaned back in the chair, smoothing her skirts. "My father is not here at the moment. When should I tell him that you'll pay a call upon him?"

Damian's brow furrowed. "Pay a call upon him for what?"

Persephone laughed gaily. "Why, to ask for my hand in marriage again, of course." She reached for her teacup once again. "My answer might be very different this time."

He remained silent at first, trying to grasp this. For months, he'd done everything she wanted, playing the role of the dutiful suitor. And now that he'd abandoned Persephone, she was suddenly willing to consider marriage? He stared at her, realizing that Violet had been right all along. Persephone only wanted what she couldn't have.

Or was he being too harsh? Right now, her face held only softness, an expression without guile. Was this what she was like without the other suitors? Had he judged her by the pretense she wore in public? Was she a different woman in private, one who actually had a heart and compassion? His instincts warned him not to believe her...but it wasn't so easy to walk away from a dowry that would give back what his father had lost.

And what of Violet? She didn't deserve to be abandoned after he'd nearly seduced her. It had been a stolen moment, and he'd surrendered to his own temptation.

Yet, what future could there be for them? He couldn't set aside his family's needs for his own desires, no matter how much he cared for her. What right did he have to entertain the idea of a marriage with a woman who had nothing at all?

A grim resolution settled in his gut. Despite everything, he had responsibilities to his family. He didn't want to see his sisters having no Season or no prospects for good husbands—not when he could transform their lives. All he had to do was agree to wed a woman he didn't like.

He pushed away the bleak thoughts of a future he didn't want. With no other alternative, he said, "I will pay a call upon the duke by the end of the week."

VIOLET HAD JUST finished her speaking lesson with the Pettifords when the earl arrived. She hadn't seen him in several days—truthfully, she hadn't expected him to return. Not after what she'd demanded as her favor in the coach. A hollow ache caught in her chest at the sight of him, though she tried to behave as if his presence had no effect.

But the moment his eyes met hers, it was like a physical blow.

Don't let him hurt you, her brain warned. It was likely he'd come to apologize.

"You're doing very well, Miss Edwards," Mrs. Pettiford praised. "Keep practicing, keep singing, and with time, your stutter will be more controlled."

Violet murmured her thanks, although all of them knew the stutter would never truly go away. She had been taking lessons every day from them, and she'd come to understand that this was about managing her condition and not becoming overwhelmed by embarrassment. Her speech would never be perfect, but she wasn't going to allow other young women to bully her. Not anymore.

After the couple departed, Lord Scarsdale greeted her. "Miss Edwards."

"I...didn't expect to see you again," she confessed. But even though he didn't smile, his presence warmed her. She drank in his handsome face, his dark blond hair and green eyes. Her cheeks burned with the memory of his hands and mouth upon her bare skin—and she couldn't deny that she wanted his touch.

"I wasn't certain if it was wise to do so," he admitted. "But Mr. Gregor suggested that I come one last time."

Something about his expression evoked an empty unhappiness. He looked as if he'd lost everything, and she sensed that he didn't truly wish to be here.

He continued, "I should never have taken advantage of you the way I did that night in the coach. It was wrong and unfair to you. Let me make up for that."

She didn't regret it at all, for she had never imagined a man's touch could feel so wonderful. Likely, she was supposed to be embarrassed or outraged. Instead, she savored the memory, thinking of him every night when she lay awake in bed.

She still wasn't certain why he'd come, and at her curious look, he continued. "We need to set a plan to reveal your progress in London. And you need to face your family."

The very thought of going home again was horrifying. Violet tried to keep her mind steady and clear, but she sensed that the moment she returned, she would revert into a pathetic shadow of herself. "I need more time," she protested. "The moment my mother knows w-where I am, she'll demand that I go to live with my grandmother."

"She won't do that if you are engaged to be married," he said.

All the breath left from her lungs. Was he suggesting that *he* would pretend an engagement with her? Her heartbeat quickened, and a wild hope flared within her imagination. Then she dared to ask, "Are you...suggesting that *you* would pretend to be my f-fiancé? That we would be courting?"

His face fell. "I…no. I'm afraid I cannot do that."

And just like that, her hopes diminished into ashes. She sank down upon the chaise longue, trying to gather control of her riotous emotions. *See,* her brain reminded her. *He doesn't want you. You're not good enough. He needs to marry a woman with a large dowry, not you.*

"Oh," she said at last. "Then…what did you mean?"

"I have friends," he offered. "One of them might be willing to step in. We will find the right man for you. Someone decent who will treat you well. And for all we know, the false engagement might become a real one, in time. That would be enough to end any objections your mother might have."

The thought of pretending to be betrothed to a stranger was so outrageous, she couldn't bear it. No. It was impossible.

"I don't w-want to tell lies," she said quietly. "I'm not going to pretend something that isn't real."

"You don't have to be alone when you face your family," he said. "Let me help you." He sat down beside her and asked, "I thought you said there was a gentleman who had caught your interest? Someone you wanted?"

"That person was you," she murmured, not looking at him. There was no point in trying to hide it anymore.

But then, Damian reached out to her face and drew her to look at him. In his eyes, instead of seeing pity, she saw raw emotions she didn't understand. Within seconds, his mouth was upon hers, kissing her as if he couldn't stand to let her go. She kissed him back, winding her arms around his neck, and tears welled up.

"I can't have you," he said against her mouth. "No matter how much I might want you. No matter how much I think about you."

At that, her tears did fall. Damn it all, she'd fallen in love with him. And his words were breaking her apart.

"I have to marry someone I don't want to wed," he said, cupping her face between his hands. "To save my family."

She lowered her hands to her lap. "I know you do." The words came out dull, lifeless.

"I am speaking with the duke tomorrow," he said. "And when I do, I must ask him for Persephone's hand in marriage."

The emptiness in her chest only cut deeper. She didn't even bother to hide the tears that fell.

Damian held her gaze for a long moment. With his thumb, he wiped a single tear away. "We both knew this would have to happen. There's no choice for me. I have the means to solve my family's problems. How can I turn my back on that opportunity?"

"All you have to do is sacrifice your happiness for theirs," she said. "I know."

It didn't matter that she would fight for him if he wasn't willing to fight for himself. She stood from the chaise longue and said dully, "You should go now, my lord."

"What about your plans?" he asked. "I meant to help you with your...debut."

"I will attend another gathering this w-week," she said. "And I will face my family o-on my own." The quiet words belied her own lack of confidence. It was entirely possible that she would fall back into the trap of doing exactly what they wanted her to do or become a wallflower once more.

But something in her rebelled against it. She didn't want to be that person anymore, someone who would retreat from the world in the midst of cruelty. She wanted to stand tall, no matter her fears, and face them all. And even if she failed, she had to try. It gave her a frail stem of hope to grasp.

"Is there anything I can do to help you?" Lord Scarsdale asked.

You've done enough, she thought. He was breaking her heart by being here. She couldn't bear to look at him while he was being kind. If he behaved like a friend or exuded any sort of thoughtfulness, she would only think of the man she wanted but could never have. It would be far easier to break their friendship now.

"Yes," she said at last. "You can leave and not come back."

His expression turned weary, as if he'd expected this. "I'm sorry, Violet. I never should have touched you. I just…couldn't stop myself." He looked as if he wanted to say more, but he fell silent.

"Just go," she insisted. "And when you see me at the ball, pretend it was the way it used to be. When you didn't notice me at all." She pushed back the surge of hurt rising within. "I don't want you to talk to me. Don't ask me to dance. Let me be invisible."

"I hope you find the husband you want," he said quietly. "Someone who sees what I see when I look at you."

And what is that? she wanted to ask but didn't.

He answered her unspoken question by taking her hands in his. "A woman who is warmhearted and beautiful. Someone far beyond what they could ever imagine." Then he leaned in and cupped her cheek, stealing one last kiss. It nearly broke her heart.

He stood from his chair and offered his hand. When she took it, he squeezed her palm. "I want you to show them who you really are, Violet. It's going to be all right, I promise you."

She offered a weak smile but didn't believe him at all. Her worst nightmare was about to begin.

DAMIAN GAVE HIS hat to a servant while he awaited his audience with the Duke of Westerford. While he sat in the drawing room, he saw a painting on the wall of a woman and her dog. The animal reminded him of Violet's dog Rupert, and the guilt struck him hard once again.

He knew what he had to do—ask the duke for Persephone's hand in marriage. It was necessary, and she had finally agreed to his suit. Somehow, he would have to make the best of the situation.

The duke entered the room, and Damian stood. "Your Grace."

"Sit down, Scarsdale," the duke said.

He obeyed, and Westerford chose a seat of his own. "So, you've come to pay a call because you have a question to ask me, I understand?" His gray eyes twinkled in anticipation.

Damian forced a smile on his face. "Yes, Your Grace. I was hoping to ask permission for your daughter's hand in marriage."

The duke gave a nod and leaned back. "Yes, she told me you were going to ask." He tilted his head to one side. "She's always been a lively one, my Persephone. Very opinionated. How will you handle her?"

In separate houses, Damian thought. *Hundreds of miles away, if possible.*

"I intend to give her the freedom she desires," he answered. "Asking Lady Persephone to remain obedient is an exercise in futility."

At that, the duke barked a laugh. "You do know her, don't you?" His face warmed with sincerity then. "Yes, I think you will do quite well for her husband." With a shrug, he added, "I will let her know you have my permission. Ask her again, and see what she says."

"Is she here now?" Damian inquired.

"Oh, no. I think she went off with three other gentlemen to Gunter's," he said. "Suitably chaperoned, of course. Her mother went with her."

Damian kept his smile, though the tension tightened. "I suppose I shall go and invite her on a drive. We can talk then."

"If you can drag her away. My Persephone does love attention."

Damian gave no argument with that, though he found it telling that she had asked him to speak with her father and then had gone with other gentlemen for ices. "Thank you for your permission, Your Grace."

The duke stood, and Damian followed suit, inclining his head slightly. After the man departed, he glanced back at the portrait with the dog, and a heaviness descended over him.

He knew what he had to do, but it didn't make it any easier.

"YOU HAVE A caller, Miss Edwards," Mr. Gregor announced.

"I don't want to see him," she answered, pushing aside the page of words Mrs. Pettiford had given her to practice. Rupert was nestled at her feet, and she drew comfort from her dog's presence. She didn't want to hear anything from the earl at all. It was easier to grieve the loss when he wasn't here.

"It's your sister."

At that, she stood immediately. Rupert woke up and began to pace, agitated by her sudden change of mood. "Charity is here?" Panic clenched her stomach, and she asked, "What of my family? Do they know where I am?"

Mr. Gregor shook his head slowly. "Shall I show her in?"

"Yes, please." Violet gripped her hands together, wondering how Charity had found out where she was. Her sister hadn't been there the night of the masquerade, so there was no way she'd recognized her.

Before she could wonder any further, her sister hurried through the door and then embraced her hard. Rupert began barking and dancing in circles.

"Oh, Violet, I was so worried."

"How did you find me?" She hugged her sister back, but she wondered how Charity had even discovered she was gone. When Rupert put his paws on her gown, she told him, "No. Down." The dog obeyed, but his tail continued to twitch with excitement.

"Grandmother arrived two days ago and told us you never arrived in Bedfordshire. We've been asking if anyone saw you."

There was only one possibility Violet could imagine. "Ashleigh told you."

"Only because I threatened her," Charity said. "I thought if anyone would know where you'd gone, it might be Ashleigh or Persephone. They're both so awful...but they do know everyone in London."

"What do you m-mean you...threatened Ashleigh?" Violet couldn't understand what her sister was talking about. "With w-what?"

"Let's just say that some of Ashleigh's secrets aren't so se-cret," Charity answered. "But I want to know why you've run away here."

Violet glanced around. "Let's take the dog for a w-walk along the Serpentine, and I'll tell you everything." She went to get the dog's lead and then she gave orders to a footman to prepare a carriage for them and join them as an escort.

When they arrived, Rupert was beyond delighted to be out-side on a walk with them. The dog's tail wagged with ecstasy, and Violet kept a firm grip on his lead to keep him from dragging her down the gravel path. Once they were a slight distance away from their escort, she lowered her voice. "I am attending Mrs. Harding's School for Young Ladies."

"The School for Spinsters?" Charity blinked at that. "I...well, I'd heard rumors, but...it's real?"

Violet suppressed the desire to roll her eyes. "Of course, it's real. And I-I am grateful to them for their h-help."

Charity linked her arm with hers and walked with her along the pathway. "Are you happy here, Violet?"

She nodded and tried to force a smile. Rupert was sniffing the ground, so she stopped to allow it.

"You don't look happy," her sister said quietly. "Did some-thing happen? Were they mean to you?"

"No." *I just got my heart broken, that's all.* But she didn't want to even mention Lord Scarsdale. The moment she thought of him, her skin blazed with color.

"You look as if you're walking to the executioner's block," Charity remarked. "Are you upset that I found you?"

Violet sighed. "No. But I'm not coming home. Not until I finish w-what I've started."

Her sister studied her as they walked. "You do look different,

Violet. And not just your gown. That color does suit you, though."

"Thank you." She glanced down at her blue morning gown, and ventured a smile, thinking of her adventure with the modiste when the woman had tried to sell her an orange gown. Now that she thought of it, a vivid shade of orange might be flattering against her brown hair. She'd been horrified at the time, but it might not be that bad.

They walked along the gravel pathway, and she told her sister about her lessons. About Ashleigh and the dancing. And how she had begun taking command of her life, starting with the dog and then finally her night at the masquerade.

Her sister eyed her and added, "There's something else. You've met someone, haven't you?"

Violet couldn't stop the color from spreading over her cheeks. "It—it doesn't matter. He's not going to m-marry me."

"You *did*," her sister breathed. "Now this is what I'd rather hear about. Who was it?"

Before she could do anything, Rupert tore away from her, dragging the lead behind him. "Oh, dear." Violet grasped her skirts, wondering what the dog had seen. Probably a rabbit. "Rupert, no!" She hurried around the corner and nearly skidded to a stop when the dog took off in a full run toward the Earl of Scarsdale...who was walking with Lady Persephone. Her mood plummeted, but then the dog jumped up on Scarsdale. His tail wagged with ecstasy when the earl reached down to rub his ears.

Rupert was delightedly licking the earl's fingers, his tail wagging furiously as if to say, *See? I found him for you.*

"Who does that creature belong to?" Persephone was already pulling away, horrified by the dog's enthusiasm.

Was it terrible to hope that Rupert would put his muddy paws on her gown? Probably.

"Violet?" Charity asked. "Is that who you..." Her words broke off, and she started laughing. "Of course, it is. I can see it on your face. How wonderful."

"It's not w-wonderful at all." She sighed and walked toward them to retrieve her dog. When she saw Damian, his expression shifted from amusement to something else. In that moment, he looked as if he wanted to take her hand and kiss her senseless.

And unfortunately, she was weak enough that she would not hesitate to go with him and enjoy the senseless kissing.

"Rupert, get down," she ordered. The earl wasn't helping matters by rubbing the dog's belly and calling him a good boy.

"Is that animal yours?" Lady Persephone demanded.

Violet took the lead and turned to face her. "Yes, he is." To Damian, she added, "I'm s-sorry he interrupted your walk. I don't know what got into him."

The look in his eyes said he knew exactly what it was. The dog remembered him and missed him. Just as much as she missed him herself.

"You should control him better," Persephone sniffed. With a sneer, she added, "H-h-he's t-t-terrible."

A sudden flash of irritation caught her. She took a deep breath and said, "You don't…need to…mock me, Persephone."

The earl's gaze held pride, while the duke's daughter grew enraged. "How dare you speak to me like that?"

"I could ask the same of y-you." She coughed to hide the slight stutter.

At that, Charity intervened. "Violet, I don't think I've been introduced to your…friends."

It was partially true that her sister had never been formally introduced to Persephone, even though she knew who the duke's daughter was. Violet understood it was Charity's desperate attempt at peacemaking. And though she recognized what her sister was trying to do, she was tired of Persephone's mean behavior. It wasn't wise to confront the woman in this way, but Violet wasn't about to retreat any longer.

The only problem was, she didn't like seeing Persephone holding the earl's arm. Jealousy caught her off guard, and she relaxed her hold on Rupert's lead. Another wicked part of her wished the dog would relieve himself upon Persephone. Which wasn't kind at all.

With a sigh, she said, "Lord Scarsdale, may I p-present my sister Charity Edwards?" She supposed she ought to have introduced Charity to Persephone first, but the truth was, she didn't want to.

"I am pleased to make your acquaintance," he said, inclining his head. The wicked look in his eyes suggested that he knew exactly what she'd done.

"And Lady Persephone, my sister Charity."

The duke's daughter raised her chin but did not extend her hand or speak a word. The earl cleared his throat and waited, studying Persephone. The frigid expression on the young woman's face said more than any words could, and she turned away.

"I am sure the lady is delighted to meet you," Damian responded. "Would you care to join us?"

I'd rather drown myself in the Serpentine, Violet thought.

"I w-wouldn't dream of interrupting you both," she responded, sending him a look. "But do enjoy your walk. I will try to k-keep a firmer grip on Rupert." Even so, she leaned down to stroke the dog's ears. He flopped to the ground in delight and rolled to expose his belly once again.

She indulged him by bending down to pet him. He might not have soiled Persephone's gown, but he was a sweet boy. He most definitely deserved a treat when they arrived back at Mrs. Harding's.

"I will bid you both a good afternoon, then." Damian tipped his hat and offered his arm to Persephone.

Charity waited until they were a good distance away before she said, "Violet, what have you done?"

"I'm petting m-my dog," she answered. Though she knew that wasn't the question at all.

"It's him, isn't it. The Earl of Scarsdale. You've gone and fallen in love with him."

At that, she stood up. "I haven't."

"I'm not blind, Violet. You were practically glowing. And he looked as if he wanted to leave Persephone and carry you off." Her sister let out a dramatic sigh. "It was terribly romantic."

Violet didn't quite know what to say. Yes, it *was* romantic. And she did care about the earl more than she wanted to admit. "But he's n-not going to leave Lady Persephone. Not w-with the dowry she has."

"You should fight for him," Charity sighed. "He's so handsome. I would fight for him if he looked at me like that."

"He doesn't look at me in that way."

"Then you're blind."

Violet ignored her sister but instead walked along the riverbank watching Lord Scarsdale and Lady Persephone. Although the young woman had her hand on his arm, the earl's posture was stiff. He didn't look at all like the teasing man she'd known. It hurt to see them, to recognize that he had chosen this course and would see it through until the end.

"I will be a-attending a musicale on Saturday," she told her sister. "Lady B-Bridgeford's, I think."

Charity stiffened. "We were invited to the musicale as well, Violet." Her eyes held sympathy. "What will you do when you see Mother? Or our grandmother, for that matter? She's coming, too."

The familiar wave of uncertainty caught Violet in the stomach, and her mood turned grim. But then again, she'd always known this time would come. It wasn't realistic to think that she had months to escape. It had always been a matter of weeks.

"I'll face them both," she said, "and then I will decide whether or not to return home." Though she wanted to believe that her mother could be reasonable, the truth was, she suspected she would have to remain at Mrs. Harding's until she could gain a marriage proposal of some kind.

"If she tries to send you away—" Charity started.

"—I'll refuse," she finished. "I promise, I'll stand up to her."

There was no other choice anymore. But oddly enough, she *did* feel as if she'd made progress. She had already confronted Persephone, and it hadn't been as terrible as she'd imagined.

Her sister's face turned pained, and she exhaled sharply. "Well. Unfortunately, you won't have to wait that long. They're here." She nodded behind Violet, and she turned around to see her mother and grandmother approaching.

Oh, dear. Not good at all. "I-I wasn't expecting to face them this soon," Violet admitted.

"Just be strong," Charity said. "And know that it's only because you're my sister that I'm not running away as fast as I can right now. Because this is going to be awful."

Violet wholeheartedly agreed, and she clenched the dog's lead, trying to gather her courage.

"They'll try to force me to return home," she said softly. "And I don't think I'm ready for that yet."

"Then don't come home. She doesn't know where you're staying."

Violet heard the crunching sound of their footsteps against the gravel but didn't turn around. Rupert sniffed the ground, his tail wagging furiously.

"Violet, what on earth are you doing here?" she heard her mother's voice. "You were supposed to be in Bedfordshire."

Her mother's face was nearly purple with fury. The familiar fear washed over Violet, but she forced herself to take a breath and calm down.

She ignored her mother's demanding question and instead took a moment to collect herself. Rupert leaped toward Thomasina, and Violet barely managed to pull the dog back before he jumped up.

"I'm sorry," she said. "He's still in training." She glanced at her sister, and Charity stifled a laugh. Her grandmother, on the other hand, did not appear amused at all. Rupert started to approach, and Annabelle tapped her cane on the gravel. The dog immediately sat.

Violet was so startled at Rupert's sudden obedience, she couldn't help her smile. "Hello, Grandmother."

Annabelle didn't return the smile. "You and I are going to have a talk later."

And suddenly, it struck Violet that she did have more power than she realized. Her mother and grandmother were controlling, yes, but it didn't mean she had to succumb to their wishes. Nor did she have to cower or let the woman berate her in public.

"How have y-you been, Mother?" she asked airily.

Thomasina looked as if she wanted to choke, but instead, she masked her disapproval and said, "We've been worried sick about you. How could you do such a thing? Your grandmother thought you could have been in an accident on the road. She sent many men to look for you, and yet you were here in London the entire time?"

"I was, y-yes." She straightened her posture and met her grandmother's icy stare. She stopped to clear her throat, masking the stutter again. "That is, I was staying w-with a friend."

"Not anymore, you're not," Thomasina snapped. "You will return with us this very instant."

Charity started to step between them when their mother reached out. Rupert let out a low growl, and Violet was grateful to both of them.

"I will return w-when I am ready," she said. "Not before." She gripped the dog's lead again to hide her shaking hands. But she didn't back down from her mother.

"I've never seen such ungrateful behavior," her mother said. "You will obey me at once."

"Or what?" Violet asked. "You'll send me away?"

Was it her imagination, or was there a gleam of approval in her grandmother's eyes? For a long moment, there was a silent challenge between them. Finally, Charity spoke up. "You look wonderful, Violet. I've missed you." She gave her a hug of support.

She warmed to her sister's words. "And I've m-missed you."

"And we'll see you at Lady Bridgeford's musicale this Saturday?" Charity suggested. "You will come, won't you?"

"I—well, of course," Violet answered. She'd already told her sister she was going, but she recognized it as a means of saying goodbye.

"I was so glad to see you in the gardens today," Charity said. "I'm sorry you have to go, but I do understand. You don't want to keep your friend waiting any longer."

Violet motioned for her footman to come closer, and she ordered him to bring the carriage. "Goodbye. I will see y-you on Saturday."

And with that, her grandmother answered, "All right, Violet." But despite the matriarch's answer, she sensed that the woman had every intention of taking her back to Bedfordshire.

Which meant that Violet had to find a husband quickly.

Chapter Twelve

DAMIAN AWAKENED IN the middle of the night to the sound of glass breaking. He shoved the covers aside and pulled on trousers before he opened the door.

It seemed that his father had arrived home from Scarsdale. And from the sound of it, Jonas was in an unholy, drunken rage.

He hurried down the stairs and narrowly dodged a marble bust that his father threw at the wall. "You made a fool out of me," the marquess snarled, lunging for him.

Damian caught his father before he could strike and gripped his wrists. The smell of whiskey made it clear that Jonas had been drinking most of the way home from Scotland. "It's late," he said. He glanced around for his mother but didn't see her. Likely, Clara had already fled to her room.

"You let me believe there was an inheritance," Jonas raged. "There was nothing. They had no idea what I was talking about. *You* wrote that letter."

"Yes, I did," Damian admitted. There was no reason to hide it anymore.

"Why, damn you?"

"Because I needed time to find out how much damage you've done to this household. You're not yourself anymore, and you haven't taken on your responsibilities as marquess. You've spent every coin we have, and even money we don't have. Melanie and Regan don't have dowries anymore because of you. And someone has to save this family before you humiliate us all." He nodded toward the footmen. "Help me get him to his bed."

"I ought to have you horsewhipped," his father shot back. "You deserve it for what you've done."

He ignored his father's rage. "I only did what was necessary at the time."

"Necessary for what?"

"I was courting the duke's daughter you want me to marry," he answered. "The one with a very large dowry."

Some of his father's ire diminished. "Lady Persephone."

"The same." Although now, he regretted the decision to ask for her hand. She was a coldhearted viper, and marriage to her would be terrible. But he saw no other choice. He had managed to pay many of the bills, but there were not enough heirlooms to pay off his father's debts. He didn't even have enough to buy Persephone an engagement ring; instead, he'd found a ring that had belonged to one of his grandmothers. He intended to ask her to marry him after Lady Bridgeford's musicale.

But God help him, he didn't want to. Even with her dowry, it wasn't enough to dig them out of debt. He'd made the one investment with Graham Hannaford, but even if that one was a successful venture, it would still take years to undo the damage his father had done.

His father shrugged off the footmen who tried to help him up the stairs. "I can manage myself. Be gone with you."

Damian ordered one of the footmen, "Go and light a fire in the hearth of his bedroom." To the other, he said, "Bring tea and food upstairs." Perhaps hot tea and sandwiches might ease the effects of his father's drinking. The truth was, he simply didn't know if it was possible to help his father anymore. Jonas was well beyond redemption. The moment his father left the house, he would start over again with drinking and gambling.

Damian led the marquess to his room, and the first servant

was already preparing a fire in the coal hearth. But to his surprise, instead of fighting back, Jonas sank into a chair and buried his face in his hands. "We're ruined, aren't we?"

Damian said nothing until the servant had finished with the fire. Then he dismissed the man wordlessly and closed the door behind him. "Likely so."

A wrenching noise caught in his father's throat, something between a groan and anguish. In a single moment, Jonas's mood shifted from anger to grief. "I'm better off dead, aren't I? You should put a bottle of laudanum in a large glass of whiskey. I'll drink it and put an end to my vices."

"That would be more than you deserve," Damian said quietly. "Why should you get to die and leave the rest of us in ruin?"

At that, Jonas lifted his head. His blue eyes were bloodshot, and the misery in them mirrored the pain in his own heart after leaving Violet. "There's nothing left for me, is there?" The dull tone of his voice suggested that he was still contemplating his own death.

"There is...something we could do," Damian suggested. "But you won't like it."

His father waited, and then he continued, "You need to stop drinking and gambling."

"I've been drinking and gambling all my life, Damian."

"You have," he agreed. "And this is the result. The question is whether you're strong enough to stop. Whether you can rebuild our home and our lives from the ashes that *you* created when you burned it all to the ground."

His father remained quiet for a time and continued to stare at the coals. Then at last Jonas spoke. "For how long?"

He knew his father could not last a single day if he reentered society. "You should remain at home for at least one month," Damian said. "Do not leave the house." He thought about it and added, "There can be no drinking or gambling. And I don't believe you're strong enough to resist temptation. Not if you go to your club or to a ball."

Jonas let out a heavy sigh. For a moment, he seemed to consider it. "Perhaps if I only went for an hour."

"No." Damian stared him in the eyes. "You know the moment you leave this house, you'll fall into temptation. You've never been strong enough."

His father appeared disconcerted, as if he wanted to argue. "Do you plan to keep me a prisoner in the house?"

Damian thought about it. Truthfully, it wasn't a bad idea.

"I could lock you in this room," he answered. "For a few days, at least. You could take your meals here. Mother would come and read to you or play cards. You can look out in the streets."

His father appeared irritated by the idea. "And why would I agree to that?"

"Because you won't like it when you're not allowed to drink," Damian responded. He fully believed his father's anger would get the best of him. "And we can't afford for you to break anything else."

Jonas stared at him without speaking. Then Damian added, "After that, you could come out of your room, but you'd stay in the house for a few more weeks."

He fully expected his father to outright refuse. Instead, Jonas turned his attention to the fire. His face had gone somber, and he admitted, "Your mother didn't come back with me, you know. She stayed at Scarsdale."

And now Damian was starting to understand why his father had remained drunk during the journey home. "Why?"

His father sighed. "Because she wants no part of me anymore."

Damian understood that feeling only too well. After the way he'd touched Violet in the carriage, she didn't want to see him again. He'd irrevocably hurt her and deserved nothing less than to lose her.

He took a deep breath. "The only way you can win Mother back is to undo the trouble you've caused. You have to repay your debts and never gamble again." He contemplated their situation and added, "I'll see to it that a servant keeps you company. Or Melanie and I will come see you. When Regan comes home from school in a few months, she'll do the same."

"I don't know if I can do this," his father said quietly.

Neither did he. Any more than Damian knew whether or not he could rebuild their fortunes. Although he hadn't caused the massive debts, he couldn't turn his back on his family. And for the first time, it did seem that Jonas had accepted responsibility for his actions.

"We'll work together," Damian said. "First, we have to get you well. And while you're recovering, start finding out if we can sell any unentailed lands. We'll cut out everything from our expenses that isn't strictly necessary."

His father turned solemn. "What if Clara doesn't return?"

Damian couldn't give him false hope. "I don't know if she will. But you'll have to give her a reason to come back."

His father's hand was shaking, but Jonas reached out to him. Damian took his father's palm and gripped it hard.

He didn't know how they would find their way out of this mess. But for the first time, he felt like someone else was sharing the burden. And it gave him a sense of hope.

VIOLET STOOD AT the entrance to Lady Bridgeford's musicale. Though outwardly she kept her face calm, inside the terror was rising. Mrs. Harding and Mr. Gregor stood behind her as silent escorts. Tonight, she would face her family and the rest of the *ton* as herself. And if the worst came to pass, she would have to see Lord Scarsdale with Persephone.

A part of her ached at the memory, though she tried to dispel the raw feelings. It was her own fault for falling in love with him. She'd known from the beginning that he was only there to be a thorn in her side. If she did see him, she wanted him to remember the time they'd spent together and regret what would never be.

But she didn't know if she could bring herself to truly look for another husband. For no man would ever measure up to him.

She wore a high-waisted cream-colored gown trimmed with rose-colored ribbons. In some ways, it felt like a suit of armor while she prepared to do battle against those who meant to harm her.

The footman announced them and, thankfully, few people in Lady Bridgeford's ballroom noticed. In one corner there stood a large pianoforte while in another corner there were several violins and even a harp.

"Find your courage," Mr. Gregor prompted, offering his arm. "Are you ready?"

"I suppose as much as I...can be." She slowed her words to keep from stuttering. He led her past Lady Persephone, who wore a sneer on her face, but Violet hardly cared. Tonight was about moving forward and claiming her own life.

She went to greet her hostess, the Countess of Bridgeford. The woman smiled warmly at her. "I'm so glad you could come, Miss Edwards."

It seemed that the countess was only slightly older than herself, and Violet returned the smile. "Thank you for your hospitality."

Lady Bridgeford inclined her head. "There are refreshments in the next room. Please enjoy them before the performances begin." Then she excused herself and went to greet more of the guests.

From across the room, Violet saw her mother and sister. Charity was crossing toward her, but then before her sister could reach her side, Lady Persephone moved in front of her.

"M-m-miss Edwards. H-how nice to s-see you."

Violet stared back at the young woman, wondering how anyone could be so cruel. She blatantly ignored the woman's taunt, keeping her face impassive while she gave a nod of acknowledgement. "Lady Persephone." She noticed that Lady

Ashleigh was not at Persephone's side, which was unusual.

Charity finally reached her side and embraced her. "You look beautiful, Violet."

She murmured her thanks to her sister and followed her deeper into the room. As they passed through the crowd, Violet kept a soft smile on her face, but it was nearly impossible to push away the loneliness building inside.

But then she saw Scarsdale standing just beyond the door. His gaze met hers, and she couldn't breathe when she saw the longing on his face. For a moment, she drank in the sight of him, the way his dark coat clung to his broad shoulders and the snowy cravat at his throat. His breeches clung to his thighs, and she suddenly remembered sitting on his lap while he kissed her.

It took everything she had to turn away from him. It didn't matter how she felt or what she wanted. He'd made his choice, and he would have to live with it.

"Are you all right?" Charity asked.

Violet smiled. "No. But I have to g-get through this."

"Are you coming home afterwards? Or are you staying longer at the school?"

She saw no reason to delay the inevitable. Steeling herself, she said, "Yes, I'm coming home afterwards. Lucy a-already packed my trunk, and it's in the carriage."

"I've missed you," her sister said warmly.

It was then that Violet saw Mr. Gregor approaching her with a friendly smile. At his side was another man, whom she hadn't met. The gentleman was quite attractive with brown hair and gray eyes. And if she wasn't mistaken, it seemed that he had an air of mischief about him. "Hello, Miss Edwards," Mr. Gregor said. "I've been wanting to introduce you to the Earl of Dunmeath, Cormac Ormond." To Lord Dunmeath, he said, "Miss Edwards is the lady I described to you earlier."

The earl bowed and said, "It's a pleasure, Miss Edwards. You look lovely this evening."

"Thank you, Lord Dunmeath." She paused and asked, "Are y-you from Ireland?"

"I am indeed. You've a good ear." He smiled and asked, "Would you care for some refreshments? I could bring you a plate. Or you could come with me and tell me what you'd prefer."

This was why she had come—to meet a potential husband. And she could certainly do worse than Lord Dunmeath.

"I w-will come with you," she answered. Though a part of her worried that it might be too soon for her bruised heart to consider another suitor, he was giving her the opportunity she needed. Persephone wanted her to hide in the corner and remain embarrassed. Violet wasn't about to become a wallflower once again.

But the moment Lord Dunmeath led her to the next room, she passed by Lord Scarsdale. Memories flooded through her, of being in Damian's arms. And despite how much she hated the choice he'd made, she couldn't relinquish the feelings in her heart. She still loved him, even after he'd decided upon a different path. So, what choice did she have, except to consider men like Lord Dunmeath?

Violet forced a smile on her face as the earl took a plate and began offering her different cakes. When she told him which ones she wanted to try, he took two of each.

"I don't think I can eat that many," she confessed, "though I do thank you."

Lord Dunmeath gave a wry smile. "I'll confess that I put mine on the same plate. I can't get you a glass of lemonade if I'm holding two plates."

"Are you planning to steal my f-food?" she teased.

"Of course not." The expression on his face held mischief once again. "If you're wanting them all, then by all means..."

She laughed. "I wasn't being serious, my lord."

At that, his expression softened. "That's good then." He held out the plate and she chose one of the cakes. "I'll be honest with you, Miss Edwards. I returned to London because I am seeking a wife. Mr. Gregor recommended you highly."

She nearly choked on her cake. Her eyes widened, and she was grateful to have a mouth full of cake to avoid answering.

His expression turned serious, and he asked, "Are you willing?"

She blinked a moment, unable to believe what she was hearing. "Lord Dunmeath, while I am f-flattered by your proposal, we've only just met. I don't know you."

He did smile at that. "There's time for that. I'm simply wondering if you would consider my suit. There's no point in wasting time if you've no interest in a man like me."

"But..." Her voice trailed off as she wondered what to say. Her heart was crying out no, while her head warned her not to answer in haste. "You don't know m-me either. W-why would you ask me to marry you because of w-what someone else thinks?"

"It's not exactly a proposal," he hedged. "More that I'd like to know you better. You seem easy to talk to," he said. "And Gregor said you have a good heart." He glanced over at Lord Scarsdale who was standing beside Lady Persephone. "So, what do you think?"

"I'm...not sure." It still bewildered her that a handsome, titled gentleman would offer his attention. "It's my first proposal. Even if it really isn't one."

He offered a wide smile. "If the other gentlemen haven't offered for you yet, then that's my good fortune. You're better off without them, I say."

His sudden defense caught her off guard, for she'd never expected this man to stand up for her. Although she wasn't at all interested in his courtship, he did seem like a kind man.

"Thank you, Lord Dunmeath."

"You're welcome." He held out the plate to her. "Would you like that glass of lemonade?"

"I w-would love that."

But before he could reach for it, Damian entered the room.

He glanced at Lord Dunmeath, then at her.

"The music is starting soon," he told them. Then to Violet, he inquired, "May I have a word?"

She didn't want to. But with reluctance, she gave a nod. To Lord Dunmeath, she asked, "Will you save a chair for me?"

He gave a bow while Damian's expression never wavered. Violet set down her plate and reached for a glass of lemonade, waiting for him to speak.

"You look beautiful, Violet." His voice was gruff, and she didn't know how to answer him. This wasn't why he wanted to speak to her.

And so, she simply nodded and asked, "Is your engagement f-finalized yet?"

"Not yet." His tone held a dull emptiness, and he took a step closer. "It's not what I want. I hope you know that."

She set down her glass and regarded him. "Don't say it."

But he ignored her and dropped his voice low. "You have to know that what I felt for you was real. That night in the carriage and in the library—"

"Stop." She took a step away, feeling the fury rise within her. "I don't want to hear about what you w-wanted or what might have been."

His expression turned bleak. "You deserve the truth. If I had a choice—"

But she cut him off. "You've made your choice, Lord Scarsdale. And it wasn't me."

He stared at her as if she'd struck him down. And yet, he knew the truth, just as she did. It did no good to grieve what would never be.

And though it broke her heart into a thousand pieces, she forced herself to turn and walk away.

DAMIAN WATCHED AS Violet went to join Lord Dunmeath, with

Mrs. Harding on the opposite side. Jealousy burned through him, and he wished he could seize the earl by the coat and toss him out. *He* wanted to sit beside Violet during the musicale. Although he'd known this would be a difficult night, he'd never imagined he would feel such helplessness. Damn it all, he despised this entire situation. He'd wanted Violet to know that Persephone wasn't the woman he wanted, but her words had forced him to face the truth. She was right. He'd made his choice, and now he had to live with the consequences.

Resentment brewed inside him at his father, at the life that had closed over him, and the sense of imprisonment. He wanted to turn his back on his family and claim Violet as his own. A reckless urge took root and began to spread. The only reason he'd considered this arranged marriage was because it had offered a swift means of changing his family's fortunes.

But the cost was too grave. He didn't want to sell himself into marriage. Surely there had to be another way. He stood by the refreshment table while in the next room the music had begun.

If he wanted to change his circumstances, he could no longer rely on others. He had to do it himself. His father had agreed to go into seclusion, essentially handing over his responsibilities as marquess. And now Damian had to make the right decisions for all of them.

In the doorway, he saw Lady Persephone approaching. "Lord Scarsdale." She smiled and extended her gloved hands. "I've been wanting to speak with you alone." She wore a gown of royal blue, and her blond hair was piled atop her head and adorned with pearls. "Do you have a moment?"

"Is this wise?" he murmured. Although he knew this was probably in his best interests, he didn't want her reputation to be compromised. Especially now, when he was reconsidering everything.

"No one will notice during the performance." She glanced over at a young lady who was playing the harp. "Just for a moment," she pleaded.

Damian didn't trust her at all. But he supposed there was no harm in hearing what she had to say. She led him to the opposite side of the room so no one could overhear their conversation. When they reached the far end, she smiled at him. "You've been avoiding me since our outing in the park." Her tone was between a pout and teasing.

True enough, he thought. And were it possible, he'd continue to do so. But he said nothing, waiting for her to get to the point.

"I missed you," she whispered with a sly smile. "You have no idea how much."

The words were practiced and fluid, as if she'd spoken them a thousand times. Again, he waited for her to continue, and she asked, "Do you still wish to marry me, Lord Scarsdale? Or have your affections dimmed?"

He knew she was expecting him to reassure her, to offer flattery and compliments that would soothe her. But he didn't want to speak any lies. Not anymore. He paused a moment and answered honestly, "I am weary of playing games and waiting, Lady Persephone."

She reached for his hands and said, "You won't have to wait any longer, my lord. I am willing to announce our engagement this very night."

Her declaration might have filled him with elation at one point, but no longer. Instead, he felt only annoyance. This wasn't what he wanted anymore, and it wasn't right to lead her on. But before he could speak, she continued. "On one condition."

His instincts sharpened, knowing she was up to something. "What is it?"

She smiled and said, "I did not like being set aside for that stuttering Miss Edwards. Really, Scarsdale, why would you lower yourself with a nobody like her?"

"She's not a nobody," Damian said. "She's kind and has more courage than anyone I've ever met."

Persephone's expression darkened. "She can't even speak a sentence without stuttering."

"Which is not her fault," he corrected. He could see that with every compliment, Persephone grew angrier. And somehow, he didn't care anymore. "Miss Edwards has more determination than any other woman here."

"Even me?" she asked. He could hear the venom rising in her voice. *Especially you*, he thought. Instead, he ignored her prompt and finished with, "I wish her nothing but the best, after all she's endured."

He knew he was stoking the fires of her anger, but he couldn't stop himself from saying what he truly felt.

Persephone's demeanor turned quiet. "Do you want to hear my condition, Scarsdale? Or are you trying to tell me you'd rather wed that wallflower instead?"

He didn't answer, and she took his silence as a response. "I want you to publicly tell everyone that you were only teasing her," she began. "That you never wanted someone who stammered so badly, you could barely hold a conversation."

He couldn't believe what he was hearing. Not only did she want him to embarrass Violet—she wanted him to ruin all hopes of Violet finding a husband. It went well beyond cruelty, and all because of her vanity.

Without hesitation, he answered, "No. I'm not doing that. It's not fair to Miss Edwards."

"Then I don't know if I can marry you." She shrugged as if it meant nothing at all. It was just another game to her.

He'd had his fill of her attempts to manipulate him. And this was the final straw. "I also don't want to marry a woman who would condone such actions." He met her gaze openly, wanting her to understand that it was over between them.

She didn't bother to hide her nonchalance. "That's what I was afraid of. Then, I suppose we are not suited to marry."

Her airy acceptance was too practiced, and he wondered if it was real or only a pretense. But he responded, "No. We're not suited at all."

"I might have guessed you would say that, Scarsdale." She let out a baleful sigh. "Then you leave me no choice. I will see to it that others spread the rumors about Miss Edwards. I will use my influence to ensure that no one will invite her to any of their balls or gatherings. By the time the gossip has circulated, no man will ever want to marry her."

What a heartless bitch. He couldn't believe what he was hearing. "Why would you do this, Persephone? She's done nothing to you."

"You chose her over me," she said simply. "And that is unacceptable."

He'd made a grave error in misjudging Persephone. Her vanity was far greater than he'd imagined, and by ignoring her, he'd incited her rage. She shrugged as if she cared nothing about ruining someone else's life. "But you *do* have a choice, Scarsdale. If I hear you insult her—with my own ears—then I will leave her alone. I might even defend her and say that she's not so bad. There might be a gentleman or two who will take pity on her."

This was about power and control. He'd infuriated Persephone by choosing someone else, and now, she was making him pay the price. He thought about walking away and ignoring her. But he believed she would carry out her threat to hurt Violet's reputation.

"So. What did you decide?" she asked. "Will you tell everyone what a mistake you made and how you never wanted her? Or will you let her pay the penalty for your mistake in spurning me?"

"You won't say a word against her." He made no attempt to hide the threat in his voice. "You will leave her alone, or I'll see to it that no man ever wants to marry you." Although he knew this was unwise, he couldn't stop himself from saying it. She'd dropped the gauntlet, and he wasn't going to stand by and let her harm Violet.

Even so, the best course of action was to get her out of here, to send her away and protect her from Persephone's malice.

A smug smile spread over Persephone's face. "Don't dare to threaten me, Scarsdale. You'll regret it, I can promise you that."

He ignored her words and crossed the room. It was best to warn Violet and bring her out of harm's way. As he returned to the ballroom, the harpist finished her performance to the sound of polite applause. Damian scanned the crowd, searching for a glimpse of Violet. At last, he spied her sitting with Lord Dunmeath and Mrs. Harding. Her family was sitting behind her.

He started to walk toward her, but Persephone caught his arm. "Are you certain this is what you want to do, Scarsdale? There's no turning back now. One word to her, and I'll end her chances of marriage."

He covered her hand with his own and took it off his arm. Then he leaned in close to whisper. "I pity the man who marries you. For you'll make his life a living hell."

VIOLET HEARD A slight disturbance behind her and turned to see Lord Scarsdale removing Lady Persephone's hand from his arm. His expression was nothing short of murderous. When he strode away from the lady, Violet saw Persephone staring back at her with a look of fury.

At one time, that look would have terrified her. She didn't understand what had happened, but she recognized the danger. Something had happened between the lady and Scarsdale. Had he called off their betrothal? Her nerves tightened as she saw Persephone staring at her with hatred, but Violet had no intention of backing down now.

Lady Persephone approached the front of the room with a smirk on her face. A moment later, the crowd quieted to hear her speak. "Lady Bridgeford, may I suggest another performance tonight?"

The countess inclined her head, and Persephone continued. "I have a surprise for all of you," she said. "Miss Violet Edwards, would you come and join me?"

Every head in the crowd turned to face her, and she felt her cheeks burning. Whatever Persephone had planned, she suspected it was meant to humiliate her. Violet's heart began pounding, but she forced herself to stand. Lord Scarsdale remained at the doorway, and he slowly shook his head.

But she had turned away from confrontation so many times before. Whatever Persephone intended, Violet was ready to face her.

"I've heard it said that you have a lovely voice, despite that terrible stutter," Persephone said. "Would you be willing to sing for us?"

From the amused look in the young woman's eyes, Persephone clearly believed Violet would refuse. Perhaps even stammer or run away. But no. She was not about to let the duke's daughter get the best of her. Although terror had seized her stomach, and she worried that her voice would quiver, she had to take her own stance. "I w-would be delighted. Thank you for the invitation."

The sudden frown on Persephone's face made her realize that the woman had never imagined she'd agree. She appeared bewildered as Violet approached the musicians. She asked them if they could accompany her and was relieved when they recognized the song.

She went to stand on the staircase to face all of them. Her mother appeared horrified, while Charity offered an encouraging smile. But this was not about performing in front of the *ton*. It was about fighting back against those who had wronged her. She knew she could sing without a stammer, and that was exactly what she intended to do.

The violinist began to play the lilting tune she'd requested, and Violet began to sing. She projected her voice to the crowd, and after a moment, she gained her courage. The lyrics were deliberate, and she sang of a handsome suitor and a woman who loved him. Her heart ached as she thought of Damian, and as she searched the crowd, she saw him take a step closer before he leaned against the door.

Her grief grew heavier as she sang to him, and she poured her emotions into the song. Charity smiled at her while their mother appeared nervous and uncertain. And when the song came to an end, there was thunderous applause. Persephone clapped slowly as well, but there was no masking the irritation in her expression. She walked over to Violet and smiled sweetly. In a low voice, she said, "You may think you've won, but you're wrong. You will never marry Scarsdale—or anyone else for that matter."

Violet straightened and faced Persephone. Amid the applause, she added, "It seems as if you won't marry him either."

Anger flashed over Persephone's face before she masked it. The young woman had intended to humiliate her even further—but Violet had bested her. And it felt as good as she'd imagined.

But it was Damian whose approval she wanted. He was watching her from the doorway. When she met his gaze, he slowly gave a single nod. She didn't know what he meant by that, but the grim finality on his face tore her heart in two.

Somehow, she managed to keep herself together. What had she expected? That he would cross the room and embrace her? That he would compliment her or declare that he loved her? It didn't matter what they'd once shared—he would never set aside his family's needs for her. And it didn't matter that she had faced down her worst enemy and won. She still wasn't enough for him.

As she walked back to her chair, she was dimly aware of compliments about her voice, and she murmured her thanks.

Charity came to her side and took her hand. "You were wonderful, Violet. I never knew you could sing like that." She followed her sister back to her mother.

Thomasina appeared utterly bewildered. "You were very good indeed."

A slow clapping sound caught her attention, and she raised her head. There, standing just behind Thomasina, stood her grandmother Annabelle.

"You sang well, my girl." The old woman's voice was rough, and she lifted her chin. "But now, I think we should return home. We have much to discuss."

She met her grandmother's gaze and risked a glance back at Damian. But it was too late—the earl had already gone.

"I don't know," she started to say, but Annabelle lifted her hand.

"Let us go and speak alone in my carriage. You can make your decision afterward." She leaned on her cane and added, "In the meantime, lift your head high and enjoy the praise…while it lasts."

Violet suspected her grandmother wanted to take her back to Bedfordshire, but she wasn't certain that was what she wanted. Her thoughts were in turmoil just now, and then Lord Dunmeath came forward.

"You have the voice of an angel," he said. "I meant what I said earlier. I believe you would make an excellent wife."

Her mother winced, but Violet wasn't about to embarrass the gentleman. "You are very kind, my lord. But m-my heart belongs to someone else. I suggest you speak w-with Mrs. Harding over there." She nodded toward the matron. "She is quite good at matchmaking."

He offered a slight smile of regret. "I will consider it."

Her grandmother pressed a hand against her shoulder and said, "We should go, Violet. Before that shrew causes any more trouble." She eyed Persephone, who was speaking again to several of the matrons.

Violet stopped to thank Lady Bridgeford for the invitation, and then she followed her grandmother outside. She searched for a glimpse of Lord Scarsdale, but he was nowhere to be seen.

Once she was inside the carriage, her grandmother regarded her. "I misjudged you, Violet."

She didn't know what to think of that, but Annabelle continued. "Your mother led me to believe that you were a shy, stuttering idiot who would never find a husband." She leaned forward and regarded her. "I was wrong."

"My mother led me to believe you w-were a sickly, dying woman who wanted me to empty her chamber pot," Violet countered.

Annabelle barked a laugh. "I like you." Then she stared back for a few long moments. "Thomasina doesn't know you at all, does she?" Without waiting for an answer, she nodded. "I can see that." She rested her cane against the side of the carriage. "I will offer you a choice, Violet. If you wish to come back with me to Bedfordshire and be free of your mother, you may be my companion for a time. Or if you'd prefer to stay in London and seek a husband, I have no objection."

Violet thought about it and answered, "I will think about it."

Chapter Thirteen

One week later

I T WAS STRANGE to realize that a single moment could upend all his plans. From the moment Violet had sung, Damian realized what an idiot he'd been. Her fierce determination and the way she had stood and faced down everyone had made it clear that *she* was the woman he wanted. He didn't care what sort of dowry Violet had, if any. He wanted to marry her, and that meant he had to take command of his own problems before he could offer her a life with him.

He'd been trying to rely on wedding an heiress instead of solving their financial disasters. It was time to change that.

He'd sent word to Graham Hannaford a few days ago, in the hopes of learning whether the new shipment of silks had arrived from India. His friend had been unresponsive, and Damian didn't know what that meant. But in the meantime, he was determined to find a way to help his family—even if that meant selling off unentailed property.

His father had kept his word about avoiding gambling and drinking, and thus far, Jonas hadn't touched any spirits. He'd remained in their London townhouse during that time, enduring tremors, headaches, and sleeplessness. But worst of all, Jonas had written to his wife, and in the past fortnight, Clara hadn't answered a single letter. It didn't bode well for their future.

"My lord, you have a caller," a footman said. "The Duke of Westerford is here to see you."

Now what did His Grace want? Undeniably it had something to do with Persephone. Damian hadn't attended any events during the past week, for he'd kept all his attention on his father's health and selling off everything possible.

He followed the footman into the drawing room where he greeted the duke. "Your Grace, this is a surprise." And not a pleasant one, he thought.

The duke stood from his chair, but Damian motioned him down and took his own seat. "What can I do for you?"

The man's expression didn't bode well for good news. "I know that you and my daughter have...not made any final decisions about marriage. Persephone told me that she hadn't given her consent yet."

Because the woman would never admit to being spurned, Damian thought.

But before he could answer, the duke continued. "I made some inquiries about your finances and learned that you invested a great deal of money with Mr. Graham Hannaford. And this concerns me."

"Why would that concern you?" he responded. "Graham has been a trusted friend of mine for years."

"The shipments were supposed to arrive a week ago," the duke said. "I didn't invest because...there was no need. But I am concerned that you may lose a great deal of your own investment. I heard rumors that the cargo was stolen. The only barrels left behind were filled with rice..." He let his voice trail off. "You can see the reason for my worry."

Damian was careful not to let his emotions show, but he asked, "Have you heard anything from Hannaford? I sent word, but there has been no reply."

The duke shook his head. "Nothing at all. But because you may one day become my son-in-law, I came to make you an offer. I will buy your shares from you. And if the shipment was lost, I can afford to lose that money. You cannot."

Damian didn't know how to respond, but the duke's offer of returning the five hundred pounds was not something he could easily dismiss. "And if the ship does return?"

"I would, of course, share the profits with you through Persephone's dowry," His Grace answered. "But I fear that this is one investment that will not pay off. You stand to lose everything, and I don't want you to take that risk."

Damian stood from his chair and went to stand by the window. The logical answer was to agree to the duke's proposition. But he sensed that if he did, it meant tying him back into a betrothal with Persephone. Which wasn't what he wanted at all.

"Your offer is fair and appreciated," he said. "If I may have time to think about it?"

"Certainly," the duke agreed. "You can give me your answer tomorrow."

He'd hoped for more time than that, especially if the ship did arrive. But he didn't bother to argue.

"There's something else," the duke said. "It's about Miss Violet Edwards. Persephone told me some troubling news about the young lady."

"Did she?" So, she had carried out her threat to try and ruin Violet. Damian didn't allow a trace of emotion to cross his face, though inwardly his fury brewed. He needed to warn her about this.

"It seems that Miss Edwards has been…a trifle indiscreet. There are rumors that Lord Dunmeath asked her to wed for an entirely different reason." The duke shrugged. "Persephone thought you should know because you were friends with Miss Edwards at one time."

Damian didn't acknowledge the duke's remark at all but instead answered, "Thank you for the information regarding the shipment. However, I believe I will keep faith with Hannaford. We've been friends for years."

"That would be most unwise," the duke argued. "Why

should you take the risk of losing five hundred pounds when I am willing to buy them outright?"

It was strange that the duke seemed to know so much about the investment, particularly the amount. And why had he paid a special visit today to ask about it? Damian questioned whether it had anything to do with Persephone. Had she even told her father that there would be no marriage? Somehow, it seemed unlikely.

"Thank you for your warning," he said. "For now, I intend to keep my shares. I will let you know if my decision changes."

The duke's face tightened, but he gave a nod. "Very well."

But after the man departed, Damian couldn't help but wonder what it all meant. He needed to send word to Violet, to warn her about Persephone's lies. God, he missed her.

She'd gone home with her family, but he wondered if she would be happy there. She'd run from them once before.

He pulled out paper from his escritoire, intending to write her a note. But what could he say to her? That he'd called off his engagement with Persephone and wanted to marry her instead, though he had nothing at all?

For a moment, he studied the empty walls where paintings had been removed. They had sold off silver, jewelry that had belonged to his mother and sisters, and even a few furnishings. It was humiliating that they had sunk this low.

Why would Violet want any part of this? Or him, for that matter?

He made a silent vow that he would dig himself out of this financial ruin, no matter what happened. And he would begin courting her in earnest.

He dipped his pen in the ink and began writing.

FOR A SINGLE day, Violet was startled to have suitors paying calls upon her. The drawing room was filled with flowers, and she'd spoken with many gentlemen. Even Lord Dunmeath had returned, despite her confession that her heart belonged elsewhere.

But then, the following day, the flowers and callers stopped. And the next day after that. It seemed that Persephone had followed through with her threat, just as she'd promised. Violet hadn't yet decided what to do, but when her maid Elsie told her that Lord Scarsdale had come to call, her heart began to pound. This was what she'd wanted—for him to come to her. And now he had.

She hurried down the stairs, delighted that he was here at last. When she arrived at the drawing room, he stood. He appeared as devastatingly handsome as ever, wearing a dark coat with a bottle green waistcoat and dark breeches. For a moment, he stood without speaking, almost as if he didn't know where to begin.

"Lord Scarsdale," she greeted him.

"Miss Edwards." He held out a wrapped package, and she took it, wondering what was inside. "I've brought a gift for you."

She pulled back the brown paper and found a deck of playing cards and a leather collar for Rupert. She smiled and held up the cards, "Were you h-hoping for another game?"

"Later, perhaps. I came to talk with you."

She had a darkening suspicion that her visions of a marriage proposal were not going to happen. Instead, he appeared troubled. "What is it?" She set down his gifts and motioned for him to sit. Then she chose a chair across from him.

"A few months ago, I invested five hundred pounds with a friend of mine. His ships were expected over a week ago, but he and his ships have not returned."

"Were they shipwrecked?" she asked.

Lord Scarsdale only shrugged. "I don't know. There's a rumor that the ship brought back only rice, no silks or spices. His Grace, the Duke of Westerford, offered to buy my shares. I refused because I think he wanted me to owe him an obligation. But now, I wonder if turning him down was a mistake. Our finances are as dire as ever."

Violet was starting to understand that this call was more of an apology. Why had she dared to get her hopes up? He wasn't here to ask her to marry him. He was here to explain why he couldn't.

She closed her eyes, and asked, "What do you want from me, Lord Scarsdale?"

"I came here because I had to see you," he answered. "I heard about Persephone's gossip, and I needed to know that you're all right."

Though it made sense, it still wounded her pride a bit. She didn't need him to watch over her like a child. "I'm fine. Persephone only did w-what she said she'd do. She's chased away any suitors I m-might have had."

"What can I do to help?"

"Nothing. I don't need someone else to solve my problems for me." She shrugged. "If any of those men believe her, I don't need them." Especially one who took the word of an arrogant debutante. She thought of standing up to Persephone once again, but she didn't have the heart to attend another ball. It simply wasn't worth it.

"You deserve far better, Violet."

"Yes, I do," she whispered.

He rose and went to stand in front of her. "I'm doing everything I can to rebuild and repay my father's debts. I only need a little more time."

Was he asking her to wait for him? For how long? She had all but given up on a life with him. Part of her didn't care how long she had to wait, so long as it meant he would be her husband. But her brain warned her to raise her defenses.

He took her hands in his and drew her to stand. Then he brought them to his waist, and he cupped her face between his hands. Without asking permission, he leaned in and stole a kiss. The moment he did, all her fears came crashing back. His mouth moved upon hers, and when his tongue slid inside, spirals of need threaded through her body. She couldn't stop herself from winding her arms around his neck, holding tight to the moment.

It was goodbye. She knew it deep in her heart, and the weight of losing him felt like drowning. She held back the tears, aching inside.

She didn't care if they lived in poverty or not. All that mattered to her was that she loved him, and she wanted him to love her in the same way. But there would always be a reason why he couldn't be with her. Whether it was his father's debts or her own insecurities, she knew they wouldn't be together.

And worse, she didn't want anyone else. Damian had ruined her for other men, for when she spoke to them, she could only hear his voice. If anyone ever kissed her, she would remember what it was like in Damian's arms. And she wanted more than he could give.

With reluctance, she broke the kiss and pulled back. "I hope your ships do return, Lord Scarsdale." Though she kept her words bright, she had already decided that it would be too painful to remain in London. She didn't want to be reminded of the things she wouldn't have.

"I wish you well," she said to him. And though her heart was breaking, she braved a smile she didn't feel. For she wouldn't see him again.

AFTER ANOTHER WEEK, there was still no sign of the ships and no word from Graham Hannaford. Though he didn't want to get involved with the duke, Damian saw no choice. He couldn't afford to lose the five hundred pounds—not if the man wanted to buy out his shares.

He waited in the Westerford drawing room, but instead of the duke entering, he saw Persephone. She wore a rose gown with matching pink blossoms in her hair. The moment she met his gaze, she smirked.

"Lord Scarsdale. What a pleasure this is."

He didn't answer, for she was the last person he wanted to see. Then she turned and closed the doors behind her.

"Open the doors," he reminded her. "We don't have a chaperone."

"We don't need a chaperone for this conversation," she said, sidling closer. She started to remove pins from her hair, and he took a step backwards.

"What are you doing, Persephone?" He didn't like this turn in behavior, and he sensed exactly what she intended.

"You haven't come to see me," she pouted. "Not in weeks."

"After the way you treated Miss Edwards, why would I?"

She set the pins down on a nearby table, her hair falling across her shoulders. "I don't know why you're so interested in that nobody. She can't even speak. I am worth ten of her, and you know it."

"She's worth a hundred of you."

He didn't know what Persephone was doing, but every instinct warned him to get out of there. He kept his distance and started to move back toward the door. Although he'd come to offer the duke his shares in the shipping, he didn't want to be caught with this viper.

But before he reached the doorknob, she screamed. "Stop it! Take your hands off me!"

Within moments, several servants arrived, along with the Duke of Westerford. Damian risked a glance back at the woman and saw that her gown was loose, exposing her corset. He didn't know how she'd managed it, but likely she'd already plotted it from the beginning.

Somehow, she'd even worked up tears, and the duke demanded, "What is this, Scarsdale? What have you done?"

"I've done nothing. Your daughter is under the mistaken impression that I intend to marry her." Damian met the duke's fury with his own grim expression. "I've had my fill of her playacting."

"Papa, please," Persephone sobbed. "Don't let him compromise me like this."

The duke blocked Damian's path. From the furious look in his eyes, he believed his daughter's lies. "I expect you to obtain a special license and marry my daughter within a fortnight. Otherwise, I'll see to it that everyone in London knows of your father's debts. Your family will be ruined, and you'll never show your face in polite society again. Your sisters will never marry."

Damian felt as if he'd taken a blow to his stomach. For so long, he'd been trying to restore his family's fortunes, sacrificing everything for them. And now, the duke intended for him to wed Persephone, chaining himself to a lifetime of misery.

He thought of Violet and the way she'd refused to let Persephone's lies affect her. She'd held fast to her courage, despite all that had happened. How could he not do the same?

He would not beg the duke to buy back his investment shares, nor would he marry a woman he despised. No, he would stand up to them—but in his own way. Let them believe he intended to make things right.

And so, he faced the duke and raised his chin. "I will obtain a special license this week."

His Grace visibly relaxed. "Good. We will make the arrangements for the wedding."

Damian said nothing but passed the duke in the doorway, not even bothering to look back at Persephone.

Bedfordshire

SOMETIMES THERE WEREN'T enough tears to cry. Violet stared outside at the cloudy sky while, in her lap, she held a wedding invitation inviting her to celebrate the nuptials of Lady Persephone and Lord Scarsdale. She should have known better than to believe he would desire her instead. All along, he had placed the needs of his family and estate ahead of any feelings he might have. It was her own fault for believing that the kiss meant something.

"What are you weeping about?" her grandmother asked.

"Nothing. It doesn't matter." Violet rose from her chair and tossed the wedding invitation into the fire burning in the hearth. She knew Persephone had sent it out of spite, not because she wanted her to attend. Rupert was curled up beside the fireplace, snoring while he lay on his back with his paws curled up.

Her grandmother leaned on her cane and moved in closer. "It's that earl, isn't it? You're in love with him."

"W-whether I am or not is irrelevant. He's chosen s-someone else."

"Has he?" Annabelle's eyes gleamed. "Well, that's a shame, isn't it? So, you've decided to simply cry and give up?"

Violet turned to face her grandmother. "It takes two p-people to make a marriage, Grandmother. And if he doesn't w-want me, there's nothing I can do."

"Humph." Her grandmother nodded outside. "I thought you were someone who didn't give up so easily. At least, that's the girl I saw in London. Why don't you go for a walk and think about what you truly want? Return when your head is clear."

Violet had no interest in taking a walk, but at least it would give her a chance to cry in private and let out her frustrations. Within half an hour, she put on her pelisse and began walking down the gravel path through the gardens.

She'd wanted so badly to believe that Scarsdale would earn his own fortune through the shipment and that he would want to marry her. The last time he'd kissed her, there was no doubt that he cared about her. But she'd wanted him to fight for them.

Violet increased her stride, punctuating her steps with the anger flooding through her. Then she started to run, letting the tears fall. Ahead, there was a thick grove of trees, and she hurried toward it. The shadows of the trees darkened her path, but she followed it along a stream to where a stone summerhouse lay at the farthest end. It was a place of peace, where she could grieve what she'd lost.

She stopped running and slowed her pace when she neared the summerhouse. The floor was made of slate with limestone walls in a circle. The shutters were pushed back on four open spaces that provided light and air with makeshift windows, and the roof held protection from the elements. There were two stone benches inside, and she entered the summerhouse, feeling the chill in the air. She leaned back against the stone wall and closed her eyes, wondering if she would ever be able to move past her feelings for the earl.

Footsteps approached, and she guessed it was a servant coming to summon her for luncheon. A shadow darkened the doorway to the summerhouse, and she opened her eyes...only to see Lord Scarsdale standing in front of her.

Shock suffused her, and she could only blurt out, "What are you doing here?"

"Your grandmother said I could find you here."

Violet let out a rough sigh. So, Annabelle had known the entire time. The conversation had only been a means of sending her away so the earl could talk to her alone.

Scarsdale sat down on the stone bench beside her. His hair was rumpled, as was his coat. It seemed as if he'd traveled to reach her and had only just arrived. He set down a blanket he'd been carrying. "I came to correct a mistake I made. You were right."

Her heart was pounding with fear and anticipation. "About what?"

"I've been allowing my father's debts to guide my future. I'm not going to be manipulated any longer. I'm here because I'm not letting you go, Violet."

His voice made her throat go dry, for she'd never imagined he would come to her like this. She wanted him desperately, but her fears started to take hold. Persephone had ruined her reputation in society, and she didn't truly believe Scarsdale could face that. She was accustomed to being overlooked and misjudged. But if he experienced that, he might come to resent her for it.

"I don't think this is wise," she whispered.

"You're right." He stood from the bench and drew closer. He reached out to touch her nape, and a shudder of anticipation flooded through her. His green eyes burned into hers as if he wanted nothing more than to spend this day with her. "It's scandalous."

He moved his mouth to her nape, and her body came alive with goosebumps. Her heart warned her brain to stop thinking, to simply enjoy his touch. "Lord Scarsdale—"

"Damian," he corrected. "After today, you will always use my name when we're together."

"Damian," she agreed. "W-what are you doing?"

"What I should have done long ago." He framed her face in his hands and kissed her deeply. It was as if she were a craving he couldn't satisfy, and her body came alive, filled with yearning. "I'm offering myself to you. Whatever you want from me, I will give. I am yours to command."

Although her heart was overjoyed, her head warned her that he held the power to destroy her already-broken heart. She couldn't trust that this would work between them. But neither could she deny him.

"Tell me what you want," he said quietly.

She hardly knew where to begin. For a moment, she studied him, wondering what to say or do. Perhaps honesty was best. "I want to trust you," she began, "but I'm afraid you'll break m-my heart."

"I've done many things I'm not proud of," he admitted. "And I haven't solved the problem of my father's debts. But I'll be damned if I allow a woman like Persephone to dictate my future." He rested his hands on her shoulders. "Will you give me the chance to prove myself?"

She nodded. And when he leaned in to kiss her, she opened her mouth willingly, tasting the forbidden desire she wanted more than all else. His tongue slid against hers, and she wound her arms around his neck. It occurred to her that he'd come to seduce her. And worse, that she was willing to let it happen. The touch of his mouth against hers, his hands sliding to her back…it was enough to unravel any common sense she might have had.

She pulled away from the kiss and faced him. For a heated moment, he seemed to drink in the sight of her, and she couldn't deny how badly she wanted him. "What do you w-want from me, Damian?"

He took her hands and bade her to stand. Then he picked up the discarded blanket and spread it upon the slate floor. "I want to make love to you, Violet. And then I want to marry you."

She grew speechless, terrified to say yes. And yet the thought of saying no was far worse.

His eyes turned heated. "You're nervous, aren't you?" She inclined her head, unable to speak. "Then I will take command. And if there is anything you don't want me to do, simply say the word. Is that agreeable?"

She gave another nod, feeling as if she couldn't speak at all. He moved behind her and pressed a kiss to her nape. "I'm going to undress you now."

His hands rested upon the buttons of her gown. One by one, he unfastened them. She felt the light breeze of the wind against her back, and when he pressed his mouth to her skin with the release of each button, she couldn't stop the sharp inhalation.

Her brain questioned why she was allowing him to touch her when there was no guarantee that he meant what he'd said about marriage. Why was she ruining herself with a man who had let her down before?

Because she loved him. The bittersweet knowledge made her heart ache, for no other man would ever compare to Scarsdale. His humor, his steadfast encouragement—all of it made him the man who had captured her heart. And even though this was wrong and scandalous and everything her mother had ever warned her about, she didn't care.

She would seize this moment for herself, even if it was only for today.

When her gown was unfastened, she let it slide to the ground. Although the air was cool, she felt the goosebumps all over. She turned around to face him, still clad in her corset, chemise, and petticoats.

"Take off your coat," she ordered. "Then your waistcoat and shirt."

He obeyed, and when he was bared before her, she reached out to touch him. His chest was warm, his muscles firm as she explored him. His expression had gone rigid as her fingers drifted over his skin.

"Is this all right?" she asked softly. She moved her hands up his chest to his broad shoulders. "I've wanted to do this for a w-while."

"Don't stop," he said in a deep voice.

She lowered her mouth to his heart, and he reached back to unfasten her stays. One by one, he pulled the laces free until he lifted the corset over her head. She wore only her chemise and petticoats now. Her pulse pounded, and she needed a distraction to keep her fears at bay.

"Kiss me," she whispered. He obeyed, tantalizing her mouth while his hands slid under the chemise and cupped her bare breasts. She gave a soft cry when he gently rolled her nipple between his thumb and forefinger. The echo of sensation caught between her thighs, making her yearn for more.

Damian untied her petticoats, letting them fall to the floor. Then he lifted away her chemise until she stood naked before him. Never in her life had she felt so exposed or afraid.

"You're the most beautiful woman I've ever seen," he murmured. He continued caressing her breasts, and she gripped his shoulders as the pleasure coursed from her sensitive nipples down between her legs.

What if he's lying to you? her brain warned. *What if he's only trying to seduce you before he leaves again?* She stiffened at the thought, and he seemed to guess what she was thinking.

"Am I frightening you?" he asked against her lips.

Yes. But instead she admitted, "I've never done this before, Damian."

"Do you want me to stop?" he asked. Before she could answer, he bent down and took her breast into his mouth, swirling his tongue around her nipple. The heat of his mouth upon her sensitive breast nearly made her knees buckle.

He'd deliberately tantalized her, and she guided his mouth to her other breast. "N-no," she answered. "Don't stop."

He rewarded her by gently nibbling at her nipple, and she grew more aroused with a rush of wetness between her legs. She gripped his hair while he continued to suckle at her, the wild frenzy rising hotter between them.

"Do you want me to show you what else I wanted to do?" he asked, trailing his mouth lower.

"Yes." Her voice grew ragged, and she hardly recognized the sound.

Damian spread his coat out on the ground and then unfastened his trousers, stripping the rest of his clothing away. She felt her nerves rising again, but she tried to push them back.

She had never before seen a naked man, but his body was magnificent, as if sculpted of pure muscle. She risked a glance at his erection, and she was embarrassed by her overwhelming desire to touch him. She had pleasured him once before, and she wanted to do so again.

He picked her up and laid her down gently upon a bed made from the blanket and their discarded clothing. Then he laid down beside her and turned her to face him.

The intimacy of laying naked beside him reminded her of what it might be like to be married to Damian. He took her palm and kissed it. "Don't be afraid, Violet."

She touched his face and against her fingertips, she felt the light stubble as if he hadn't shaved in a day or two. He kissed her again and then brought her hand to his rigid length. "Do you see how much I want you?"

The rigid heat of his manhood fascinated her. He tensed when she explored him, circling the tip with her thumb. He'd liked it when she'd touched him before, but from the fierce expression on his face, she wondered if she was hurting him.

"Is this all right?" she murmured.

"Yes," he gritted out. "You can do whatever you want to." He closed her hand around his shaft, and she moved it up and down, stroking his length. "God above, that feels good."

She smiled, marveling at the power she held over him. She continued to squeeze him, and then he moved his hand between her legs to touch her intimately. As she caressed him, he did the same to her.

She could hardly breathe from the tantalizing wickedness of his touch. A moan broke free from her, and she stilled her hand. He spread her legs apart and when he found the tight bud above her entrance, he began to circle it with his thumb. From deep inside, she could feel the shocking sensations, and she couldn't stop herself from trembling.

"Do you like that?" he murmured, moving his mouth back to her nipple. He suckled at her breast while he penetrated her with a single finger.

She gasped at the pleasure that ignited within her, her arousal growing desperate. She squeezed his erection with her palm, moving her hand up and down faster.

"God above, Violet, you're making me lose control." He entered her with a second finger, and she felt the bead of moisture upon the head of his shaft. Already, she was at the brink, her body craving so much more. For a moment, he moved his fingers in and out, preparing her for lovemaking. She was arching her body against him, moving in a silent rhythm to his penetrations.

Then without warning, he withdrew his fingers. He palmed her hips and raised her to his mouth. With his tongue, he tasted her intimately, and she shattered, the waves of immense pleasure crashing over her. Her hands dug into the blanket as she arched, the eruptions of need so violent, she could scarcely breathe.

He lowered her again, a satisfied smile on his face, though she knew he was still aching.

But she reached for him and said, "I'm not finished with you yet, Damian."

Chapter Fourteen

DAMIAN WAS SURPRISED when Violet sat up and pressed him back to the ground. She straddled him, her wetness against his shaft. He nearly shouted when she moved against him. She leaned down to kiss him, and he plundered her mouth, his body riding the razor edge of need.

Then she moved her mouth to his neck, her tongue flicking against his skin. Heat blazed through him, and he wanted so badly to guide his shaft inside her.

But he'd sworn to let her stay in command. Instead, as she kissed him, he drew his hands down her spine, massaging her bottom so that she continued to move intimately against him. He fought to keep from losing control.

Then she continued moving lower, backing away from him until her mouth was near his erection. "Will you like it if I kiss you in the same way you kissed me?"

He didn't know if he had that level of control. But nothing in heaven or earth would make him deny her. "Yes," he gritted out.

When her mouth closed over him, he nearly lost it. Her wet tongue stroked the blunt head of his erection, and when she sucked at him, his hands clenched into fists.

He was struggling to breathe, his body aching for release. Her hands cupped his balls, and he knew he wouldn't last.

"Violet, wait," he said. "I want to be inside you. I won't last if you keep doing that. Please." He didn't care if he begged. But if she didn't stop, he was about to spill himself inside her mouth.

Thank God, she listened. She pulled back and guided his shaft to her opening. Never had any woman claimed him like this, and as she guided him into her tight wetness, he gritted his teeth to hold back his shout of pleasure.

She was a virgin, and he could tell she was starting to struggle. "I—I want this," she said. "Will you...help me?"

"Let me make it easier for you," he said. Gently he moved her to her back and lifted her knees. He didn't move any deeper, but instead bent to suckle one breast. As he'd hoped, he could feel her clenching against him. Slowly, he moved in and out. He moved his tongue around her nipple while he caressed her other breast with his fingers. She was breathing harder, and he continued to push a little deeper with every thrust. Then he pushed past her innocence, and she gave a slight cry when he was fully embedded within her. For a moment, he didn't move, wanting her to get adjusted to his size. She appeared stunned, and after a moment asked, "Is that all?"

He nearly laughed. "Not by half." With his thumb, he circled her hooded flesh, and she tightened against his shaft.

"Th-that's better," she said. He could feel her pushing back against him as if she wanted more.

"God, you feel good, Violet." He continued to caress her and added, "but I'm going to make you feel even more pleasure."

He deepened the pressure of his thumb against her clitoris, while he began shallow thrusts in a steady rhythm. She closed her eyes, her breathing starting to match the penetrations.

"I want your mouth on my breast again," she demanded. He obeyed, suckling at her as she clenched his length. Although he tried to keep it together, she made it impossible. Her wetness surrounded him, and every time he entered and withdrew, her inner walls squeezed him.

She started to lift her hips to meet his thrusts, and a keening cry broke forth from her. He found a rhythm that made her body seize up, and she gripped his shoulders hard, arching against him as she came. He felt the tremors clenching all around him, and he let go, the release coursing through him as he spent his seed deep inside her.

Damian continued a few more strokes until he collapsed against her, feeling as if he had been given a lesson of his own. Never in his life had sex been like this. This woman was the missing part of him, and he rolled to his back, keeping them joined while he cradled her body upon his.

He continued to stroke her back, running his hands down her spine, against her soft bottom, and against his chest, he could feel the curve of her breasts.

"I love you, Damian," she said.

Her confession evoked a warmth he hadn't expected. He couldn't remember the last time anyone had said they loved him. Surely his mother or father must have at one point. Possibly one of his sisters. But his past relationships had been for mutual pleasure, not much else.

Her words reached inside him, filling up the years of loneliness until he had to tell her his own feelings.

"I love you, too," he answered. "Will you marry me, Violet? Even if I can't give you the life you deserve?" He wished to God he could find a way out of his father's financial mess, but it seemed that poverty was their only option.

She smiled at him, running her hands down his back. "You might need to convince me a few more times."

IT FELT AS if her emotions were tied up in knots of joy, nerves, and fear that she was only dreaming. On her wedding day, Violet wore a simple, high-waisted, forest green gown made of silk, with short sleeves. Her grandmother had loaned her a diamond and emerald necklace that matched the color of the gown exactly.

"Stop pacing, Violet," Annabelle demanded. "You're making me dizzy."

"I'm sorry. I'm j-just nervous." Violet rested her hands on the back of a chair. "It doesn't seem real that this is happening." Beneath her gown, her skin tightened with the forbidden memory of that stolen afternoon in the summerhouse. And although she was truly happy that the earl had proposed, she worried about their future together. After all that had happened, what if he regretted his decision to marry her? She had no doubt that Persephone would attempt to make their lives miserable after Scarsdale had spurned her.

"You do want to marry him, do you not?" her grandmother asked.

She nodded and smiled. "More than anything. I'm just w-worried about what will happen when we return to London."

"You will remain out of the public view for a time," Annabelle said. "Stay at the Scarsdale estate while you make your plans. Ally yourselves with the important folk."

"You make it sound as if w-we are preparing for war." Violet held back her amusement, for her grandmother's expression was quite serious.

"Oh, you are, make no mistake. And if you want to help the earl's sisters, you will need to be strategic. The more allies you have, the less likely it is that anyone will spurn you." She leaned against her cane and stood. "Now, I believe it's time for you to be married, my girl."

Violet reached out to embrace her grandmother, and the old woman patted her back. Annabelle had become such an unexpected support, and she was so grateful to her.

"I arranged for a few guests," Annabelle said. "I hope you don't mind."

"No, not at all." The wedding had been planned in such haste only a few days ago, Violet had fully anticipated only servants in attendance.

Her maid gave her a nosegay of roses and summer flowers.

Then she opened the door to the hallway, and Violet followed her grandmother toward the stairs. With every step, her nerves increased, but when she reached the drawing room, she saw her sister Charity smiling at her. Her mother wasn't there—likely a deliberate decision by Annabelle—but Violet didn't mind. She much preferred to have her sister there.

To her surprise, Damian's mother was also in the drawing room, though the marquess was absent. The marchioness's face paled when she saw Violet, but then she managed a smile as she reached for her handkerchief.

But it was Damian's expression that caught her heart. He was staring at her with disbelief, and then his face shifted to longing. She walked toward him, and he took her gloved hand in his. The comfort of his hand soothed her fears, and then the rest of the wedding ceremony became a blur. They spoke their vows, and he gave her a simple gold wedding ring with a pearl before he kissed her lightly. Then he leaned to her ear and said, "I'll give you a better kiss later."

She blushed at that, and he lifted her hand to his mouth while the guests applauded. As they led the others toward the wedding breakfast that awaited them in the next room, Damian asked, "Where in the world did you get that necklace, Violet?"

It was a curious question, but she answered, "My grandmother loaned it to me. Do you like it?"

He paused a moment. "It reminds me of one that once belonged to my mother. It was lost for many years."

She sensed that there was more about the necklace, but there was no time to ask him about it while other guests approached to wish them well. His mother, Lady Trent, came forward at that moment to wish them well. She hugged her son and smiled at Violet, taking her hands. "I am so happy for you both."

Violet murmured her thanks, and then asked Lady Trent, "Lord Scarsdale said that you had a necklace like this one, long ago. It's not the same necklace is it?"

The marchioness hesitated. "It certainly looks like it. But that was long ago, and even if it was once mine, I am glad you have it now."

Damian's hand moved to Violet's spine. To his mother he said, "My father lied, didn't he? He probably lost it in a wager but made me think I had lost the necklace in the river."

Clara's face tightened. "Let us not speak words that will darken your wedding day. It doesn't matter how she got the necklace." She managed a smile and said, "I am so glad to see it on you, Violet. I can think of no one better to wear it now."

Damian walked with them both toward the wedding breakfast, offering his other arm to his mother. "Have you spoken to Father?"

She shook her head. "Not since I left him. And if you're asking me to return to London, the answer is no. I've had my fill of his gambling and drinking."

"He is trying to stop," Damian admitted.

Although his words suggested that he'd forgiven his father, Violet hadn't missed the slight note of resentment—probably about the necklace. But since it still belonged to her grandmother, they could not sell it to pay off debts.

"He'll never change," Lady Trent remarked. "I've known that for years. And I would rather live the rest of my days at Scarsdale than face him again." She turned back to Violet. "That is, if it's all right with you."

"Y-you may stay as long as you like," Violet assured her. But even as Damian echoed her words, she didn't miss the tension on his face. He was still worried about his family, and their marriage had not brought much of a dowry at all. She didn't know what could be done, but she took his hand in hers and brought him to one side of the room.

"Damian," she murmured. "It's going to be all right."

He ventured a smile and bent down to steal a kiss. "In time, I suppose."

She understood that he was trying to solve the problems of everyone, a burden that was too much for any man. "Look at me," she bade him. "W-whatever may come, I have faith in you."

He took her hand and raised it to his lips. "I only hope you don't come to regret this marriage one day."

She met his gaze. "You're the only husband I could ever want."

DURING THE FIRST week of marriage to Violet, Damian could hardly keep his hands off her. He'd spent every waking hour with his new wife, and she kept surprising him in new ways. But now, it was time to return to London and begin the Herculean task of resurrecting his family's finances. They had packed their belongings and had traveled most of the day south.

"You look w-worried," Violet said. She was seated across from him in the coach, but after he gave a single nod, she moved to sit on his lap. With her arms around him, she asked, "What are you thinking of?"

His hands moved around her waist, and he admitted, "I don't know whether I've lost five hundred pounds and have to begin all over again or what land can be sold or…"

She cut off his words with a kiss. Then she said softly, "Whatever happens, we'll face it together."

He kissed her again, and the sensation of her bottom pressed against his arousal had evoked a painful desire. "Do you know, we have hours before we'll reach London."

"Is that so?" She offered a knowing smile at him. Then she reached down to his trousers. "I wonder what we can do with all that time?"

He began unbuttoning her gown, trying to reach her stays to loosen them. "We could sing songs."

She laughed at that, and when her hand moved to caress his aching shaft, he let out a hiss of air. "Violet…my God."

"We could play cards," she suggested.

She moved out of his lap, still stroking him. He fumbled to

get his trousers down and then tore at her laces to loosen them.

"Have you decided how you w-want to pass the time, then?" Her voice held wickedness, and he wanted to taste her skin, to push her close to the edge and fall into her release. She lifted her skirts and straddled him with her knees resting on the coach seat.

Damian pulled down her chemise, baring her breasts. "I need to think about it." He marveled at the sight of her gorgeous skin, and when he took her nipple into his mouth, she moved against him. The familiar warmth of her wetness slid upon him, and then she guided him deep inside. He groaned at the exquisite sensation, rewarding her by swirling his tongue around her erect nipple.

The rhythm of the coach's wheels upon the road made her bounce against him, and he moved to the edge of the seat, clasping her hips.

"I think I like riding in a coach with you," he said against her skin, and she laughed, guiding his mouth to her other breast.

While he suckled her, she threaded her hands in his hair. "I do love you, Damian. And if we lose every last penny, it w-won't matter at all to me. We'll have each other."

He kissed her mouth again as they rumbled along the road. Her hair had come loose, and it tumbled across her shoulders.

Damian moved his hand beneath her skirts, finding the hooded flesh that brought her pleasure. He stopped his thrusts and began to circle her there. She gasped, her fingers digging into his shoulders.

"Please," she whispered. "It feels so good, Damian."

The motion of the coach caused him to penetrate her in shallow thrusts. She leaned back, her face contracted with need as she clenched his length. The sensation of her body surrounding him was pushing him to the brink of his own control. He loved watching his wife come apart, and it only spurred his own desire. Her breaths were coming in quick gasps, and he knew the moment she cried out as she trembled all around him with her orgasm.

The coach hit a sudden bump in the road, and it plunged him deep inside her. At that, Damian couldn't stop himself anymore. He gripped her hips, penetrating her hard, and she drew her legs around his waist. He reveled at the sensation of joining with her, knowing that they belonged together. Violet would never care if they were poor, nor would she worry about servants. She meant it when she'd said they would face the future together.

"I love you," he gritted out, holding her fast as he gave in to his own release and emptied himself within her body. "So very much."

Her body quaked with aftershocks, but she held him close, smiling as she kissed him.

And for now, it was enough.

THERE WAS NO question that Damian was thoroughly distracted by the lack of news on the shipping investment. He spent hours poring over his father's ledgers, and though Violet tried to help him, he kept shutting her out. She tried to occupy herself in his London townhouse, but her very presence had sent the household into an uproar. Even his father appeared confounded at their marriage.

She sat across from Lord Trent at luncheon, and the marquess remained silent. There was only the clinking of their utensils as they ate. Violet tried to think of a way to soothe the awkwardness, but how could she speak to someone who didn't wish to converse?

At last, she decided that she could only be honest with him. "My lord, I realize that m-my marriage to Lord Scarsdale was sudden, but—"

"It was irresponsible," he answered. "Damian was supposed to get a special license to marry Lady Persephone."

"But he got the special license for his marriage to me, my lord." Her heart began pounding, but not out of fear. She'd never thought about the marriage license. But if he'd obtained the marriage license before he'd come to see her, then it meant he'd intended to marry her for weeks. And not Persephone.

A warmth spread over her heart as she suddenly understood what Damian had done to defy everyone. No, he hadn't married an heiress. He'd married a wallflower with a terrible stutter. But he loved her—she had no doubt of it. And she loved him. That was more than enough to build a marriage upon. And somehow, she was going to help him out of his financial straits.

She had her own purpose now, and she set down her fork. "I am sorry the w-wedding was so rushed. We thought we could have a smaller celebration for my f-family and for you…"

"We cannot afford that." The marquess dismissed the idea and cut into his meat. The blade scraped across the plate, and Violet tried again.

"I meant a small gathering at the house with food. Nothing so expensive as a ball."

"There will be no celebration," he snapped. "Now an annulment, on the other hand—"

The dining room door opened, and the marchioness entered the room with her head held high. The moment he saw his wife, Jonas stood from his chair, a joyous smile breaking over his face. "Clara," he breathed. "My dear, I'm so glad you're home."

"Not because I want to be," she snapped. "But I've come to bring Melanie back to Scarsdale. Then I will go and fetch Regan from school before we return north."

She took a seat beside Violet, and the footman brought her a plate. The marquess's expression held confusion, and he sat down again. "But this is your home. I thought—"

"You thought wrong." She sliced a bit of meat and ate. "I am done with this marriage and with you. I will no longer live with a man who squanders every penny. I am taking the girls with me, and next year, Melanie will have her Season."

Violet was beginning to feel like she was caught in the middle of their argument, and it wasn't at all productive. "Instead of fighting, could we w-work together instead on solving this problem? Perhaps we could go over the ledgers."

Clara ignored her. To her husband, she added, "You don't care a whit about Melanie or Regan. But I will no longer wait for you to gamble away more of their futures. Instead, I will take care of our girls. Without you."

The marquess's face grew stricken, and Violet suddenly felt sympathy for the man. She knew what it was to love someone and be left behind.

"Let me try to make it right, Clara," he said quietly. "I haven't touched spirits in weeks, and I haven't played cards, either." He met her gaze with utter honesty. "Give me a chance."

She shook her head, tears brimming from her eyes. "I gave you fifteen years' worth of chances. You didn't change then, and you won't now."

Violet felt her own tears rising, and more than anything, she wished Damian were here to stop them. A marriage was crumbling apart before her eyes, and she was helpless to stop it.

"It will be all right," the marquess said. "Damian and I will do everything in our power to restore our fortunes."

"No, it's not all right." Clara swiped at her tears and glared at her husband. "You wanted our son to sacrifice his own happiness for the mistakes you made. I, for one, am glad he ignored your orders."

Lord Trent paled, but he said, "I am sorry, Clara. For disappointing you."

"This is well beyond disappointment, Jonas. You're the one who caused this mess. It's your turn to solve it."

With that, she tossed her napkin on the table and stood. Then she glared at her husband and left the room.

For a moment, Violet didn't dare to speak. The marquess had his hands pressed to his temples, his head lowered. More than anything, she wished she hadn't witnessed his humiliation.

Damian had told her about the weeks his father had remained sober, locking himself away from the world. Jonas *was* trying. But

Clara had already made up her mind that he was a failure.

"I'm sorry," Violet said to the marquess. At first, she thought she should go. But then, that was what she'd always done, all her life. When problems arose, she'd hidden from them, hoping they would go away. Was Jonas not doing the same thing?

"Lord Trent," she said. He ignored her, and Violet tried again. "I want to help you."

Several moments passed before he finally raised his head to look at her. "There's nothing you can do."

But she didn't believe that. Even if there were no answers to be had, the marquess needed to feel like he was making progress. And so, she said, "Here is what we're going to do. W-we will go over the household ledgers during the last five years. You will write an accounting of any losses f-from gambling. Whatever you remember." In the meantime, she planned to look through the books to determine if there were any discrepancies in the accounts.

"Then w-we will talk together and discuss what else can be sold." Violet cleared her throat and added, "We will cut our expenses down to the minimum and f-find out what to do next. Are we in agreement?"

The marquess stared at her as if he didn't know what to think. Violet simply nodded and said, "Good. We will begin immediately."

DAMIAN WAS STARTING to put together the pieces. His friend, Graham Hannaford, had been missing for weeks now, and the ships had not returned. But from discreet inquiries, he'd learned that the Duke of Westerford had coerced nearly every investor into selling their shares. Which Damian found entirely suspicious, in his mind.

On a whim, he'd sent word to Cedric Gregor. The man seemed to have connections all over London. The gentleman had agreed to meet him here, at Swan's Tavern, to let him know what he'd learned.

But when Cedric joined him at the table, his expression was grim. Without a word, Damian handed him a tankard of ale.

Cedric sat down and admitted, "Graham Hannaford isn't missing—he's being held in prison."

"What? For what reason?" Damian hadn't heard anything about this. "He's done nothing wrong."

"They are holding him on charges of attempted sodomy," Cedric said softly. "He is to be flogged."

From the tone of his voice, Damian sensed that there was a deeper undertone of fear. And it was likely that Cedric knew more. "Tell me what you know so I can help him."

"I don't know if that's possible. The Duke of Westerford claims that one of his men was attacked by Hannaford. And who would dare to stand against His Grace's accusation?"

Damian released the breath he hadn't realized he was holding. They would need power over the duke in some way. Some means of quietly manipulating the man to drop the charges. "I will need to make more inquiries. We need leverage over His Grace. Some scandal or secret that he doesn't want revealed."

And then he would demand the release of his friend. More and more, he was convinced that the duke wanted control over everything on those ships. But why would he care so much about silks or spices? It made little sense.

Cedric studied him for a long moment. "I am glad I chose you to be a match for Miss Edwards. You look happy together."

"We are." Damian thought of his wife, and how she made him want to be a better man. She gave him hope that they could find happiness together. And that one day, they might have children of their own. "I am grateful for your matchmaking." He finished his drink and put down a few coins. "I will see what can be done for Hannaford. In the meantime, find out what you can about those ships."

Damian bid farewell to Cedric and went back to his carriage

to return home. He wanted to talk to Violet, to hear her thoughts. Ever since he'd brought her back to London, he was aware that he'd been distant. It had been too easy to fall back into old habits. The only exception was at night.

He'd refused to give Violet a separate room but had ordered the servants to place all her belongings with him. Then after he'd spent most of the day out of the house, he could return to find his wife in his bed.

Often, she would be asleep, but he could lie close to her, feeling the warmth of her skin against his. She brought him comfort, and not only when she awakened and welcomed him into her body. It went far beyond that. He needed to see her each day and, knowing that she was waiting for him, only made him long to be with her.

It was growing dark, and he returned inside his London townhouse, giving his hat and walking stick to one of the footmen. He'd expected to find his wife and parents at supper—instead, one of the servants informed them that his family was inside the study.

Damian had no idea what to make of that, but he pushed open the door and blinked at the sight in front of him. His father was writing, while his sister Melanie was busy reading through ledgers. Violet had two ledgers open in front of her, and there was an array of sandwiches, cups of tea, and even biscuits.

"I've found another one!" Melanie said. "On the fourth of September. Twenty shillings that were paid to the grocer."

"Only they weren't," Violet answered. "Here's another bill f-for the same amount." She checked her ledger and added, "The secretary changed the amount in the household account."

Damian could hardly believe what he was seeing. "No one thought to invite me to your party?"

Violet set down the books and beamed at him. She stood and held out both hands. "You're home. Come and see w-what we've learned. Would you like tea? We started hours ago, and the f-footmen keep bringing us sandwiches and biscuits. There's plenty if you're hungry."

He took her hands in his and leaned in to kiss her cheek. Against her ear, he murmured, "I'm always hungry."

She gave him a sensual smile that promised she would fulfill that desire later. "Let us show you what we've learned."

She pointed to the ledger she'd been reading, and he leaned over her while she explained the discrepancies between the household accounts and the bills. "It's all very small amounts, nothing significant. But it appears that it's been happening for years."

He leaned over her shoulder to study the accounts and as he did, he rested his hand on her shoulder. It hardly mattered what they'd found—knowing that his family was working together with him made the burden easier to bear.

"Did the secretary steal the money?" Melanie wondered aloud.

"I dismissed him months ago," Jonas noted. "He came to me many times, asking me about the household accounts and whether I had taken money from it for my gambling." He shook his head and sighed. "I grew tired of him asking and sent him away. Now, I think he may have been trying to help."

Violet held out a piece of paper. She'd written out a summary of the amounts during the past few years, along with the dates, showing how much money had gone missing.

"Someone has been embezzling money from your father," she said, "and though Jonas has admitted his gambling, this goes back f-further than I ever imagined."

Damian took a sandwich and ate it, thinking to himself. He tried to remember which of the servants had been with them the longest. It might have been one of the maids or a footman, someone who was struggling for wages.

"It's getting late," he said. "Melanie, has Mother talked to you about going to Scarsdale?"

His sister sighed. "She has. But I don't want to go." She glanced over at Jonas. "Papa, you need to talk to her. I would rather be here than hidden away at Scarsdale."

The marquess turned grim. "I can order you to stay, and I can write to Regan's school, forbidding her to go with her mother. But Clara has already lost so much. If I take you from her, she'll never forgive me."

"You're not taking anyone," Melanie said. "I'm simply refusing to go."

Damian decided they might as well speak to Clara and explain matters. He rang for a servant and ordered, "Tell my mother I wish to speak to her here." He didn't want Melanie caught in the middle of their parents' marital problems.

In a quarter of an hour, Clara arrived. The moment she saw all of them, her face twisted with annoyance. "Damian, what is it you need?"

"We've been going over the accounts, and I hoped you could shed some light on missing funds."

She rolled her eyes. "The only missing funds are the ones that your father gambled away."

"No, that's not it. Money was taken in small amounts from the household accounts." He took a breath. "Do you think your maid could have been stealing from us?"

"She would never." Clara straightened and shook her head. "She's been with me since I married your father. Why would you ever think she could do such a thing?"

"Because we've had to decrease her wages, along with the rest of the staff," Damian said.

But his mother was already shaking her head. "Leave Florence out of this. The only person guilty of stealing from us is your father." She turned to Melanie. "I've told Florence to pack your trunk. We're leaving in the morning to get Regan."

"You'll do no such thing," Jonas answered. "Melanie wishes to remain here. And so, she shall."

"I am not leaving her with you," Clara began.

"Mother, enough." Melanie stood and walked to stand beside Jonas. "I want to stay here and help. And leave Regan alone. She's perfectly happy at school." With a pained smile, she added, "I know there won't be a Season for me next year. But there are still more gentlemen here. Damian could introduce me to some of them."

Clara stiffened. "There *will* be a Season for you next year, Melanie. I promise you that."

"Mother, you need to face the facts. There is no money for a Season. Not when we have servants to pay and bills." Melanie shook her head. "Even when we do receive the rents, we haven't enough for gowns or frivolous expenses."

"And whose fault is that?" Clara demanded.

"Leave it be," Damian said at last. "I know you must be tired after all that's happened. I can have Florence bring you tea or warm milk to help you sleep."

His mother's expression turned weary, and she shrugged. "Do as you will. But the girls are coming with me."

After she departed, Melanie sighed. "She just can't seem to face the truth of our poverty."

He agreed with his sister, but right now, there was nothing he could say to their mother. She'd made up her mind to leave London, and it would be a battle to prevent her from taking his sisters with her.

"You look tired as well, Damian," Violet said. "I think w-we've done enough for today." She took his arm in his, and they all left the study together.

But just as they reached the stairs, the marquess called out, "Violet. I owe you an apology."

"You've done nothing wrong," she said.

"No, I didn't realize that you meant what you said to me earlier," he admitted. "Even though we aren't your family, I see now that you do want to help. And it means a great deal."

"She *is* part of this family now," Damian corrected.

But his wife startled him by reaching out to his father. She took his hand and squeezed it gently. And the marquess gave a nod as if a silent conversation had occurred.

VIOLET HAD TROUBLE sleeping that night. Damian's naked body was twined with hers, and though he slept soundly, she kept thinking about the stolen money.

There was a connection of some kind between her husband and the Duke of Westerford. It went well beyond the arranged marriage with Persephone that hadn't taken place. No, it felt as if someone were deliberately trying to sabotage the marquess and his family. It wasn't only his finances that had fallen apart—the very fabric of his marriage had been torn asunder.

She shifted beneath the covers, and her husband stirred beside her. "You're thinking too much, aren't you?"

"I am." But against her backside, she felt his body harden with desire for her. She grew wet simply thinking of how it felt to make love to him. He cupped her breast and began to stroke her nipple. Then he slid his length between her legs, making her ache for his touch.

"What are you thinking about?" he asked. He took her hand and guided it low, pressing her fingers to the hooded flesh that made her body shiver. Lazily, he circled, showing her how he wanted her to touch herself. He guided his hot length to rest at her entrance, but he didn't move. She pressed herself against him, taking just the head of him inside.

"I can't remember what I was thinking about," she confessed. "Something about the household accounts."

He wet his fingertips and then caressed her nipples. Violet rubbed herself the way he'd taught her, and the delicious sensation began to rise and ebb within her.

"Tell me," he urged.

"You're tormenting me." She closed her eyes, trying to guide him inside her, but he pulled back.

"Not yet. Not until you've told me what's bothering you," he teased.

She could hardly keep a single thought in her mind with the way he was touching her, and as he continued, she felt herself drawing close to the edge of release. She was craving him, but then he took her and pinned her to the bed beneath him. She spread her legs, and her heart was pounding with need.

"Damian, I can't think right now."

"I'll reward you if you tell me," he promised, leaning in to kiss her lips. "Something has been keeping my clever wife awake, and I want to know what it is."

He had her trapped, and she bit her lip. "The duke," she said. "I wondered if there is a connection of some kind. Something about your father and whether His Grace caused him to be ruined for a reason."

"The duke needs nothing from my father," Damian answered. "And as far as I know, there's no enmity between them. The only person furious with my father is my mother."

Violet went motionless at that. They hadn't even considered Clara's role in this. "Damian," she whispered. "Do you think your mother…?"

And then he understood, without her having to say a word. "She kept telling me my sisters would have their Seasons. I always thought she was in denial."

"But what if she's been setting aside money for years?" Violet breathed. "It only stopped when she left with your father for Scarsdale."

"You are brilliant," he said. He kissed her deeply, his tongue swirling against hers. Then he moved his mouth to her breasts and, finally, he kissed a path down between her legs. He slid one finger deep within, stroking her from inside while he worked her core with his tongue. It took only moments for the quaking pleasure to rise higher until she was sobbing from the pleasure breaking over her. A white-hot crest made her tremble, and she bit back a scream as he joined their bodies together. She met his thrusts by lifting her hips, crying out as another wave claimed her, and she orgasmed around him.

"I love you Violet," he said, plunging hard until she felt him tense, and he found his own release.

"I love you, too," she whispered. And as she started to fall asleep, she cradled him against her body, so thankful for the gift of this man.

Chapter Fifteen

HIS FRIEND GRAHAM was exhausted, his body bruised and beaten, but at least Damian had arranged to have the charges dropped. Cedric Gregor had loaned him money to bribe the magistrate, and thankfully, the bribe had worked. Corruption had worked in their favor this time, but it hadn't hurt that Hannaford had a sound reputation in London for his honesty, as well as his tendency to turn a profit.

In the carriage, Damian had given his friend food and drink, along with a blanket for warmth. But it was the hopelessness in Graham's eyes that bothered him.

"They had no proof," he said quietly. "Only the word of a duke against mine."

"Why did he have you arrested?" Damian asked. "There was no evidence or reason for it."

"Because we didn't find the silks we were expecting." He lowered his head, and Damian let out a breath of air.

"So, you lost the ships? There was no cargo?"

Graham faced him, and his eyes held weariness. "Oh, there was indeed a cargo. But I had to stop and change the crew because I couldn't trust the men. Then I had to hide our goods in barrels of rice, so no one would discover the truth. But, as it turns out, someone did. The duke, that is." His expression tightened. "I did manage to set aside your portion of the profits, though that was why he had me imprisoned. Because he wanted all of it. He bought out all the shares, except yours."

"What was your cargo, Hannaford?" Damian asked quietly.

"Diamonds and rubies. I had intended to buy silks with the investment money, but one of my friends advised me to buy shares in two of the mines." He gave a thin smile. "It was the right choice. But, as you can imagine, we had to hide our goods. I bought barrels of rice and hid the pouches of gemstones in the rice. Though we tried to keep it a secret, someone sent word to the duke."

Damian could hardly believe what he was hearing. "Do you mean to say that I paid you five hundred pounds, and you brought back a shipment of gemstones?"

"I did," Graham agreed. "I chose a different port for my ships because I wanted to deliver the gemstones myself. We traveled by wagon to London, and I have yours in a locked room in my house. I delivered the duke's portion, and he had me arrested when I refused to give him the remainder that included my portion and yours."

It shouldn't have surprised him that the duke had a ruthless, greedy side. But more than that, Damian felt a sense of anticipation for his own good fortune. If he had enough profits from the sale of the gemstones, it was possible that he could pay off some of his father's debts and let his mother quietly retire to Scarsdale with a small portion while his sisters kept their dowries.

Damian didn't blame his mother for setting aside the money. It was necessary for the girls, and he didn't begrudge them any of it. He only wished Clara had trusted him enough to tell him her secret.

"I am glad I was able to free you," Damian said. "And that the bribery worked."

"I'll repay you for it," Graham promised. "But the charges were false, and the magistrate knew it," Graham said bitterly. "After this, I won't allow the duke to invest in my shipments again."

The carriage arrived at Graham's house, and Damian helped his friend out of the vehicle. They went inside the dwelling, and Graham withdrew a key from a hidden part of his desk. Then he unlocked another room and revealed a barrel. "I had it sealed, so you'll have to break it after you bring it home."

"Thank you, my friend," he said. "I am grateful for your help."

"As am I for yours," Graham answered. "I hope you and your new wife find happiness together."

Such a strange turn of events, for a simple barrel to hold life-changing riches. Damian could hardly wait to show Violet. He had no idea whether it was a small pouch of gemstones or more, but after the carriage arrived at his townhouse, he gave orders for an axe to be brought out.

Violet came to greet him and asked, "What on earth do you need an axe f-for, Damian?"

"You'll see." He helped the footman roll the barrel into the drawing room. "There's more inside this barrel of rice. We'll find out once we've opened it."

Violet ordered one of the maids to bring out a sheet and lay it beneath the barrel. "There's no need to waste the rice," she pointed out.

Damian nearly laughed, but said, "I appreciate your practicality, my wife." Then he hefted the axe and began chopping at the barrel. He took turns with one of the footmen until, at last, the rice spilled all over the sheet. There, at the bottom, he spied a simple leather sack tied shut.

"Hold out your hands," he bade Violet. Then he used a knife to cut the leather ties. His own excitement built, and when he poured the gemstones into her hands, she uttered a cry of shock.

"There are so many," she breathed. "I can hardly believe it." A smile broke over her face as she admired them.

It was then that his mother entered the parlor. "What's all this, Damian?" Then her gaze settled upon the diamonds and rubies, and she covered her mouth.

"It's the fortune I earned for my wife and family," he said.

"Oh, my goodness," she breathed. "I can hardly believe it."

"Just as I could hardly believe you stole money from your own family." He couldn't stop the accusation, for she never should have done it.

She blanched at his words. "Damian, I—"

"I know why you did it," he said. "But it was wrong. I nearly married a heartless shrew of a woman to help my sisters when it wasn't necessary."

"I couldn't tell you," she whispered. "Jonas would have learned the truth. And I couldn't risk their futures."

But she was willing to risk his. A hollow ache caught his stomach, and Damian didn't know what to say to that.

"I was helpless," Clara said. "I saw our fortune crumbling before my eyes, and it was the only thing I could do." With a heavy sigh, she said, "I knew you would be all right, Damian. You've always managed to find your way. But I was so worried for the girls."

"Give the money back, and let me put it into trust for Melanie and Regan for their dowries," he said. "If you do, I won't tell Father what you did. I'll let him believe the money came from my investment."

She gripped her gloved hands together and closed her eyes. "Thank you."

Violet poured the gemstones back into the bag and came to stand beside him. Though she didn't say a word, he took comfort from her presence. Damian took the pouch of gemstones and kissed her lips lightly. "I'll arrange to have these sold, and we'll begin again. You can spend every penny I own if it makes you happy."

"We are very lucky," she agreed. "But even if we still had nothing, I could not be happier." With a smile, she added, "I don't need a fortune to be happy, Damian. I only needed you as my husband." She rested her hand on his arm and added, "After we've settled the debts, can we return to Bedfordshire? I want to tell my grandmother of our change in fortune. And…I'd like to offer some comforts to her."

"Annabelle Edwards needs nothing at all," Clara scoffed. "The woman has more money than a Byzantine emperor."

"What are you talking about?" Violet exchanged a glance with him. "My grandmother has nothing at all."

"Bah. She lives like a miser, but she had money of her own from before she was married. She simply chose to live as a pauper." Clara dismissed the thought. "It wouldn't surprise me if she was buried with her fortune. She certainly didn't want Thomasina to have it."

Damian saw his wife tense, and he suddenly realized there might have been an entirely different reason why Annabelle had wanted Violet to live with her. It was possible that her grandmother intended to make Violet her heiress.

"I never realized," Violet said softly. "Still, I would like to visit her. Perhaps we could see her if we are traveling to Scarsdale?"

Damian nodded. "If it makes you happy, we can invite her to visit." To his mother, he added, "I know you want to live at Scarsdale, but you should consider what will make Melanie and Regan happy. Somehow, I doubt either will want to go." Clara fell silent, and he could see the disappointment in her eyes.

"You should talk to Father. I don't expect anything to change, and if you wish to go to Scarsdale alone, that is your choice. But he has been trying to be a different man. You might find that you like this one better."

He didn't wait to hear Clara's argument, but instead took Violet with him upstairs. He stopped to lock the jewels away in his desk and then pulled out a crumpled dance card from the drawer.

When she saw it, an incredulous smile broke over her face. "You kept this."

"I did." He lifted it up and read it aloud. "The first thing you wrote was 'Smile'."

Her smile widened, and she asked, "I suppose I have many reasons to smile now. W-what else?"

"Drop fan." He didn't quite know what she'd meant by that, but Violet pulled up her handkerchief and pretended it was a fan. Then she dropped it before him and gave a wicked smile. She started to lean over, but he bent down to pick up the handkerchief and could see the daring curve of her breasts beneath her bodice.

He stood up quickly, but she laughed and took a step backwards. "And the third thing I wrote?"

"Confidence," he read aloud. To his delight, Violet pressed him to take a chair, and then she sat upon his lap. She took his face between her hands and kissed him deeply. For a moment, he indulged in the sensual touch of her lips, savoring her mouth upon his.

"I'm confident I can please you," she said. She slid her hands over his shirt, down to his waistcoat. "If you give me the chance."

He stood from the chair and swung her into his arms. "Then let's get started, my love," he murmured against her lips.

"What was the last thing I wrote?" she asked.

"Money. But that one doesn't matter." He let the dance card fall onto the desk, kissing her again. Never in his life had he imagined that he could love anyone as much as he loved Violet. She meant everything to him. "I'd rather you showed me your confidence."

"Somehow, I think you'd rather I showed y-you other things," she teased. "Behind closed doors, of course."

A laugh broke forth from him, and as he took his wife to their bed, he thought of what she'd said before, that she didn't need money to be happy. Violet was right. He would still be grateful for her, even if they had nothing at all.

"I love you," he murmured against her mouth. "And yes, I do want you to show me other things."

Her eyes twinkled as she smiled at him. "You first."

About the Author

Michelle Willingham has published nearly fifty romance novels, novellas, and short stories. Currently, she lives in Virginia with her children and is working on more historical romance books in a variety of settings such as: Regency England, Victorian England, Viking-era Ireland, medieval Scotland, and medieval Ireland. When she's not writing, Michelle enjoys baking cookies, playing the piano, and chasing after her cats. Visit her website at: www.michellewillingham.com.